THE SENSORIANS

Awakening

Brigitte Morse-Starkenburg

PROLOGUE

The girl covered herself with blankets and a high pitched scream came piercing out from underneath. Any attempts by Alice to comfort her child were met with violent lashes and kicks and even more screeching. Alice had no idea what triggered this particular melt down, but it was one of many and there was little she could do apart from wait until the girl had got past most of her distress. Even then, it was difficult to console her. It made Alice feel like the worst mother in the world. She just didn't understand the creature.

"Please help me out," she sighed in desperation to her partner as the girl was now scratching her own arm so hard it started to bleed.

He had tried his hardest to stay out of it. Not to undermine Alice. It had always been a sensitive issue between the two of them.

He approached the little girl slowly and sat beside her for a while before saying anything. His voice calm and soothing, but nothing different from what Alice had tried countless times before.

"Lizzy."

Just hearing his voice made the girl pause for a

second and a little eye peeked out from under the blanket. Rick spoke softly to her, repeating the words he'd used a thousand times before, over and over again.

"I'm here for you, my sweet. I love you." Eventually, the girl relaxed and stopped thrashing about. Rick tried to put his hand on her back to rub it a little, but she jerked back like a scared animal.

"Too much?" he asked gently.

The girl, little as she was, didn't have the vocabulary to answer him but her eyes looked relieved by his understanding. They didn't need words to connect. They had an immensely strong, intuitive bond and it was something Alice envied. She'd tried the same method, the same words, but it didn't have the same effect and that made her feel excruciatingly frustrated.

After Lizzy had calmed down sufficiently Rick took her to bed, about two hours after she was meant to have gone. Alice poured herself a glass of wine to help her unwind. Rick came down and nestled next to his beloved on the sofa. He kissed her furiously, his eyes dark and tempting.

"I love you more than anything. You know that, right?"

That's how plenty an evening unfolded. She was

nothing like him, just a 'Dullard' as his friends liked to call her and tease him with, but he loved her deeply.

One evening, though, it ended very differently indeed. Rick went up to say goodnight to little Lizzy, but the moment he walked in to the room, she froze. She looked at him with accusing eyes and her lip started to tremble slightly. Rick realised he couldn't hide anything from his daughter. He gave her a tender hug, and looked deeply into her eyes. She pulled away slightly, distrusting.

"This isn't your fault. Remember that. I love you. Always."

He kissed her softly on her forehead and then left. He didn't say anything to Alice, who was in the kitchen at that moment. He just put his letter on the coffee table, got his coat, and disappeared.

*

The psychiatrist sat behind his desk, Alice opposite him whilst Eliza, now 5 years old, played with some Lego in the corner.

"Everyone just stop talking, pleeasy, pleeasyyy!" she piped up, getting slightly agitated and grabbing at her ear defenders that she wore full time.

Both adults ignored her, deep in conversation.

"We have come to the conclusion that, even though it is rare in such a young child, Eliza is presenting with a form of schizophrenia with paranoia. The fact that you have commented she can often feel, see or smell things that nobody around her can, is indicative to the condition....."

Alice zoned out and could only concentrate half on what the doctor was saying.

"... few characteristics of children on the ASD spectrum, so we will further investigate..."

Alice felt relief.   It wasn't her fault her baby girl was the way she was. Then guilt.

"...with a real danger of self harm..."

How could she have wished for anything to be wrong with her daughter.   So selfish.

"...starting her on medication, including some sedation..."

Suddenly she felt overwhelmingly protective over Lizzy.

"How do you feel about that, Ms Howlett?"

Alice was aware she was meant to answer but couldn't think of anything useful to say. It was as if this wasn't happening to them, but to someone else. She was a mere spectator.

6

"Sorry, could you please repeat that?" was all she managed to say.

How she longed for Rick to have been there to support them. He would have known exactly what to say.

CHAPTER 1

My eyes are open,
Seeing, but nothing makes sense
I can feel the motion, slow and fast at the same time
like a giant, striding with purpose
I can hear the rustling of the grass, or is it the sea?
Then this all encompassing sense of dread
fills me from deep inside
A lifeless shape being carried
or is it me?

I woke up drenched in sweat, with a mouth as dry as the Sahara desert. I hated these mornings, feeling drained as if I hadn't slept at all, slightly confused and a feeling of imminent danger lingering. I could never quite put my finger on what I actually dreamt but I knew it was always the same. Very frustrating. I always slept badly when exams were looming at school.

I dragged myself out of bed, put on a dry t-shirt and glanced at the clock on my phone which read 6:45.

"Shit." I muttered.

There was no point going back to bed so I had a

shower. I grabbed my towel and sauntered to the bathroom. I wished my head wasn't so foggy in the morning. My vision so blurry, I could hardly see where I was going. Those damned meds, I thought grumpily, full well knowing that without them I would not be living at home with my mum but instead in some mental institution, or worse....

Our bathroom was small and functional but mum had used some colourful tiles to brighten the place up. It had worked. Sort of. I loved having a shower or bath in there, listening to music whilst getting ready, to the great annoyance of my mum as it would usually take me forever to finish, making the room so steamy you could hardly breathe.

A vague memory of when I was little crept into my head. I used to feel elated coming in here. The pinks, yellows and greens of the tiles evoked such intense happiness I told my mum once that it felt like they were singing to me. In fact everything around me I would absorb like a sponge. I used to feel the colours and sounds around me and they would engulf me with such a mixture of emotions that I could hardly make sense of them. I would look at someone's smile and it would make me burn inside with happiness. An angry glance would make me crumble inside and I

9

would sometimes cry out in pain. More often than not, especially when outside of the house, I felt so overwhelmed with all the stimuli around me that I would crawl up in a ball and hide or scream, to the despair of my mum who just didn't understand.

The sounds too had changed. Voices everywhere, and loud, used to be all around me. I could remember the shower sounding like a downpour, footsteps as billowing as a drum and my mum's reassuring breaths like she was right next to me, wherever she was in the house. I could always work out where she was when I tuned into her. I knew the sounds of her like the back of my hand. It had made me feel safe. But what I missed the most was all the smells around me. I remembered every season had their own distinctive scent. Spring had been my absolute favourite. More bizarrely, I was always able to work out exactly what mood people were in by just a whiff of their scent. It used to reassure me.

I could feel my mouth turn into a sad smile. Confusing as they sometimes were, I really missed those intense feelings, but I could always tell they had frightened my mum.

I heard my phone ping in the distance.

Probably Kasper. He always got up early to try and catch a wave before going to school. He, so far, had failed to convince me to come on these early outings but I loved watching him in the afternoon. He was the typical surfer dude, with long blond hair which he, more often than not, wore in a messy man bun. He had the most gorgeously warm smile which was always reserved for me. The thought of him was enough to make me feel more optimistic about the day ahead and I was able to shake off the feeling of unease which the dream left me with.

Pick u up laters babes xxx -

I quickly towel dried my hair as I usually let it dry naturally with a bit of texturising wax rubbed in to get that slightly tasselled bob look. I threw on some reasonably smart clothes for school. In Sixth Form we didn't have to wear a uniform, but we had to look presentable as if we would be going to work in an office. I never seemed to pull off that smart casual look very well somehow.

I heard some clanking noises in the kitchen which was mum getting a coffee ready to start the day. She recently started working in a solicitor's office in town and she loved it. She used to do all sorts of odd jobs, just to earn some extra money, but her main focus had always been me. Her new job had given her some new opportunities to develop her career into something more long term and rewarding, and she was thriving on it. I never knew for sure how she was able to support us, but even though we weren't rolling in it, we never seemed to be short of money either. She always avoided the subject, but I managed to extrapolate that my father had made promises to her when he left, albeit in a letter. I gave up asking as it upset her, though she always tried her hardest not to show it. I understood as, little as I was, the pain I felt when I realised that my daddy had gone was as if he was physically ripped out of my body. It had left a gaping hole, never to be completely filled again.

"Have you had breakfast Eliza? I think we are a bit low on milk so can you get some on your way back from school today?" she asked in a hurried voice.

"In a minute. Might wait for Kas, as he might want some too" I added quickly.

Mum liked Kasper, but was not too keen on the amount of time I spent with him. I should concentrate on my studies, she constantly reminded me. I got some cereal out the cupboard and watered down the tiny amount of milk that was left.

Kasper did join me for some breakfast, wolfing

down some toast. He would never say no to the offer of food.

We walked to school and Kasper was in a buoyant mood, unlike myself.

"Looking forward to Soph's party tonight? It should be fun. Loads of our crowd are going to be there and I think there will be food and live music too!"

His face shone with joy. I could literally feel his anticipation ripple through my body.

"Wow Kas, you really do want to go tonight, don't you?" I said, lacking the enthusiasm he was looking for.

He looked at me in a slightly peculiar way, though I doubted he realised that.

"You are coming, aren't you Eli? It won't be the same without you."

He looked at me with his gorgeous bright green eyes. It was clear he was going to go with or without me, but he was desperately hoping I would come. How could I refuse. I was sure I would love it once I was there.

"Of course! Wouldn't miss it for the world" I said, still with a hint of sarcasm.

Kas didn't notice.

"Love you babes. It's gonna be great," he smiled happily.

We met up again after school in our local coffee shop. Usually five or six of us went, giving each other the low down of our school day, whilst drinking our cappuccino's and hot chocolates and having a sneaky snack or two. Today, everyone was particularly animated about some incident that had happened between some mates of a mate.

I wasn't particularly interested in the event so my mind wandered, looking at everyone's faces and making mental notes on their little quirks and expressions. In my mind I often played a little game awarding people their soul mate animal based on their facial expressions. It sometimes made me giggle out loud, immediately being punished by being thrown odd looks. My small group of friends were used to my quirks now, but it had taken me a long time to establish a solid friendship group. I had always been a bit of an outsider, especially till my early teens.

As I was sitting there, pondering over my childhood, I first noticed him. Or actually, not really noticed him but rather felt him watching me. I brushed it off thinking I was imagining it, being paranoid. A recurring theme in my life which I had to address with my psychiatrist next time I saw him.

14

CHAPTER 2

I knew instantly she'd registered my presence. Her body stiffened, imperceptibly to most people, but abundantly clear to me. I also noticed she dismissed the feeling and tuned out immediately, suddenly engaging with some boring conversation about some to do at school. I knew she hadn't been interested before, but she was now trying very hard to look part of the group again. If only she knew how wrong that was. I almost felt sorry for her.

I had argued with Markus, saying at seventeen she was too young and not ready for whatever Markus had in mind for her. Especially as she had no idea who and what she really was, having lived most of her life amongst common Dullards.

However, Markus saw it differently. He believed it was perfect timing. Her mind would still be open and malleable enough to let us in, but at the same time grown up enough to deal with the inevitable shock of finding out that her life up to now was basically a lie, or at best, not lived to its full potential. Markus can be incredibly persuasive when he has to and he's not scared to use his authority to the full. At nineteen years old, I had no fucking chance.

"Zack, you will see it my way sooner or later, but for now you just have to be satisfied with the knowledge that I have done this before and it worked."

Markus had looked at me sternly when he was trying to persuade me to drop it and just get on with my mission.

"This is different, she has absolutely no idea. She's on medication and will probably blame her perceived mental illness and run a mile!" I had tried, but Markus wasn't having any of it.

"I have absolute trust in your powers of persuasion. You will meet her and draw her in." he said, convinced of himself.

"She has a Dullard mum and friends though, she's settled. She has no knowledge about her gift. It could be dangerous. What if she confides in someone who's not in the know? What if her mum won't let her go..."

"Stop the arguing Zack. This is your job. You have to remind yourself we *need* her here, with us, so do whatever it takes, I will take care of the mother. And please don't call ordinary people Dullards. It's derogatory."

He walked off. There was no budging him. I just had to do it.

I tracked her down and laid eyes on her for the first time in that coffee shop. My misgivings were confirmed. She seemed so young, a typical fucking teenager. However, I was encouraged by the signs of her latent powers. They must be strong to work through the haze of the meds she was on.

The group was talking about a party they were going to attend in the evening and I made a mental note on whose party it was. I was just contemplating how I would make my first approach, when some of the kids were starting to make signs of wanting to leave. Kas was one of them. I presumed that he was her boyfriend as he had been displaying some slightly possessive moves all afternoon. He looked like a laid back kind of guy, but where Eliza was concerned I saw a different side to him. Protectiveness with a slightly possessive streak to it. I wondered if Eliza was the annoying type of girl who people tended to mollycoddle. I fucking hoped not.

I saw him looking at Eliza, getting up and fishing some money out of his Jeans. I had to move quickly otherwise the moment would pass but I could feel I was to be in luck as I noticed Eliza needed to go to the ladies before they'd leave.

As she stood up, I manoeuvred my way into her

path, bumped into her and spilled my coffee all over her arm and chest.

"Fuck, I'm so sorry! Are you okay? Sorry, I..."

"Ouch, yeah, no. I'm fine," she lied.

"Let me get a cloth."

"No, no it's fine. I need to go to the toilet anyway. I will sort it. Don't worry."

She went bright red as she briefly looked into my eyes.

I apologised again, trying to keep eye contact as I let her pass. I needed her to remember my face for when I was to approach her next time. She certainly did notice me. I could hear her heart quickening slightly and I got a glimpse of her pupils widening before she lowered her eyelids coyly.

"Thanks." she whispered as she hurried on.

That's when I decided to make my move sooner rather than later, and that party at Sophie's they'd all been talking about seemed to offer the perfect opportunity. All I needed to do was gate crash it, which wouldn't be too difficult as it seemed to be promising to be quite a big and open affair.

CHAPTER 3

I noticed Kas wanted to make a move and I wanted to go with him. We both loved having a bit of time on the beach to relax.

"Wait for me Kas, just need to pop to the loo before we go." I mouthed to him.

As I walked to the toilet I could sense movement and before I knew it I was wearing someone's cup of coffee as some guy bumped into me. It hurt like hell as it landed mostly on my bare arm, and I looked up ready to give him a mouthful for being so careless. He was most apologetic and, not to mention, gorgeous! I caught his eyes and, annoyingly, only managed to squeak out that it was fine, but he really had me flustered, which took me by complete surprise!

I wasn't in the habit of ogling other boys since Kas and I had been together, and I felt a little guilty, but this specimen of the male variety was stunning! His dark intense eyes bored into me when he let me go past and I had to look down as to not make a complete and utter fool of myself. How come I had never noticed him before! This dude with his closely cropped black hair and muscular physique certainly stood out. He must be new to the area. Then I realised that earlier on I half imagined him watching me, but again felt I was being paranoid. I took a moment in the toilet to compose myself and get the stain out of my top. I didn't hurry, and successfully avoided running into him again when I exited the toilets.

Kasper and I took a stroll to his parents' beach hut where he stored his surf kit. He'd bought me a beach chair and a little fridge that could hold drinks plus a kettle of course, for the days were more often cold than warm. I loved kicking back there, watching Kas strutting his stuff on the board. I also took the time to read or have some phone time as at home it was tricky with mum on my case to do my homework. Unfortunately, mobile coverage wasn't great on the beach but with a bit of luck you could get some free WiFi from the campsite nearby.

Kas was putting his wetsuit on and I looked on. Never could I have imagined that, one day, I was going to be the envy of many girls at school, having landed Kas as my boyfriend. He has an incredible body, athletic and lean, perfectly proportioned. I longed to explore it a bit more and I sidled up to him, planting a kiss on his arm. He turned around, took my face in his hands and gently kissed my lips.

"Mmmmm, love you babes" he mumbled.

"Sure you don't want to join me in the water?" His eyes sparkled mischievously.

"You can but try!" I said wrapping myself up more.

"But I am perfectly happy to sit here for a bit, then ravage you later." I laughed.

We had only just recently had our 'first time' together, which had been far from perfect, with lots of awkward fumbling due to our lack of experience, but it had left us wanting more. Something had awakened inside me and I was keen to experiment, and I have to say, so was Kas!

After an hour or so we left to go home, have some dinner and get ready for the party. We agreed to meet each other there, like we usually did. I remembered to pick up some milk on the way back and popped it into the fridge as a text from my friend Bella arrived, asking if I could come to hers. She was having a crisis about to what to wear. As if I would be any good advising her! But I agreed of course, and said I would be over at about 8pm.

It forced me to think about what to wear myself and had a look at my collection of clothes. I always opened the wardrobe door expecting something to jump out and say "wear me"! But I knew that it was always the same old stuff in there and wasn't going to be surprised with some fantastic outfit that I'd forgotten about. I chose my trusted black skinny jeans with a crop top and a little jacket over the top. I knew I looked good in it, but sometimes I wished I would choose something more feminine and outgoing. As a child I used to love bright colours and flowery patterns as they made me feel happy, but it just didn't have the same effect any more.

"Eliza, are you home?" I heard my mum calling, interrupting my contemplations. I heard her footsteps approach my door and a gentle knock preceded her entering my room. She perched herself on the edge of my bed.

"How was your day then, sweetheart?" she looked at me with that always slightly worried face, which I used to get annoyed about, but now just ignored. It was easier.

"I have a party to go to this evening. Is that okay?"

I hadn't actually considered asking for permission, so it came as a bit of an afterthought. I hoped it was fine to go.

"Whose party is it? Will there be alcohol and are the parents there?"

I rolled my eyes at mum and sighed.

"It's at Sophie's. Her dad will be there, and I suspect there will be alcohol, mum. Don't worry though, I'll be sensible!"

It was mum's turn to sigh.

"I'd rather you didn't drink at all, Eliza. You know it can trigger bad things in you. Is Kas going?"

I chose to ignore the first comment and nodded. I knew she was alluding to last summer when I'd drunk half a bottle of vodka at a party and worried my friends sick by hallucinating I was kidnapped and that my mum was not my real mother. I got myself into such a state that I hid away and lashed out to anybody coming near me, convinced they were out to get me. Everyone thought I had lapsed into a mental break down and ever since, understandably, mum was extremely nervous about me drinking any alcohol. I wasn't that worried. I had been fine the next day, I'd just been drunk.

"What are we having for dinner?" I said trying to change the subject.

Mum got up from my bed and muttered something about pasta, and left me alone.

"Hey Eli, you look amazing!" Bella gushed when she opened the door for me.

"I love your eye make-up! You so got to help me out, hun!"

Her room looked like a bomb shell had gone off. Clothes were strewn across the floor, bed, chair, in fact, everywhere I looked!

"OMG Bella, really?!" I laughed sarcastically.

"I just don't know what to wear!"

She gesticulated wildly and pulled a sad face.

"And I think Jimmy will be there and I have to look good! I have to wear something I haven't worn before!"

Her desperate expression made me laugh again.

After about an hour of trying different combos on, we finally settled on a little dark blue dress with some funky heels, which showed off her figure perfectly. I could see Bella felt good about herself in it, which made me happy.

"Come on Bells, let's go. I'm sure the boys will be there by now!"

I started pushing Bella gently towards the door. Her mum waved us out with a string of 'be carefuls' and 'look after each others' as we walked up the road. I felt quite excited now, and was glad I'd decided to go.

When we got to Sophie's house, the party was already in full swing. I spotted Kas and Jimmy with a group of girls and a drink in their hand. Bella and I approached them and were met with hugs and kisses.

"I thought you had changed your mind Eli! What took you so long!" Kas exclaimed, only a touch disgruntled.

"However, you look absolutely gorgeous. Worth the wait!" I glanced at Bella and whispered in Kasper's ear.

"It was Bella's fault, she couldn't decide what to wear. She really has got it bad for Jimmy!"

"He would have liked her had she worn a plastic bag!" he laughed.

"Let me get you a drink Eli, what would you like?"

"Cider for me, thanks." I said with a fleeting thought of my mother's warning and dismissing it straight away.

A girl has got to have some fun right, I convinced myself.

I stood people watching for a minute whilst waiting for Kas to return, when the guy's face appeared out of nowhere with those eyes that had slightly unnerved me earlier in the day, looking straight into mine.

"Hey." he half exclaimed.

"Fancy bumping into *you* here. Your arm okay?"

He looked at me inquisitively.

"Yeah, fine." I mumbled.

I knew pretty much all of Sophie's friends and he definitely was not one of them. He must have seen my confusion as he started to explain his connection to the party.

"I know Joe, he mentioned the party the other day..."

I didn't know Joe that well so that would make sense.

"Who are you here with?" he asked, looking around to see where my friends were.

"I..uh.. sort of know most people here but I came with Kas, Bella and Jimmy. Do you know any of them?"

I couldn't keep myself from staring at his beautiful face. He had near black, thick eyebrows and very dark blue eyes, not a colour I'd ever seen before. When I saw him last I could have sworn they were brown, but having had a close look now, they were definitely blue.

I saw him looking at me questioningly, expecting me to say something but I had missed his answer completely!

"Oh, sorry didn't catch any of that...the music, too loud!" I blabbered.

"Never mind, I think either Kas or Jimmy is here with your drink." he said looking over my shoulder.

I looked up and saw Kas approaching.

"Oh yeah, that's Kasper." I breathed a sigh of relief.

Kas handed me my drink and looked inquisitively at the rather imposing stranger.

"Thanks Kas, this is..." I realised I didn't know his name, but he didn't leave me hanging.

"Zack," he paused a second.

"Nice to meet you."

CHAPTER 4

I shook Kasper's hand whilst looking at him with wide open friendly eyes. I knew perfectly well he thought I was hitting on his girl, but I also knew all the signals to emit to say I was no threat. I had noticed though, that Eliza had not introduced him as her boyfriend. I wondered if Kasper had noticed that too. It didn't look like it, as he visibly relaxed whilst I made some casual conversation about the food, the drinks and commented on some of the girls who were walking by, paying little attention to Eliza. Then I left them to it with an excuse to find Joe and his mates, but not without casually touching Eliza's arm with the promise to return later.

I purposely had chosen Joe, as my background research had revealed he was one of Sophie's friends who didn't mingle with Eliza's friendship group. I now needed to socialise with Joe's group for a bit, to then return to Eliza and get her to relax a bit with me. She was too tense and suspicious of me. She relaxed somewhat when I talked to Kas, though. I had to move quickly, but not too fast for fear of scaring her off. I needed her to trust me enough so we could talk alone. I didn't want to have to take drastic actions if I

28

could avoid it.

I had spotted Joe and his friends and observed them for a while before I approached.

"Hey Joe." I started, having chosen my moment perfectly when his friend was about to leave to get some drinks.

Joe looked at me a bit puzzled but open enough for me to continue.

"We met at some gig a little while ago. I think it was The Psychos or something? It's Zack..."

I looked at him with confidence. Most people will accept that, as they don't trust their own memories, especially when alcohol was involved. I knew Joe went to lots of gigs so I could afford to be a little vague about it.

"Oh yeah, that gig was ace! They're performing near here soon. Was thinking about seeing them again."

Joe turned out to be an easy going bloke and we soon were discussing the finer details of the bass line and awesome guitaring of The Psychos. Just as well I'd listened to some of their tracks beforehand. I had done my homework well.

Joe's friends joined us and Joe introduced me as one of his mates. My plan was working out rather well

at the moment and I was feeling a little smug about it.
I mentioned an upcoming music festival, and they
were all up for it. Brilliant. One of the guys had
handed me a beer which I wasn't planning on drinking
as I had to keep my wits about me, but accepted it
cheerfully.

I kept an eye on Eliza and her friends in the mean
time. She and Bella had a little dance before, and I
had to stop myself from staring at her so I wouldn't get
distracted from my job in hand. That proved fucking
tricky as Eliza intrigued me. She didn't dance in that
overtly sexy way that her friend was displaying, but it
was sexy none the less. Different, as if she was in her
own little world. Maybe it was more cute than sexy.
No, definitely sexy too. Anyway, I had figured out that
Eliza was about to get the drinks, so I made my
excuses to Joe and his mates and walked across to
the drinks area. Sophie's father was there, keeping
an eye on the alcohol consumption. I turned my back
on him and tried to catch Eliza's eye.
I could smell her from a mile off. In the heat of
the party, the scent of her body had managed to
escape the masking effect of the perfume she wore. It
was an uncomplicated, quite musky scent, but mixed
with whatever meds she was taking, covering her true

scent. I managed to tune out my sense of smell a bit as it wasn't the best sensation at a hot and sweaty party like this. Nevertheless, Eliza's scent was distinctly recognisable as one of our own.

We could work out family connections several generations apart, just by the sense of smell if we really tuned in. There are about fifteen family lines within the Sensorians in our country, all with their own distinct scent. Eliza was part of the Mankuzay clan, that was more than clear.

"Hi Zack, enjoying the party?" she asked, pouring herself another cider.

"Yeah, it's a great crowd and good music. You? I saw you having a little dance earlier."

She looked up at me at that, one eye brow raised. She lowered her eye lids and looked at me through her lashes.

"Do you fancy one later?"

She was flirting with me. Her pupils were enlarged, she was touching her hair and moved her hips slightly whilst talking to me. I had to put her off as I didn't want to antagonise Kasper. I didn't need a fucking fight.

"Not much of a dancer, me." I declined.

I definitely shouldn't encourage her, but I did feel

a little tingle in my stomach. I was attracted to her, but nothing could come of it. There were too many important things riding on me successfully persuading her to join us and train her up to be a worthy member of our Sensorian community. It would mean I would have to be strict with her. I could be an extremely hard task master if I had to, and I got the feeling she wasn't going to like that much.

However, we needed her, desperately, in our upcoming mission. And at that moment, as if Markus was watching me, a text came through from him to ask about my progress, reiterating to not waste any time. I reassured him, it was all in hand.

"But I love music. Joe and I and some mates are going to this music festival next weekend. Do you and your friends want to come along? The more the merrier!" I restarted the conversation after our slightly awkward moment.

I turned slightly away from her to get a drink as I had ditched my beer earlier to have the excuse to come up. There was some movement behind Eliza and I saw Kasper, Bella and Jimmy approaching. Eliza turned towards them.

"Yep, sounds great! Here they are, so run it by them now if you want."

I smiled broadly at Kasper and Jimmy and gave Bella a nod.

"I was just telling Eliza about this Music Festival next weekend at Lakeside. Anyone up for it?"

They looked at each other and were all enthusiastic about it and said they would have to check but wanted to go.

"I will set up a Whatsapp group for it, if you want. Just pass me your numbers" I suggested.

They all got their phones out, including Eliza, whose number I was really after. Dullards were so fucking easy to manipulate.

Mission accomplished, I was keen to leave, but hung around the boys and had some banter with them for a while, trying not to pay too much attention to Eliza, or Eli as her friends all seem to call her. She seemed to have gotten the message and was mostly talking to her girlfriends. She certainly still was apt at reading people's signals I thought again, which boded well for her abilities. It'll be a shock for her when she realises what she has been suppressing all these years with the medication she was on. I hoped she would be strong enough.

I said my goodbyes with assurances to let them

know the details of the festival and went to see Joe and his mates for a bit before I left the party. I needed to have some time to think about the next stage of my plan.

CHAPTER 5

OMG I cannot believe I asked Zack to dance! I don't know what came over me, but I was definitely coming on to him! What was wrong with me! I loved Kas, what was I doing! Luckily Zack wasn't having any of it so that saved me from an argument with Kas. Lovely as he was, he didn't like me chatting with other guys, unless we've both known them for ages. He wouldn't stop me, but he'd definitely be in a mood for quite some time, which would then upset me.

Still, a little part of me was a little disappointed that Zack hadn't shown more interest. I'd gotten the impression to start with that he was drawn to me in some way, but his actions had given a different message, so that was that. Anyway, why was I even thinking about this. I was happy with Kas.

Soon after Zack had set up this Whatsapp group for the Festival, he'd left, but our group had stayed till the end. I loved that part of parties, where most people had gone and only the hard core was still there, chilling on the sofa. We had a good deep and meaningful putting the world to rights, before helping Sophie clear up somewhat. We walked home to get some fresh air, me cuddling up to Kas.

Having got home, I was lying on my bed mulling over the evening, not quite ready to go to sleep. My face was twitching a bit, another sign I should talk to my doctor about readjusting the dosage as it seemed to be getting worse lately. Mum would blame it on the alcohol though. Still, I would ask her to make an appointment soon. Then I drifted off to sleep.

A door creaks
Soft footsteps approach
Warmth envelopes me
A dark figure bends towards me
A sigh in my ear
I stop breathing.....

I woke up with a gasp of air. Sweating again. I really hated those dreams. This one was different but they were connected somehow. It was still dark outside so I tried to go back to sleep after a sip of water. I turned my radio on to help distract me enough so I wouldn't dream again. In the end I fell asleep, however, a very restless one. Not surprisingly, I woke up with a bit of a headache and was glad I hadn't arranged anything this morning and could just hang around a bit. I decided not to mention the headache to mum as she would start on one of her

36

tirades against alcohol again.

I just came out of the shower when I heard my phone ping. Probably Kasper. I went to check it but it showed an unknown number, which aroused my curiosity.

Hi. I have something to ask u. Meet me @Copper Cafe for a coffee? I'll be there from 11am. Hope ur hangover's not too bad. Zack

That took me by surprise. I didn't think he was interested in me yesterday. Maybe he genuinely had something to ask, I thought a little naively. I sent him a text saying I'd pop round there a little later. It wouldn't hurt meeting him there to find out what he wanted, would it? I was kidding myself, I really wanted to go and see him and not only to satisfy my curiosity, but I stubbornly brushed that feeling aside. It could do no harm popping in there. I didn't even have to have a drink if I thought better of it once I was there. I carried on getting dressed and stuck some wax in my hair, suddenly a little more preoccupied by what to wear and my appearance.

It was eleven o'clock and I started getting ready to go, when Mum put her head around the door of my bed room.

"Hi sweets, what are you up to today? Don't forget to fit a few hours revision in, please."

She smiled as she knew I hated being reminded about the revision, but she always did anyway. Couldn't help herself she always said.

"Just popping out for a bit. Will do later." I sighed.

I grabbed my phone and bag and made my way over to the cafe.

He was sitting by the window, casually drinking a cup of coffee and reading the paper. *Who still reads a paper nowadays?* My stomach lurched. I nearly turned round and walked straight out. But I couldn't, as he had clocked me already. He stuck his hand up to acknowledge he'd seen me and I walked over, scanning the room at the same time to see who was there, as if I was doing something wrong. How come I felt so guilty about this? I knew deep down why though. I wasn't doing anything wrong...yet, but I was opening doors to roads that could lead to unhappiness one way or another.

"Hey Eliza. Come over. What would you like to drink?" he said, leaving me no choice but to sit and ask for a mint tea.

He folded his paper away and signalled to a waiter who came straight over.

"A mint tea and another coffee for me, please."

"Fancy anything with it?" he addressed me.

I declined. The waiter scuttled off to get our drink whilst Zack looked at me intently. I wasn't sure where to look but decided to look straight back at him. I wasn't the demure type of girl and was curious to find out why he wanted to see me, so I asked him straight up. He actually broke his intense stare for a second and looked down. When he looked up again I noticed a slight hesitation but then determination shone through in his eyes.

"I have some information that may shock or upset you."

He paused to see my reaction I suppose. I sat still, my heart beating a little faster. What the hell was this going to be about? I considered getting up and leaving, running home and forget what I had started by coming here. But I couldn't now. I needed to know.

"Go on." I encouraged him, to my own surprise. *How could my voice come out so confidently?*

"Okay, here it goes..." he seemed to mumble more to himself than me.

He moved his upper body forward so our faces

39

were nearly touching.

"I know your father and he needs your help."

His eyes took on a more guarded look and he was watching me closely. I looked at him, my stomach turning, a wave of sickness hit me.

"What are you saying?" I managed to whisper.

I must have looked panicked or about to be ill as he grabbed my hand as if to make sure I wasn't going to bolt. Part of me wanted to do just that, but I knew I had to find out more.

I hadn't thought about my elusive father for a long time. And when I did, the hole he left gaped open a little wider, so I usually banished him from my thoughts pretty quickly. All I knew was that he disappeared when I was about two and a half years old. I always thought he left because of my weirdness, that it had chased him away, even though mum always assured me that it had nothing to do with me. That, in fact, we had had an extremely strong bond and that he had loved me very much. She'd told me he was never one for commitment. They had a very happy time together which she never had expected to last. He was quite a few years older than her and she had always suspected there was a dark side to him that she'd never seen and never wanted to either.

She practically knew nothing about him, just that she'd loved him deeply and that he had seemed to love her.   She never saw him again after he disappeared one evening, but he had left her that letter, telling her not to worry about him and that she would always be cared for financially as much as he could.

I don't know how long I had been sitting there in silence, staring into space but I suddenly became aware of his hand, still wrapped around mine.

"So, how, why....what do you mean?" I stuttered.

Still not completely sure whether I really wanted to know, or whether I could even trust this Zack, who had come out of nowhere, suddenly claiming he knew my father. And not only that, but that he also needed my help! I couldn't really wrap my head around it. I could see Zack was trying to speak, but suddenly felt the need to get up and go. I didn't owe my father anything. I felt anger growing inside me, like a fire from the pit of my stomach, panic engulfed me.

"Do you know what. I can't do this!" I managed to squeak out.

I got up, needing to get away and get some air, but I had only made half a move when Zack, still holding onto my hands, more firmly now, moved

41

closer and told me to sit back down at once. His eyes demanding and in no way could I disobey them. He had such a force field around him, but still, it was hard to explain why I stayed.

CHAPTER 6

I could see she started to panic and I had to take charge before she ran off. If that happened, it would fuck up my chance to talk to her before she had time to think too much about it. She might decide not to want to listen to the rest. I told her to sit the fuck back down and she responded as expected. It shocked her but she was lucid now and I could reach her again. I wouldn't have to regret my decision to be upfront with her.

I had a little smile to myself with the prospect of telling my sister Zaphire, who'd find it extremely annoying. She hated that side of me. She frequently told me I was a dominant dickhead.

"Right, nice to have you back Eliza. Are you ready to listen to what I have to say?"

She nodded almost imperceptibly. I could see she was having a little internal struggle to understand herself. Probably wondering why she was still sitting here, but definitely willing to listen.

"It's going to be difficult to take it all in, but bear with me. It's very important that you know what's going on. Not only will you be able to help your father if you decide to, it will also help you understand yourself better."

I paused to gauge her reaction. She looked less shocked and more curious now.

"Good." I thought out loud and I carried on.

"Your father used to be an important man in our community..."

"What community, what...." Eliza interrupted me.

I had to be strict.

"No questions for now Eliza, let me speak first." I said firmly.

A glimmer of defiance sparked in her eyes, but I carried on nevertheless.

"He then decided he had enough of our way of life and took a break from it. Controversial in our community, but he did. He hooked up with several women but seemed to stick with this one girl, several years younger than him. That was Alice and fairly soon she fell pregnant with you. The leaders of our community kept close tabs on him but never interfered. He'd had a tough time before he left, when he had to deal with the death of a close friend, who had gone off grid and committed a crime. The type that in our community carries the death penalty."

Her eyes nearly jumped out of her face on hearing that, but I quickly continued.

44

"Our leaders felt he needed some time away from us and that in time he would choose to return, which is what happened when you were about two and a half years old. They had expected him to bring you with him, but he didn't. He pleaded for you not to be involved with us and he said he didn't think you had the Sensorian gift anyway. That you were just a Dullard, like your mum. The leaders took his word for that, rather foolishly in my opinion, but he'd been a very well respected member of our community so they left you with your mum. Everything was going fine for years up until last week. Your father disappeared without a trace and that's highly unusual. We're extremely good at tracking people down and it is almost impossible to shake us off, hence we are expecting foul play. We think Rick could have been abducted by a criminal organisation or is somehow involved. All our best people are on the case because, if someone is using your father for criminal or terrorist activities, it could be disastrous. Your people wouldn't stand a chance. And this is where you come in, Eliza."

She had been listening intently and I could see she was dying to ask some questions.

"You look confused." I offered.
She closed her eyes slightly.

"Confused? You are kidding me, that's the understatement of the year!"

She let out a big sigh.

"I don't even know where to begin!? Zack. You sound like someone out of a flipping spy film! I have no idea what to make of this. What 'community'? What do you mean 'your people', Dullards!? What 'Sensorian gift' am I supposed to have or not have according to my father? It makes no sense what so ever! I..." I interrupted her.

"Do you want me to answer any of these questions? If you do, you need to let me do so, so slow down a little."

I could see she was really struggling to keep it together again, but she did stop and looked up at me.

"Yes, yes of course." she sighed.

"It better not be some sick joke though" she looked at me fiercely.

This was going to be tougher than I'd thought.

"Look Eliza, this is no fucking joke. I promise. It's as serious as it gets, so let's start again. What question would you like me to answer first?"

CHAPTER 7

I looked at the guy in front of me with bewilderment. He'd just thrown my world into turmoil. What I'd expected to be a bit of a flirtatious chat about the upcoming music festival trip he said he was organising, turned out to be a life changing event. I could not get my head around it at all. I had wanted to leave, run away even, after Zack had told me he knew my father and that he needed my help. Somehow he managed to make me stay, in fact, I was rather annoyed at myself that I let him talk to me like he was my superior or something.

Even though it all sounded so ridiculous, with all this talk about 'our community' and 'Sensorian gifts' and everything, part of me felt he was telling the truth. But I had to be sure. I wasn't going to be targeted by some weirdo from a commune or something, so I wanted to ask question after question, not hiding my scepticism.

"Okay, fair enough." I said after his rebuke of me firing questions like a machine gun at him .

"Tell me about this community of yours to start with then. Is it like a commune?"

He briefly smiled at that, looking at me quizzically,

or was it a glimmer of admiration? I hoped the latter. I was still quite keen to impress him somehow. He took a deep breath and started to explain.

"The people in our Community, Sensorians, have a special gift. One that we suspect you harbour as well, but is concealed by the medicines you are taking.

We have a heightened sense of everything around us. We can feel and smell other people's emotions, their moods and feelings. We can see things in minute detail, we pick up on every micro movement people make, their body language, facial expressions, things that people are not even aware of themselves.

Our sense of smell is almost as good as a dog, and our hearing rivals that of an elephant. The best amongst us can predict near future events with quite some accuracy, based on interpreting all the information coming into our brain at an incredible pace."

I had to stifle a little snigger. It sounded all so ludicrous. He looked at me a little annoyed but carried on.

"As you can imagine, all these skills make us quite unusual. Dullards are often scared of us, as we fall outside the norm. In the past people like us were at best social outcasts, but in extreme cases have been burnt as witches, put into asylums, even prisons.

48

Some of us were forced to work for corrupt kings, governments, criminals, even the mafia. A group of us started our Community to protect our people, train people so they know how to disguise their gift and function in society without being persecuted or used. We like to stay under the radar. It evolved into our secret Community as it stands now."

He paused, and I took the opportunity to react.

"So, you are saying that quite possibly my mental illness is actually not an illness at all?"

I thought back of my early childhood and the amazing albeit overwhelming feelings and sensations I used to get, all dampened down after I started taking medicines when I was diagnosed. It used to feel breathtaking and I sometimes longed for those very intense experiences. Maybe now, with Zack's help I could experience them again.

On the other hand, this could all be the inventions of a maniac. I needed to know more. Zack observed me closely before he answered my question.

"We believe you have the gift. But there is only one way of finding out for sure and that is to come off your medicines. Of course we can't do anything without your mother's permission, so we have to bring your mum into this too, which is unprecedented. Some of the Sensorians in our community weren't in favour of this decision, fearing it to be unsafe. Markus, our Number One leader, persisted and managed to persuade the majority. He really must think you are worth it..."

"And you?" I interjected.

"Do you think I am worth the risk?"

I understood it must have felt incredibly risky for these people to expose themselves to people outside their community, if it did even exist.

"My opinion doesn't matter. As far as I'm concerned I have no opinion on this case. I do what I'm ordered to do and I do it to the best of my ability."

But I saw him look away slightly and felt he wasn't speaking the complete truth. It didn't matter anyway. As he said, he was just doing his job.

"So, how many of these 'gifted' people are there in the world? And where are they all? Do you all live together or something? How does it..."

"Whoa whoa, you are bombarding me again, Eliza."

He fixed his eyes on me to calm me down.

"About seven hundred and fifty in the world that we know off. There are ninety seven of us in our country, ninety eight with you included, and most of us live together in a compound. We run businesses and services there to make our money, but not all of us work there. Some of us work in the outside world. There are a couple of us who work in a private hospital as well. We have our own rules that we abide by, and we have a very accomplished team of lawyers who manage our slight indiscretions as we do have some rules and laws that are not recognised under the national law."

I raised my eyebrows at him

"Like the death penalty you were talking about?"

He nodded. I think I should have felt outrage, but I didn't. I still scorned him.

"Slight indiscretions, hey?"

My voice dripped with sarcasm. He came back quite harshly, obviously feeling defensive.

"It has to be like that! For our own good!"

He almost spat the words at me. I could see he wasn't going to say more about the matter so I didn't push him on it any further.

"Why me? Why do you need me in all of this?"

How could I, a slightly awkward misfit of a girl, be of any help for them whatsoever. I didn't even know my father. I wasn't even sure if I *wanted* to know my father.

"You're the key to establishing contact with Rick.

You need to agree to come to our Community. Meet Markus, and he will explain all."

"He better do." I mumbled.

"So.... "Dullards"...?" I questioned mockingly. It actually made him go slightly red in the face.

I felt a bit useless, I really didn't know what to do with all the information I was given. I needed to talk to my mum, if she even would believe any of this. It was eerie how he intuitively answered my unspoken worries. But then I should really have expected that considering what I just learned about his gift.

"Don't worry about your mum. Markus is already on the case. I wouldn't be surprised if he has managed to arrange a meeting with her as we speak. We'll work through all of this together Eliza."

I believed him. His calm and matter of fact approach had made me feel I could trust him. He just exuded confidence. It was hard to not be swayed by whatever he said.

CHAPTER 8

I decided to take Eliza home. I felt she'd had enough. She had been on an emotional roller coaster, and was saturated with new and frightening concepts. She needed to process everything to make a sensible decision. However, that was not to be. I had been right about Markus' proactive decision to contact Eliza's mum as I saw his car outside of their house. I told Eliza and she didn't take it very well. She looked scared. I gently took her hand in mine and turned her face towards me, so I could look into her eyes.

"It'll be fine. Markus is amazing and I'm here with you. We'll work it out together. You're not alone."

She took a deep breath and relaxed a little as we walked up to the door.

I could hear Markus talking.

"We believe she's ready for this, Alice. Zack will be with her every step of the way, and he's our best trainer and coach. He will protect and guide her. She'll be in good hands, trust me."

Alice was not in a receptive mood. She was on the defence, like a lioness protecting her cub.

"How can I trust you! Coming in here under false

pretences and then landing *this* on me!"

She was wildly gesticulating to underline her words. Suddenly, she realised Eliza and I were approaching the house and started working Markus towards the door.

"Please go now, I don't want her to see you or know anything about this!"

"That's a little too late." Eliza said when we entered.

"It's okay Mum. Let's hear them out. I need to know more, and I would like you to help me decide."

She walked over to her mum and gave her a hug.

"Don't you want to know?" Eliza pleaded.

I could feel the hostile atmosphere dissipate. Alice relented and motioned us through to the living room.

"Take a seat," she offered.

"And you must be Zack." she said with a sideways glance to Markus.

I could tell she thought I was a little young to be the 'best coach' so I had to convince her to trust me.

"Yes Ma'am, I am." I said as I shook her hand.

"Pleased to meet you. You've done an amazing job raising Eliza. She has impressed me in many ways, but mainly with her open mindedness and willingness to listen to me, but with a healthy dose of

54

scepticism."

I could see Alice wasn't having any of it. She raised her eyebrows at me and turned back to Markus.

"So this *boy* is meant to protect and train my daughter? You have *got* to come up with something better than that!"

She looked me over again; her lips forming a mocking smile. Markus took over and reassured her that I was indeed the best *man* for the job and that, though still young, I had proven myself in numerous occasions, even saving people's lives.

I started feeling a little awkward. I had never really heard Markus sing my praises before, as normally he just expected the best and that's what he got out of me with hardly a word of appreciation. I caught his eyes and they bored into me. They told me not to get used to it and not to get cocky. He didn't have to worry. I knew my place.

"So this is my plan," Markus broke the impasse.

"Eliza will come with us straight away as time is of the essence. She'll start her mission and training on the job soon after we have weaned her off her medication and when we have received a bit more intel on the last movements of your ex-partner." He turned towards Eliza.

"Your father."

I implored Eliza not to interrupt by touching her hand, but I hadn't counted on Alice butting in. I should have. Eliza clearly didn't get it from a stranger. She shuddered and spoke with confidence.

"That can't happen. Eliza is in the middle of her exams! Her father will just have to hang in there. I won't allow him to ruin this for her, or you for that matter."

I checked out Markus. He wasn't used to being spoken to like that and I dreaded his reaction. However, he looked calm and I didn't feel any tension coming from him. I truly loved watching this man at work. He'd taught me so much.

So instead of losing his patience, like he would have done had it been one of us, he calmly took Alice by the hand and spoke.

"Look Alice, everything will be fine. Eliza is not going to miss out on her exams. We'll make time for her to study and we will arrange for her to do her exams in our compound. It has been done before and it won't be a problem. If the timing is wrong and interferes with our mission, she'll be allowed to do them at any time as we can guarantee she won't have contact with anyone who has sat the exams, until she's sat them too."

Eliza looked troubled by this and I could feel her tensing. Why can't these people just fucking listen and do what they're fucking told. They can trust Markus. He knows best and the sooner they accept that, the better! I knew it wasn't going to be like that though, they were brought up in a different type of society than us. I took a deep breath to calm down and made myself ask Eliza what was bothering her. At least she had waited to be asked.

"Uh..., how exactly are you going to make sure I don't see or contact any of my friends or indeed anyone of my age sitting these exams?"

She looked at Markus, but I answered.

"I will be with you 24/7 Eliza, strict orders. No contact with the outside world unless it's part of our mission or training. No socialising or access to computers and mobiles."

I saw the horror in her face, bless her. She really had no idea how far our powers and influence stretched.

"However, it's only temporarily and hopefully we'll find your father safe and sound soon." Markus tried to reassure, obviously not happy with my abrupt answer.

I was sure to be reprimanded for that later.

Markus continued.

"Listen Alice, we'll take good care of your daughter.

We always look after our own. We need her and I'm sure Eliza wants to help her father and keep him safe. With her on board, our chances of contacting him sooner and find out what is going on, are so much better. She'll be able to tune into him better than we can due to their genetic bond. If we don't get to the bottom of this as soon as possible it could spell disaster either for your father or for our whole Sensorian community."

Alice looked at Eliza and nodded.

"I suppose I owe you and your father that. There certainly seemed to be more than just a normal connection between the two of you, and it does explain how he always understood you so well. But Eliza, (she took both hands in hers) only if you're sure you want to do this. Remember this is the man who caused us both a lot of pain, but we also loved him deeply. So, if you do, I will support you a hundred percent."

Then she looked at me with fierce passion.

"And *you*, you better look after her with your life."

I looked straight back into her eyes, not shirking away from my responsibilities.

"Her life will be mine."

And I meant it.

Eliza sighed a deep sigh.

"I do want to find my father. I'm not sure how I'm going to react, but I want to have the opportunity to confront him. So yes, I'm in."

Eliza had decided. Clearly with ulterior motives, but that didn't matter for now.

And that was that. Markus and Alice worked though the paper work, procedures and signatures whilst I took Eliza to her room to pack her stuff. There was no turning back now.

Eliza looked up at me lost, looking around for the things she needed to pack, her face an open book. Something was bothering her majorly. She needed to work on hiding her feelings I thought, before asking if she was okay.

"I need to see Kas and Bella before I go."

She was struggling with her emotions when she uttered their names. They meant a lot to her and she wasn't going to like my answer. Remembering Markus's disapproval of my previous bluntness I tried to be more gentle when I answered. Something that didn't come naturally to me at all.

"Eliza, I know these people are very important to you..."

"I love them, Zack!"

She nearly choked on her words.

"I know Eliza" I said as gently as I could muster.

"Your mum will talk to them. She'll tell them your dad has made contact and is ill and wanted to see you as soon as possible. You took a plane this evening to see him. You can't see them now, but they'll understand and they will be there for you when you come back."

Eliza shook her head violently.

"No, no, you don't understand! I need to see Kas! I need to say goodbye! What if something happens! It will destroy him!" she pleaded desperately.

I sighed before answering, losing my gentle tone already.

"He'll be fine, and Bella too. Nothing is going to happen to you, remember, I'll protect you. You just can't see them now."

She looked distraught so I softened the blow a little.

"But I'll ask Markus if you can have permission to FaceTime them later."

She carried on packing but couldn't hide her feelings, silent tears rolling down her face. I wanted to give her a big hug, she looked so vulnerable. I didn't of course. I had to tune out somewhat (or shield as we call it) as her intense emotions were physically hurting me.

"Don't even think about it!" I glared at her.

She'd spotted her phone on her desk, and her guilty scent spoke volumes. I picked it up and slotted it in my pocket. Eliza was furious.

The sooner we'd be on our way, the better. But by the time Eliza had packed all her belongings and Markus had gone through all the paperwork with Alice, it was late in the afternoon already. Alice had provided us with a lovely lunch earlier and did invite us to stay for dinner too, but we had to leave eventually. Seeing Eliza say goodbye to her mum was heartbreaking. It surprised me how sad I felt for her. Markus on the other hand looked stoically on and decided to break up their everlasting hug. He had booked a hotel for us to stay in for the night, and he wanted to get a move on. I knew he was right. Eliza needed to get off those drugs and start her training. That would give her something to focus on and help her deal with her feelings. I couldn't wait to start working on her. Maybe a little too eager, I wondered.

CHAPTER 9

Saying goodbye to my mum was the hardest thing I'd ever done in my life. I couldn't think about her without bursting into tears. Both Zack and Markus had done their best to distract me but as soon as there was a quiet moment I fell back into my dark hole, and eventually they had given up and left me to wallow.

After a very awkward journey and night in the hotel, where I had to share a room with Zack, we arrived at the compound. Zack took me to the room I would be staying in. I looked at my surroundings with awe. My room looked like something straight out of the Good Homes magazine. Everything beautifully modern with a perfectly made bed and furniture arranged in such a way it looked like no one had ever even touched it. Still, it felt more homely then a hotel room. Another opening led to a little room which housed another bed and a kitchenette hid in the corner.

The whole journey here felt like a dream. I could still not quite fathom how this all happened. The whole thing had gone so fast. Everything had started to feel real when I'd seen Markus, a tall imposing man in his late forties whose age was only given away by his slightly greying side burns, talking to mum in our house. Up to that point the whole thing could've just been the ramblings of a slightly deranged guy, but that was undisputedly not the case. Now I found myself here, in this place, far away from the comforts of home and my mum. My calm exterior completely belied the inner turmoil I was feeling.

I clocked Zack sitting nonchalantly in one of the chairs, leafing through some magazine or the other. I think he really meant it when he said he would be there 24/7. He'd been at my side nonstop. The dude didn't seem to need the toilet, ever! Or anything else.

His promise to talk to Markus about a FaceTime call with Kas and Bella hadn't materialised yet, so I decided to ask. I really wanted to speak to them, mostly to make sure they wouldn't worry. Zack looked at me, but I couldn't work out his expression at all. That was unusual for me, so he must be hiding it from me. That wasn't good. It made me think he wasn't planning on asking Markus at all.

"You *are* going to ask him, aren't you?" I stared at him hard.

He was fidgeting now.

"It's very important to me and I won't be able to focus if this call wasn't to happen..." I laid it on thick.

"I don't think Markus will let you, but let's go and ask now. Get it over and done with."

He stood up reluctantly and motioned me to follow him.

"Please let me do the talking though," he said curtly but with a pleading look in his eyes.

Zack knocked on Markus's door and I was surprised to hear a woman's voice inviting us in. His room was light and airy, not at all what I had expected, and in the middle of the room stood a striking looking woman. Her gentle eyes exuded confidence, and looked straight into mine. There was no hiding from her. Her blonde hair pinned up in an immaculate bun, something that I could never achieve with my hair.

"Hello, you must be Eliza."

She took my hand in hers and gave a firm shake.

"I'm Laura, Markus's wife and co-leader."

She smiled at what must have been my surprised face.

"Did no one tell you? Typical men!"

She flung an accusing glance at Zack, who looked sheepishly back at her.

"I suppose Zack hasn't told you either that I'm

also..."

She stopped mid sentence responding to a poignant look Zack had thrown her. I couldn't work out what it meant and she quickly continued, changing the subject.

"Anyway, nice to meet you at last. I've heard a lot about you. Have you settled in okay in your room?" she asked kindly.

"Getting there," I answered a little hesitantly.

She immediately picked up on that and asked if there was anything else I needed to help me feel comfortable. I looked at Zack who was shaking his head menacingly. I ignored him.

"Well, there was something I was promised to get access to, but it hasn't happened yet and it would make me feel so much better and more relaxed if I were able to."

I saw Zack rolling his eyes at me, looking grim.

"Laura, Ma'am, nothing was promised. I can assure you. I'm sorry, we shouldn't be bothering you with this anyway. Where's Markus? We'll talk to him."

He looked apologetically at Markus's wife and accusingly at me. However, Laura waved his comments aside and addressed me again.

"Okay honey, what is it that you so desire to make you feel comfortable?"

I took a moment to consider but decided to go for it and ask her straight out if I could have some FaceTime with my boyfriend and best friend. I wasn't prepared for her reaction as she looked such a kind and sensible lady. But now I understood Zack's reaction. She stared at me, her furrowed brow making her look quite fearsome.

"You really have no idea, do you?" she hissed through gritted teeth.

"Has no one informed you of the gravity of the situation and the need to be totally off grid? No access to any communication devices at all! If the wrong people found out you, the daughter of Rick, were here? It could endanger everyone!"

Then she turned her attention to Zack.

"I'm disappointed in you, you of all people should know better than to promise things that are not possible".

Zack straightened his back and got ready to defend his actions.

"Ma'am," he started, but was interrupted by Markus entering the room.

He felt the tension and somehow managed to diffuse it in an instant. I could see why Zack admired this man. He immediately noticed something was off

66

and took charge.

"Right, Zack and Eliza, come with me. You can tell me about what just happened and we'll find a solution. Laura, don't worry. Whatever Zack did wrong, he'll learn from it. Remember, we were young and inexperienced once. Can you brief the team please and find out if anything else has been discovered?"

Laura had regained control over her emotions and swooped out of the room, still glaring at Zack.

"Zacharya, what the hell was that about?" Markus started when he closed the door to his office.

It was a spacious, modern looking room with a bookcase full of books, making the place a little less sterile. I felt a bit sorry for Zack now and was about to say something, but he was quicker than me.

"Sorry Sir, I apologise. I told Eliza that I was going to ask you if she could use FaceTime to talk to Kasper and Bella, knowing full well that that was going to be impossible. I felt it necessary at the time as Eliza was ...."

And he looked at me when he said this

"...inconsolable and rather insistent."

He stared at the floor, not wanting to look Markus in the eye.

I didn't understand what the big deal was. They

were behaving as if he'd broken the law! All I wanted to do was reassure my friends, which probably would stop them bothering my mum or get suspicious. I decided to make my case to Markus, but when I looked at him I couldn't get my words out. What was it with this man? In any case, it wasn't necessary as, to my and Zack's surprise, Markus had decided for himself it might actually be a good idea.

"Under strict supervision, you may make a call on FaceTime. You must tell Zack exactly what you plan to say and if any awkward questions arise you must defer a straight answer. Never be precise, just leave it open ended. Remember it's for your own safety and for all of us that you remain underground."

Decided, just like that. I wondered what he was going to tell Laura, as I guessed she wouldn't be pleased. Markus wasn't finished yet. He beckoned Zack.

"A word please. Now."

He motioned for one of the girls working just outside his office, to come and 'look after' me, though I was never out of his field of vision.

I took the time to have a good look around the place. Computers were everywhere and people tapping away behind them. One area was busy with people congregated around a big screen, quietly but urgently talking. I wondered what they had found out, but I didn't dare leave the seat that Karen had put me on whilst she was dealing with a phone call. I could see Zack coming out of the office with a stoic look on his face, clearly not in the best of moods.

"Let's go to our room and talk about this fucking call you want to make. We need to get this over and done with so you can concentrate on coming off your medicines, as that's our priority now."

I stood up and glanced at the girl on the phone.

"It's okay Eliza, Karen knows you're supposed to come with me."

He signalled something to her and she smiled and nodded.

"Are you okay? What did Markus want? You're not in trouble I hope?"

I tried to read his face, but it gave nothing away. He ignored me anyway.

"Are all these people working on my father's disappearance?" I dared ask after a few minutes of silence.

"The majority is." Zack said, but didn't seem to want to expand any further on that.

I persevered though.

"So, are they any closer to locating him?" I continued.

He looked at me and sighed.

"For fuck sake. You are a curious pup, aren't you? We'll fill you in with all the details later, when you're ready. First, we need to see how you deal with coming off your meds. And if you..."

He stopped, but I knew what he was going to say.

"If I really do have the gift?" I finished the sentence for him.

"Yeah, and that." he reluctantly admitted.

"But I am fairly sure you have. We just need to be careful."

"And what happens if I haven't?" I genuinely wanted to know, but Zack just grunted.

"Really Eliza, focus on what we're about to do and stop wondering about the 'what ifs' and so on. Think about what you will tell Kasper and Bella."

God, he was annoying. Why does he have to be so evasive!

"Zack, I can deal with the truth, just tell me what would happen if it turns out I can't help you."

He just looked at me and wouldn't budge.

I had to concentrate now on what I was going to say to Kasper and Bella. This wasn't going to be easy.

Once I had 'explained' what happened, or rather told our fabricated story to Bella, under the careful eye of Zack, she was really supportive and said she would visit my mum to keep an eye on her. She didn't understand why I couldn't keep in contact, but seemed to accept it. Kas, on the other hand, wasn't having any of it. He wouldn't drop it and urged me to at least send him a text. I mumbled something about my phone playing up but in the end I had to say I would definitely try again, suffering a disapproving scowl from Zack.

It was going to be hard for Kas. He didn't like to be away from me for long, and I wouldn't put it past him to try and contact me or even try and find me. I wasn't going to tell Zack that, as it would worry him and I feared they would take some extreme measures to prevent him from doing that. I didn't think they would hurt him, but with the grim look on Laura's face still lingering in my brain, I couldn't be absolutely sure either. I didn't want my choice to help these people to have a negative impact on the people I loved.

"Done?" Zack broke my thoughts.

I wanted to know what all the stress was about with Laura as Markus seemed to have taken my request quite calmly as opposed to her.

71

"Hmmm..., yeah." I stalled.

"What is Laura's story? Why was she so uptight? She seemed so kind, but turned quite ferociously towards us. It felt a bit weird."

I fully expected Zack to deflect my question again, but to my surprise he didn't. Instead he sighed and explained.

"Laura's just careful; she's been through a lot and is extremely protective over us. She can't help but overreact sometimes when she feels we are threatened, but it's all born out of a deep caring for our kind. She's an amazing organiser and leader and will do anything to protect us. And I do mean anything."

He spoke with absolute reverence in his voice.

"She'll probably come and find you later and explain."

That filled me with dread, as no matter what Zack had said, I was scared of her. Zack took me by the hand and reassured me.

"Don't worry about it. You need to fully concentrate on your 'detox' now. Let's grab some food and then look at the paperwork about what to expect."

Food sounded great, I suddenly remembered how hungry I was! I hadn't exactly eaten much since Zack and Markus had burst into my life.

CHAPTER 10

Eliza was reading through the notes and occasionally asking me for some clarification, but seemed to take it all in, not particularly phased. I really liked her for that. So down to earth and ready to try anything she needed to. Her apprehensive feelings about the Laura incident had dissipated as she was concentrating on the task in hand. I could really feel her worry about Laura earlier, but she wouldn't have anything to fear from her as long as she didn't endanger us.

"So, everywhere it says to reduce the withdrawal symptoms of Risperdal you need to taper off usage slowly over a period of months. I take it that's not what we're doing?"

She didn't look at me and I knew she wasn't looking for an answer.

"It's going to be a tough time Eliza. You're going to feel ill, possibly vomit, feel hot and sweaty or cold and shivery. Basically, flu like symptoms, which will last for about five days maximum."

I tried to make it sound as if it was something that she's experienced and conquered before, not to worry her unnecessarily.

"What about the delusions and hallucination and a possible return to psychotic illness? That scares me."

Now, she did look at me, unsure about what to make of that.

"As you probably are not suffering from a mental illness, that won't happen. You'll be confused and overwhelmed with the return of your gift, though. It may feel like you are going mad, but I can assure you, you'll be able to tell the difference. You're in safe hands and I'll be here for you."

I hoped I was reassuring enough. Maybe I should get Zaphire; she was so much better at this touchy feely stuff. She'd be able to support Eliza and I could focus on the practical side of things and the discipline to make it work. We always make a great team and I decided to text Markus for permission to ask her. He answered almost within minutes saying; if I really felt I needed her he would let her, but it would have to wait till the day after tomorrow. That wasn't too bad, probably just when it would be worst for Eliza. She hadn't taken any medication since her last dose the evening before we took her, and I could see little signs starting to appear in Eliza's body.

"Err, it says here that the effects of the drugs may not totally go for weeks and that I might not feel 'normal' again for months!"

Eliza glanced at me with a slightly panicked look in her eyes. The girl needed to fucking relax.

"You will be able to cope with it. You might not be able to use your gift to its full potential but it'll be good enough. There's so much to learn, but let's just get through the initial obstacle of getting the drugs out of your system. Then we'll deal with the next step."

"Okay," she sighed.

"It's just... it's a big thing, you know."

She looked a bit lost.

I kept forgetting she was new to all of this. Her head must be spinning, besides the withdrawal symptoms. She isn't like us who have been living in this set up since we were little. It was time to take some control. It makes people feel safe.

"Right, enough of the reading now. You need to take a shower and go to bed. You must sleep whilst you still feel reasonably good. It will help you cope better."

I gave her a towel and ushered her into the bathroom.

"You have 10 minutes. I'll come in if you're not out. There's a clock in the bathroom. Don't be late. No locking the door either."

"Hang on a minute..." she started, but I cut her off.

"The ten minutes start now."

I heard her mumbling under her breath that she hadn't been told to shower like this since she was little and we were definitely going to have words over it. She kept forgetting us Sensorians can hear far better than Dullards and mumbling and whispering will hold no secrets. It's quite funny really.

"Don't waste your breath Eliza, it's non-negotiable." I shouted through the door.

I could hear her grunt in frustration.

After ten minutes exactly, she poked her head around the corner of the door and asked sheepishly for her pyjamas. She nodded at the bed where she'd put them earlier and I obliged.

"Good time keeping." I said appreciatively.

She just snorted. I smiled a bit to myself, she has so much to learn, poor girl. She snuggled into her bed and was literally asleep within ten minutes. I took the opportunity to grab a shower myself, but not without locking the bedroom door first. She wouldn't like it if she found out, but I was under no circumstance going to have her wandering around on her own. Even if she was fast asleep now, you never know what would make her stir and wake up. I'd been admonished enough in the past days and wasn't going to risk another bollocking.

The hot water of the powerful shower felt good and I felt my muscles relax and realised how tense I'd felt. There was a lot riding on this mission and how well Eliza would do. Not everyone was backing Markus's actions, but I knew it was the only way. It wasn't just finding Rick, we could just about handle that ourselves. It was figuring out what Rick was up to that was going to be the part where Eliza would be important. We hadn't worked out yet whether Rick was taken against his will and hence vulnerable, or whether he'd disappeared by choice and was mixed up in something criminal. I wasn't quite sure how or when Markus was intending to make Eliza privy to these suspicions and that it will be her task to find out.

With any normal person it's fairly easy for us to work out whether someone is lying, or deceiving us, but Rick is a master at disguising his intentions. He would know exactly what we'd be looking for to catch him out. It would be much harder for him to do this with his daughter. Blood relations are extremely difficult to fool. However, a lot depends on how well I train Eliza and with that thought I could feel the tension creep back into my body. I told myself to keep focussing on one step at a time and not to ponder about what would happen next and what the implications would be. I really should listen to my own advice for once!

I put some clean clothes on and went back into the bedroom, where Eliza was still asleep, however, a bit fitful and she was mumbling in her sleep. She was talking about Kas, telling him not to come. As I thought, she was worried about him not listening to her request not to contact her. I noticed it during their FaceTime, though Eliza had done her best to hide her worry. I might have to take care of that, before he can jeopardise our mission. I didn't think I needed to do anything drastic. If he tried, we would intercept anyway, and just a stern warning that any contact might make her fail all her exams as it is our duty to report any breaches of her isolation, would probably be enough. Anyway, I was aware of the possibility he might try to contact her so that made the risk almost negligible. I would deal with it if it happened.

Eliza tossed and turned and sweat was dripping from her forehead. I got a cool wet cloth from the bathroom and dabbed her face with it. I thought she might have woken up, but she seemed to be fast asleep. I decided to just sit at her bedside for a bit longer, before I'd take a nap myself.

CHAPTER 11

I hear heavy breathing in my ear
I feel my legs and arms gently swaying
from side to side
Am I scared?
My heart is beating hard or is it his?
I try and look up to see his face
but my eyes won't open
I try and try
Who is this man with his familiar smell
carrying me like a rag doll
Am I in danger?

I woke up but not in the panicked state I'm normally in when I wake from these dreams. It was different this time. I was somewhat aware that I was dreaming and I didn't feel as threatened as I normally do. There was something familiar about it, like it was a memory, not a scary dream. I felt hot, but noticed a damp cloth covering my forehead. That felt nice. I focussed on what was around me and saw Zack sitting on the edge of my bed, looking like he might need some sleep himself. His eyes searched my face presumably for signs of trouble or illness.

"How are you feeling?" he asked a bit brusquely, but I knew he was concerned for me.

"Fine." I grumbled.

I was feeling a bit queasy and dizzy, but not too bad. The answer didn't satisfy him. He pressed on asking what exactly I was feeling and I thought it better just to say as he would know anyway if I were trying to hold back. I was slowly realising there was no hiding my feelings from him. He just knew when I wasn't exactly truthful.

It was scary to think I was going to be able to do that too when I got through this and if I had the gift. I hadn't noticed any changes in my awareness of things though and suddenly felt a wave of panic engulf me. What if it turned out I didn't have this gift and would just start hallucinating again. What would happen to me? I started to sweat again and felt hot and cold at the same time. Zack noticed my change of relative calm to feeling out of control.

"Eliza, lay down and breath. Just try and relax and let it happen."

He got up to change my damp cloth for a fresh one and when he moved his scent suddenly overwhelmed me. I hadn't noticed it before, but he smelled divine if you could say that about a person. It wasn't a chemical smell, it was earthy and fresh at the same time. It made me feel comfortable but something else awakened in me as well. The fancy I took to him when I first met him and made me want to flirt with him, came flooding back but a hundred times stronger. I wanted him and I wanted him now.

When he came back and tried to put the cloth back on my brow, I couldn't help myself. I sat up a bit and grabbed his face. I needed to kiss him so badly! My urge was rudely interrupted by two hands pushing my face away and I was pushed back down on the bed.

"Eliza, control yourself!" Zack said firmly with a stern look on his face.

"You need to calm yourself down, girl."

His eyes now looked amused and a little smile played around his lips. It suddenly dawned on me what I had just done!

"Oh no, Zack, I don't know....I am so sorry, I, I didn't mean to.... your scent, I...."

That's all I was able to stutter. I couldn't quite make sense of it in my head. What on earth had just happened? I was so embarrassed; I turned around and wouldn't look at him again. I could feel my whole face go completely red.

"I..., I need to sleep." I mumbled as I pulled the

duvet up to hide under.

I wanted to crawl away and forget the whole thing. But I couldn't. His smell was right there and driving me absolutely crazy. I decided the best thing was to breathe through my mouth to try and avoid it. It was kind of working. However, I was uber aware of him, sitting next to me on the bed.

"Could you just move away from me? Please?" I pleaded with a small voice.

What on earth must he think of me. This was excruciating.

"Sure." I heard him say and felt him move away.

"Go back to sleep. We'll talk later."

I wasn't sure if I ever wanted to talk about any of it. I just wanted to pretend it never happened.

I must have dozed off after a while because when I woke next, some light peeped through the blinds and Zack was asleep on the other bed. Though, as soon as I moved, he opened his eyes too. He didn't move or say anything, probably waiting to see whether I'd doze off again. I suddenly remembered what I had done last night and quickly closed my eyes again. I couldn't look at him.

I felt so unwell though, I had to go to the toilet so there was nothing for it, I just had to get up and go. I told myself to breathe through my mouth, but I couldn't help taking a little sniff, to see if it was still there. I stopped breathing straight away as the smell made me dizzy instantly. Was this it? The gift of enhanced senses didn't seem so enticing any more. I told myself to focus and go to the bathroom

I managed to get there but felt as sick as a dog. My head was spinning and saliva filled my mouth. I knew this feeling and got to the toilet just in time. I hate being sick and was crying with it. God, I felt rough. I felt very sorry for myself.

I noticed movement behind me and then a hand stroked my hair and moved it out of my face. I wasn't sure if I could handle being near him, but I had no strength left to say or do anything, so I just let him take care of me. I heard him breathe as if his face was right near my face, but in fact he wasn't all that near. He had put my hair in pony tail and had moved away a little, I presume to give me a bit of privacy. To me, however, it felt like he was right next to me still. Another wave of nausea came over me and for a moment all I could do was retch and not give a damn about where he was.

"Hey, here's some water. Take a swig." I heard

him say to me, but I couldn't move.

Next thing I knew I felt the water touching my lips and I took a little swig.

Then everything went black.

CHAPTER 12

"Fuck!" I cursed when she collapsed.

She didn't lose consciousness for very long, but it totally disoriented her. She looked at me with dozy eyes, I wasn't sure if she registered who I was or whether she even noticed someone was there at all. I lifted her up and put her back in bed. I called the resident doctor to come and check up on her. He looked her over and managed to talk to her a bit to which she responded. A good sign. He took me to one side and reassured me she was fine, just a bit dehydrated and slightly low blood sugar levels. I was just to keep an eye on her and make sure she drank and ate.

As if I wasn't going to do that anyway.

In the mean time Eliza had fallen back to sleep, so I decided to text my sister to keep her up to date. I also ordered us some breakfast, for when she woke up. Whether Eliza felt like it or not, she was going to have to eat it. I wasn't having her pass out again.

Zaphire texted straight back, sounding worried. She was going to try and come over this evening rather than wait till tomorrow, if Markus would allow it. I welcomed that but I found myself feeling slightly annoyed too. She probably thought I wasn't looking after Eliza properly.

After about forty-five minutes breakfast arrived which was perfect timing because Eliza just stirred to wake up. It smelled gorgeous; I could really do with some food myself. There was scrambled egg, grilled tomatoes, deliciously smelling bacon, fried mushrooms and some toast. I looked forward to tucking into that.

"Zack?" I heard Eliza mutter.

She hardly dared look at me, I suspect she was still feeling embarrassed about trying to kiss me and then fucking puking in front of me. Poor girl. I would let her know what's happening to her as soon as she woke up a bit.

"Hey, sleepy head. How are you feeling?" I tried to coax her out of her shyness.

"I ordered us some breakfast and before you even think about saying you don't feel like it, it's doctor's orders. You will feel better after, I promise."

She sat up a bit and looked at me from under her big eyelashes.

"What's happening to me? I feel...overwhelmed, I think is the right word."

She looked quite lost.

86

"Your senses are awakening, Eliza. Everything will be magnified and I'll help you deal with it. Zaphire will join us later this evening as well, to support you through this." I tried to reassure her.

"I'm scared, Zack. I'm scared I won't be able to deal with it. Everything is so weird."

Her eyes started to get moist. I needed to make her focus on something else.

"Close your eyes for a minute, Eliza. Concentrate on the smells around you. Try and sort out in your head what it is you can smell and tell me."

She closed her eyes and sniffed in deep. Then I saw a slight panic on her face but quickly followed by a smile.

"Mmmmm, I can smell tomatoes, bacon, toast , mushrooms, egg, but not fried egg, there are herbs in it."

She opened her eyes and I smiled at her.

"Fantastic, isn't it? But what made you panic to start with?"

I needed to know exactly what went on in her head. I could hazard a good guess, but I wanted her to talk through her worries. Her nose wrinkled up and she looked at me furtively. Her cheeks went rosy and it was obvious she didn't want to tell me, but I insisted. We needed to talk about this to avoid it standing between us, like the proverbial elephant in the room.

"Do you enjoy making me feel awkward?" she said accusingly.

I had to nip this in the bud. I couldn't allow her the freedom to question me on every occasion.

"Eliza, I don't need to explain or defend myself with everything I ask you. I have no ulterior motives, apart from getting you to deal with the return of your senses. Just answer the bloody question."

I looked her straight in the eyes which glimmered with defiance. She wasn't going to budge easily. But I just held my stare and waited. I had time. She broke first.

"It's you. Your smell drives me mad! Don't you dare smile! It's not funny. You saw what it made me do!"

She looked exasperated.

I had to really suppress the smile forming on my lips. I had to stay professional or else my words would mean nothing.

"Don't worry. It was a perfectly normal reaction. It's your sense of smell picking up male hormones and pheromones. It's not me specifically; it could have been any male in the room that you would have gone crazy for. You'll be able to tune out and get more

88

discerning in what you like once you've got used to the scent."

It was a little white lie, which she hopefully won't pick up on yet. She definitely has a physical attraction to me and me to her, but that did not mean we had to act on it. In fact we couldn't, so it is better she dismissed it as a purely scientific reaction to men.

"Oh, I see."

I distinctly noticed a little disappointment in her voice. I needed to halt this emerging crush for sure.

"So, it is probably better if you don't inhale too deeply around men at the moment. Though, you are already controlling yourself remarkably well."

I hoped that would put an end to it and we could move on.

"Let's eat. It's going cold. Take little bites, your taste buds will be on fire so you might not want to overload them with too many tastes at the same time.

I nodded encouragingly when she hesitantly put a bit of food in her mouth.

"OMG, this is incredible! I can't remember food tasting this delicious! It's amazing!"

Her face lit up like a light in a cave. It was beautiful.

I could see she was absolutely revelling in the new sensations. Good, it would take her mind off any negativity. It took her quite a while to eat her breakfast and I had to keep encouraging her to eat a bit more. Even though she loved the taste, she wasn't feeling all that hungry, but she needed to keep her strength up so I kept at it until I was satisfied she'd had enough to eat.

"I *am* seventeen you know, I *do* know my own body and what I can do or not. I've looked after myself for ages. Even my mum doesn't nag me as much as you do." she sulked.

I chose to ignore this one. She'll just have to get used to it. She might think she can cope but it is a huge thing coming off the medication and on top of that having all your senses return to you all magnified. It was clear she had the gift and she was dealing well with it at the moment, but she was not nearly done yet.

"You need to focus on the positive, Eliza. Do you think you have the gift, based on what you are experiencing right now?"

I smiled at her, trying to look as friendly as I could. I wished, once again, Zaphire was here.

"Yeah, I think so...it must be. I've started to recognise some of the feelings. It reminds me of my childhood before..." she paused.

"Before my mum decided to drug me." she smiled ruefully.

"I need to go back to bed, I feel exhausted."

Just then, Laura came to our room, as I'd expected she would at some point. She wanted to have a word with Eliza, but I warned her she was exhausted and maybe not receptive of what she wanted to talk about. Laura insisted though, claiming it would only take a minute, so of course I had to allow her in. She was in there for no more than ten minutes, and came out looking relaxed. Whatever they had discussed it had obviously gone well, which was a relief.

"I think she understands where I'm coming from, although she still feels scared of me. She tried hard to disguise it though. I suppose I will have to earn her trust, which I will." Laura commented when she closed Eliza's door behind her.

She was always so damn sure of herself. She came over and gave me a hug.

"You're doing well with her."

She gave me an approving smile.

"Keep up the good work, Zack."

"Will try my hardest, Ma'am." I said trying not to

look too pleased with her encouragement, but failing miserably. She smiled and ruffled my hair before she left. I really savoured this rare display of affection, and locked it into my memory.

CHAPTER 13

I didn't really need to sleep, but I felt exhausted. I just wanted to stop talking and thinking about everything that was happening. Laura's visit hadn't particularly helped either. I started to feel a bit nauseous again. Damned Zack. I knew it wasn't the best idea to eat that much. Though it wasn't too bad, as long as I didn't move too much. The food did taste absolutely fantastic. What had I been missing out on for so long! I felt myself getting cross with my mum, but how was she to know. I should be angry with my father, having left me on my own with no one explaining these sensations to me. Leaving me and mum to think I was a paranoid schizophrenic for years and years. It made me feel sick again. If only he had stayed and taught me to deal with it, like any other child born into this community.

So even though I'd slept for ages before and I thought I didn't need any more, I felt myself slip away again into that state right between consciousness and deep sleep. It felt quite relaxing up until I could hear someone talking in the back ground. I tried to concentrate on what was being said and work out who was talking.

"I'm not sure Markus. She might still hear me, I can feel her senses are still semi alert. But the whole process is exhausting her so it won't be long." I heard Zack whisper on the phone.

Why do they want to talk about me when I'm not supposed to hear. That really worried me. Was something wrong? I had to somehow convince Zack I was fast asleep, so he would talk. I concentrated deeply at breathing rhythmically, slowing it down.

"Yes, she definitely has the gift, don't worry. She's doing fine...yeah....uhuh..I would like Zaphire here though...Yes Sir, I know...but....No, she's still listening Markus. Yes, will phone later."

He turned around to look at me.

"You need to practice your disguising of your feelings more, Eliza. I'm not that easy to fool."

"So, what is the problem? Why do you need to talk about me in secret?" I tried.

He looked a bit piqued, but I thought it was a fair enough question.

"You really can't help yourself, can you? Did I not ask you not to question me about everything I do or decide?"

He actually looked cross now. He didn't wait for an answer and carried on telling me off.

"All you need to do is to concentrate on getting

better. Leave everything else up to me. I'm losing my fucking patience with you Eliza. You'll hear everything you need to know soon enough. Get through this phase first. The sooner you accept that we'll look after your best interests the better."

Jeez, he was so infuriating. Being spoken to like that made my heckles stand on end and I really wanted to shout at him. But instead I turned around with a humph and didn't speak to him again. How could he be so caring and yet such an arse with it!

The day passed away slowly with periods of being awake and asleep, having a late lunch, (still not talking to him), reading a bit of a book and generally feeling a little bit better at the end of the day albeit still exhausted with all my senses being over stimulated. The lights and colours around me were so bright, I could hardly keep my eyes open and Zack passed me some sun glasses. They helped but I barely acknowledged him. I was still annoyed with the way he spoke to me and I wasn't going to let him off the hook easily.

Unfortunately, he didn't seem that fussed with me not paying him any attention. In fact, rather frustratingly, he seemed quite at ease with it all and made no effort to make conversation with me. Not once. I tried to work out what he was feeling but it was like he was wearing a mask. I couldn't tell a thing from looking at him. I needed to ask him to teach me that as soon as possible. I couldn't quite see how I was going to broker that question, since he seemed to get so annoyed with being asked anything. I could almost imagine his answer.

Finally, our silence was broken by a soft knock on the door. Zack stood up and with that I could smell his gorgeous scent again. Mmmmm, so sexy...This was going to be so hard to control.

"Hey sis! Am I glad to see you!" Zack exclaimed.

God, I must have been hard work for him if he was that relieved. Then I got hit with the most exquisite smell, even better than Zack's. And when I laid eyes on Zaphire, I couldn't help myself from gasping. She was the most gorgeous human being I had ever seen! She had intensely dark blue eyes, even more so than Zack's. Beautiful plump lips and long raven black hair. I could feel my heart beat speed up and beating so loud, it was embarrassing. They were sure to notice. I could feel the blood rise to my cheeks and I could hardly breathe. She had literally taken my breath away. Was this normal too? It felt like I'd fallen head over heels in love with her, but that couldn't be possible? I had never, ever felt anything like this for another girl. It must have looked bad, because Zack ushered Zaphire out of the room before we even had a chance to say hello. I did notice them throwing each other knowing glances, before he closed the door behind her. Then he turned to me.

"What happened there? Your heart is pounding like a herd of elephants! Breathe in deeply and count down from ten whilst slowly exhaling."

I did what he told me to do. I felt so confused; I needed to calm down as fast as I could. But every time I thought about her and her amazingly deep blue eyes and luscious smile, my heart started racing again. I couldn't talk even when I tried. I was just a gibbering wreck, butterflies battering my stomach.

"Eliza, look at me. You need to calm yourself down. Keep breathing in slowly and exhale slowly. Keep counting. Focus on the numbers, nothing else. Empty your mind."

Finally, I could feel my body reacting to my will to relax. I kept my eyes focussed on the floor and kept counting down from ten, over and over again. I think I must have done that for over half an hour or so. Then

I heard Zack's voice in the distance, drawing me back to reality again. I desperately needed a hug. I wanted my mum and I told him that.

CHAPTER 14

I couldn't give Eliza her mum but I would fucking love to give her a hug. She looked so fragile and confused, bless her. However, I couldn't do that and now it looked like Zaphire wouldn't be able to go near her for a while either. At least until she's in better control of her senses and urges. This was incredibly frustrating as I really needed Zaphire to help her with her emotions and that clearly wasn't going to work for a while yet.

However, Eliza learned quickly so maybe not all was lost, as long as she dampened down that stubborn defiant streak of hers.

I was in awe of her determination to control her feelings though, sitting there counting over and over again. I could see it was working, she was calming down. We needed another day or two to make sure all those damned medicines were mostly out of her system to really start her training.

At least Markus would get his way. He wasn't all that keen on my reliance on Zaphire to deal with sensitive issues. He's said before that we rely on each other's strengths too much with the risk of neglecting our own weaker ones. He thought if we never challenge our weaker traits we would never be a whole person and wouldn't be able to survive on our own. He had got a point, of course. But it was a habit we had fallen into and I could do with not dealing with that now, whilst working on such an important case. Markus didn't see it that way though and I bet he'll be glad when he finds out it worked out this way. He saw every case, important or not, as a learning opportunity for me and would always treat it that way, but the mission would still come first, and if he had to intervene, he would.

I offered Eliza some peppermint tea, which she gratefully accepted. She might have been in a mood with me, but I hoped she knew deep down that I cared for her. I was a bit put out by her strong reaction to Zaphire, though. She obviously had fallen head over heels with her, just by the sight and smell of her. I didn't know quite what to make of that, but at least it would put a brake on the emerging crush on me. That was good of course, but I couldn't help feeling a little disappointed. I had secretly hoped for something to blossom after this mission was completed. But then, though there was chemical attraction for sure, I wasn't quite so sure about whether she actually liked me as a person. I could come across as a bit of an unfeeling, fucking arrogant bastard. I was aware of that.

But hey, it wasn't to be anyway and I would have to guide her through these confusing feelings she was experiencing as there was no one else to do it. She needed to find a place to put them, so she could fully concentrate on her task. Mission comes first. Markus had drummed that into me from when I was little, but I wasn't deluded that it would be easy to convince Eliza of our motto. She was raised with very different values than us. It was a shame really. Had her father guided her she would have been an outstanding member of our community. I had already seen her gifts were exceptionally strong. She just needed to learn to work with and control them now.

It felt like Eliza was ready to communicate with me again so I gave it a go, treading carefully as I didn't want her to shut me out again. I had made quite a good show of not caring when she decided to ignore me, and I think she really believed it, but I was dying for her to get over it and move on.

"Hey Eliza. You're doing amazing. You're getting it under control. I'm genuinely in awe of your efforts."

I really meant it. She looked fragile, but she was strong.

"Thanks, but I really don't feel it. I feel like a slave

to my senses. It's not fair. I haven't been born into it like all of you. You don't understand."

She ventured a glance at me and I could read the envy in her eyes. It was time I told her the story of my sister and I.

"Contrary to what you think, I do know a little bit about what you are going through Eliza."

That caught her attention, though scepticism was the first feeling she showed.

"Zaphire and I weren't born into it either, but unlike your mother who looked after you, ours abandoned us when we were about five years old. So instead of being put on medication to try and deal with our 'weirdness' she just gave up on us. Left us, without a second thought."

I could hear my own bitterness seeping through, which I'd never learned to fully control. The pain of just being dumped outside the police station with my sister was still raw, even after so many years. We both felt completely lost and bewildered and with our heightened senses it felt like we were being crushed. We'd understood what she had done. She'd told us to wait until the nice policeman was going to take us inside and that she'd pick us up later. But we knew we would never see her again. Many years later,

102

Markus had managed to track her down to Brazil, but we decided we didn't want to see her. She didn't deserve us. We had found out that our dad was a Sensorian, but he'd died, never even knowing we existed. There was no other family left, his mum and dad had passed away long before and he'd been an only child.

"Oh how awful." Eliza whispered.

"What happened then? How did you end up here? What happened to your mum?"

There she went again with her thousand questions at once but this time she apologised straight away, realising she was rushing me. Something of what I was trying to teach her was beginning to sink in, finally.

"Thank you for apologising. I was beginning to think you would never learn to just listen!" I couldn't help but exclaim before carrying on.

"We ended up in a police station where one of our people just happened to work. He'd heard some rumours about the strange twins who'd been left on the door step and who apparently had given the assigned social worker 'the creeps'. We weren't deemed suitable for being fostered as they suspected we were suffering from multiple mental illnesses. Things had been set in motion to have us assessed and we stayed at a secure children's unit temporarily. Our mother wasn't found by them. Disappeared; without a trace."

I paused for a moment to check if Eliza was handling this new information and emotions that it would undoubtedly evoke. She was internalising. Probably counting herself lucky about the way her mum had dealt with her.

"At this point, the policeman, a Sensorian, had alerted Markus about us as he suspected that we had the gift, and were far from insane. A plan had to be put into place quickly to prevent us from getting lost in the system and put into a mental institute. I won't bore you how they managed to pull it off, but Markus and Laura eventually were allowed to be our guardians and we never looked back. That's when we learned to control our gift, as like you, we were none the wiser and certainly not in control of our senses. So, even though I was much younger than you, I still remember the struggle and the feeling of being overwhelmed. It wasn't a pleasant feeling. So you see, I do have a little inkling of what you are going through. That's why I want you to talk to me. Don't be embarrassed."

I hoped my story would help her realise she

wasn't on her own in this and that we would do anything to help her, as long as she abides by our way of life. I could see she was in deep thought, so I left her to ponder for a bit and see how she would react.

CHAPTER 15

I felt happy Zack had opened up to me about his past. Sad as it was for him and his sister, for me he did the right thing telling their story as it helped me come to terms with what I was going through. At least my mum had been there for me when I was little, and she dealt with my abnormality the only way she could have whilst still supporting me. My heart bled for the abandoned twins and could hear the pain in Zack's voice when he talked about his mother.

It also made me understand his relationship with Markus and Laura a bit better. They saved them from a fate worse than death, being locked away forever, never understood and alone. The authorities would have certainly split the twins up and that alone probably would have destroyed them emotionally. No wonder he treated his carers with such respect and deference.

Deeply sunk into my own thoughts, I'd been silent, and hoped Zack didn't interpret this as dismissing his story. I decided I needed to take his advice and talk to him about my wholly inappropriate response to Zaphire coming into the room. It would be the only way for him to help me control these ridiculous outbursts. And I still had trouble being near him too!

"Zack?"

I wasn't quite sure how to start, but he was ready for me. His eyes instantly looked at me expectantly. I had to work hard to ignore my arousal.

"I'm sorry, I still can't look at you without wanting to jump on you. And why did I react so strongly to Zaphire?"

I shrugged my shoulders apologetically.

"I can't seem to help it."

"Yet." Zack interjected.

"You will be able to control theses urges. They won't go away, but you will feel in control of them. Not the other way around. It's hard work to start with, but it'll become easier. What you need to do now, is decide on a word, a colour, or even better, an object you can visualise that evokes a feeling of calm for you."

That wasn't too difficult. I immediately thought of the sea. Remembering all those times I had been sitting on the beach staring out over the sea, feeling utterly relaxed. Watching the waves and Kas surfing elegantly on them. Even just thinking of it now calmed me down and so I told Zack, apart from the Kas part. I didn't think he would appreciate that.

"That's brilliant," he said enthusiastically.

"Very strong imagery for you to focus on when you need to. As soon as one of your senses is starting to overwhelm you, and this can happen very quickly remember, your mind is going to focus on the sea. Then slowly you let in the feeling, smell, sound or whatever it was that was too much. So, you're not ignoring your senses but giving yourself more time to figure them out, without acting impulsively. You can use the waves as a visual aid to let some in wave after wave. Not all at once. Does that make any sense to you?"

"Yeah, I think it does." I admitted hesitantly.

It kind of did actually. Although I doubted I could put it in practise. I could feel his eyes bore into me.

"Okay, well that's good."

He sounded encouraging.

"Let's try something then. Are you happy to give it a go?"

"Sure, what shall I practise on?"

I don't know what I expected but I certainly wasn't expecting to be thrown into the deep end. But of course that was exactly what Zack had in mind. Really, I should have known. I could feel him moving closer into me. My heart immediately started beating a little louder. My body was still reacting to his presence, even though I could not stop thinking about

108

Zaphire. I hadn't worked out what that was all about. Not only had I never fallen in love with a girl before, I didn't know Zaphire at all! I had just caught a glimpse of her, so it must just be a weird chemical reaction due to my heightened senses. I tried to dismiss it as just that. Though I had noticed Zack hadn't answered my question as to why I reacted so much to Zaphire's presence. He'd ignored it.

Zack brought me back to the task in hand.

"Right Eliza, I want you to face me when I've counted down from three, and look me in the eyes. Don't move yourself away from me. Force yourself to stay where you are and start visualising the sea and the waves. Imagine you're on that beach, relaxing, staring out over that beautiful water."

He paused for a second or two and then counted down.

I forced my eyes to look into his. His face only a few centimetres away from mine. His beautiful full lips within touching distance of mine. It took all my strength not to act on my first impulse to kiss him, touch his face, stroke his closely cropped hair. *Sea, rolling waves, beach, Kas. Sea, rolling waves, beach, Kas.* I wanted to move away, run away. My head was screaming to get out; my body didn't want anything else but get closer.

"Count the waves." I heard Zack say.

I tried my hardest to keep focussing on the waves and counting each one rolling on to the beach. I took little breaths as to minimise the overwhelming, deliciously sexy, scent. I was managing it, I wasn't trying to kiss him or touch him. I looked at his face, inches away from mine, but my mind was firmly on the waves.

"Good. Keep focusing and now normalise your breathing. You're well in control."

Zack's encouraging words gave me the strength to try it. I kept counting the waves and visualising Kas on his surfboard riding them. With each wave I let a bit more of the scent in, like Zack had told me to do. Eventually, I took a good sniff, challenging myself and I was surprised to feel in control. Maybe I would be quite good at this, I dared to think. Then the scent distinctly reduced in ferociousness, and I realised Zack had moved away from my face to the back of the room. He looked at me intensely.

"How are you feeling now? Are you okay?"

He studied my face as I answered.

"Yeah, I think so. I really do think so. That was actually awesome, knowing that I will be able to be in control again."

110

I was feeling genuinely elated and relieved. Moments later though, I was overcome with tiredness and started shivering again. Zack felt my head and shook his head.

"No more now, you have a temperature and need to go back to bed. I'll get you a cool cloth. Do you feel sick?"

"Just really tired," I whispered.

I was grateful to go back to bed and it didn't take me long to doze off.

The next couple of days all seemed to melt into one with practising my controlling techniques, eating, showering, sleeping. The medication was leaving my body and I felt better by the day, getting back to normal strength. I still struggled with the impulses reaching my brain so powerfully. The noise of everything around me, the brightness and intensity of my surroundings were immensely uplifting and draining at the same time. Zack was trying to teach me to filter the senses by concentrating on the one I wanted to use and turning down the other ones, like a radio. But I really struggled with that. At times it did feel I was going absolutely crazy, but luckily Zack was there to help me through those moments.

Amazingly, he'd managed to introduce Zaphire to me in small doses at a time, without me turning into a gibbering mess. She was beautiful, caring and smart with a cheeky sense of humour and getting to know her was not doing anything at all to lessen my crush on her. She seemed to like me too, as I started to notice little signs like her heart quickening when I brushed past her, and catching her staring at me when she didn't think I was looking. However, nothing escaped Zack's watchful hawk eyes and I swear they'd had words about me. Anyway, I wouldn't have time to explore those feelings for a while as Zack had devised my training schedule and was about to go through it with me. I was sure there wouldn't be a lot of free time.

CHAPTER 16

Eliza made excellent progress in the last couple of days. I noticed she smelled different, a cleaner scent without the medication in her system. She was growing stronger and less tired and ill, so I decided to increase her training schedule to include physical fitness as well. She needed a bit more time away from Zaphire as I had noticed her feelings for her were increasing in strength, even though she was in better control of them now. Zaphire had been brilliant with her, though and I appreciated her help. She just knew how to make people believe in themselves and grow their confidence. Eliza really had blossomed with her attention.

However, I had to have a strong word with Zaphire about being professional, as she had displayed signs of attraction to Eliza, which I'd noticed were no secret to Eliza either. She was getting better at picking up people's signals and she was encouraged by Zaphire's, albeit subtle, signs. Zaphire was a master at controlling her signals and I'd been surprised that she'd let her guard down. She wasn't particularly happy with being ticked off by me, and had given me lip, but I knew she understood I was right about this. We shouldn't distract Eliza with emotional issues right now. It would have to wait till after the mission.

"Right, let's have a look at my timetable for you."

Eliza looked a bit apprehensive. She looked over her schedule for today and looked a bit surprised.

"Boxing?" she asked incredulously.

"I haven't got a violent bone in my body, Zack. That's not for me." she said determinedly.

"Don't write it off before you've tried it Eliza. You don't have to be violent to enjoy boxing. It's fantastic for stamina and coordination. And on top of that, being able to throw a good punch is not a bad skill to have in our line of work."

She looked shocked, but I carried on.

"You'll also have self-defence lessons, to give you confidence in awkward situations you may find yourself in. I personally am looking very much forward to those lessons."

I had to smile at the look on her face. It said it all. She'd never expected that any physical violence might come into play in our mission. Markus had conveniently been vague about that, but she should be prepared for anything.

"There's s no need to be scared of it Eliza. It's just

better to be prepared. We rarely use physical force in our missions, but you never know who or what you're going to have to deal with, so we must train to prepare for the worst."

I had to be matter of fact about it to try and break through her reluctance and it seemed to work as the stubborn frightened look on her face slowly disappeared and was replaced by a look of resolve, which impressed me.

"Okay. I'll do my best, but I can't guarantee that I'm going to be any good at it. I'm not the sportiest person after all."

She threw me a little smile, which made me feel soft inside. She was cute. Undeniably fucking cute. I focused on something else before she noticed my thoughts. I was relieved Zaphire wasn't here as she would definitely have picked up on my lapse. She would've given me a hell of a lot of grief for telling her off for showing signs and now doing it myself! *For fuck sake; be professional Zack,* I scolded myself.

"You'll be fine. Anything is possible with enough practice and training." I said gruffly, to hide my earlier indiscretion, whether she'd seen it or not.

"Get changed then we can make a start today. Mornings will be for exercise and afternoons for working with your senses."

She looked at me awkwardly.

"What's up?"

"Uh, I didn't pack any sports gear." she said, obviously embarrassed.

I let out a sigh, but said she could probably borrow something from Zaphire. I texted her to bring a selection down. I knew Zaphire's clothes collection was vast, so it wouldn't be a problem. As I predicted, Zaphire came down with an armful of clothes.

"There should be something in here for you, hun. Just try and see what you are most comfortable in. Fancy not packing any!"

She giggled to which Eliza's cheeks went very pink, bless her. She scuttled to the bathroom, holding her breath I noticed. She was struggling with both of us in her vicinity. The exercises I'd planned for this morning will keep her mind off things. Sometimes sport is the best remedy. I sent Zaphire out the room to give Eliza a chance to control her impulses whilst she got changed.

"Agh, you get all the fun these days," she grumbled on her way out.

"Don't worry, you'll have yours soon enough!" I shouted after her.

I had some good self-defence lessons in mind later on in the week, where Zaphire would be extremely useful. She was amazingly quick and flexible and had learned to use that to her advantage with great effect. I would have to see where Eliza's strength lies but as she was so slight of build, it would probably be those two. Zaphire was a great all rounder and so was incredibly strong too. She was quite a sight to behold when she was in full fighting mode. It would give Eliza confidence to see a woman so able and not scared to fight.

"I'm done! Ready to kick some ass!" Eliza laughed mockingly at herself.

She had put her hair up in some sort of pony tail, with wispy dark hairs peaking out everywhere as her hair was just that little bit too short. Cute. Sexy. She didn't seem to care though. She was ready to give it a go.

"We'll start off with some circuit training, then some boxing."

I saw her flinch with the last suggestion, but I ignored it, not wanting to draw attention to it. Better to let her experience it first, so she'll realise it's nothing to be scared of.

"We'll start off slowly, but I will have to push you, to find out what your basic fitness level is. Then we can work from there to improve."

CHAPTER 17

"Hey...I..thought you said we would.....start slowly!"

I could hardly talk without having to catch my breath. Sweat poured off me and my clothes were soaked. We hadn't even done the boxing yet.

"Yep, but I also said I'd have to push you. I know what your limit is now and what we can work towards. Go stretch and take some water. Then I'll teach you some of the basics of boxing. We won't do a full session. I can see you are not strong enough yet."

"I didn't think I was doing *that* badly." I grumbled.

I felt a bit dejected. I'd worked really hard I thought, considering I had never done any sports before. I didn't know any of the moves Zack was talking about and he had to show me everything. Burpees, lunges, planking WTF. Pure torture is what it should be called!

"You *have* worked hard, but you've gone through a lot and your body is weak. Put these gloves on. I'll show you some simple moves."

As he moved closer I was suddenly overwhelmed with his scent again, intensified by the sweat he'd worked up doing his own exercises. I pushed him away and forced myself to focus on the sea and the rolling waves. I was getting the hang of this and felt

more in control almost immediately. At least I was
making good progress there.

"Sorry Zack, you were too close." I apologised.

"Are you in control now?"

He actually looked concerned for the first time this
training session. He'd been uncompromising to say
the least, barking instructions at me continuously.
However, he had stopped just when I felt it was
getting too much for me. Of course he knew what he
was doing. He could read me like an open book,
picking up all my vital signs constantly. I kept
forgetting.

"Yeah sure, just don't come too near."

That really wasn't what my body wanted, but my
brain had won this battle.

Zack kept his word and just showed me a few
simple techniques as to how to place my legs and
body, and how to hold my fists together and in front of
my face. He showed me some punches, which I
practised the move of, but without the power behind it,
as instructed. Then he signalled to do cool down and
I was looking forward to a well deserved long hot bath.

"You can have a bath today, but don't get used to it.
The first couple of days I will allow you to take a two
hour break, to let your body recover as we are

supposed to take it easy. After that, it will just be an hour in which you will have to shower and have lunch. Today I'm expecting you to be ready to learn at 2.30pm."

The uncompromising trainer was back. I didn't understand why he had to talk to me like I was in the army or something! It really annoyed me, but there wouldn't be any point saying anything, I was sure. What hope did I have, I heard him talk like this to his sister and although she wasn't happy about it, she didn't defy him either. Although, I did get the feeling that, if she really disagreed with what he had decided, she would give him as good as she got.

"Well? Are you going to acknowledge my instruction? I need to know you understood."

Zack looked at me sternly.

"Yes I understand perfectly well, Zack." I sneered.

"Do you want me to salute you too?"

Oops, I couldn't help myself. It was out before I knew it.

"Less of the attitude, please." he said calmly, but his jaw clenched, whilst he motioned me towards the door exiting the sports hall.

I could feel my cheeks starting to burn again. So bloody annoying. At least it could have been the

121

exercise that had turned my face red. We walked in silence back to my room where I retreated into the bathroom to have my bath. Zack gave me a half hour time limit, which I was going to use up to the last minute. I needed to calm down and relax to give my senses a bit of a break. I dimmed the lights right down and used the tiniest amount of bath oil so as to not stimulate myself too much. I sunk into the luscious warm bath and really relished the sensation. Just what I needed I thought, feeling satisfied.

CHAPTER 18

I used the time Eliza was in the bath to prepare for this afternoon's session. She needed to work on fine tuning her senses and blocking them so as to be in better control and not get so overwhelmed with them. To be honest, she had made excellent progress with it already and I was going to give her some difficult exercises to challenge her. She was going to be exhausted this evening so early bed time, though I knew she wasn't going to take that very kindly. She wasn't used to her life being controlled and I had to remind myself to be patient with her reaction to my orders. Had it been any one else speaking to me like she did earlier, they fucking would've had an afternoon of isolation cell for sure.

Eliza got out of the bath, drops of water littering the floor, loud as clattering stones. I had to stop thinking of her, naked in the bathroom. It was dangerous territory. She stepped into the room, smelling divine, hair up in a towel.

"How are you feeling? You look refreshed." I answered for her.

"I'll order us some lunch. I think it's carrot soup and a roll, or ham and cheese Panini with salad.

What do you fancy?"

"Wow, I get a choice?"

Her eyes glinted mischievously.

"Yes, smart arse, but be quick about it or I'll make it for you."

Fucking cheeky. That made my mind up to tell her more about us, so she would understand to take things more seriously. I couldn't put up with her bloody childish insubordination much longer.

"Carrot soup then please and oh, maybe lighten up a bit. You are no fun!" she carried on.

I chose to ignore it and went ahead with the order. It should be with us soon.

"Just get yourself ready." I barked frustratedly at her.

I took the opportunity to have a quick shower myself and was just getting out of the shower when I heard the knock on the door. I jumped out and wrapped a towel around me as Eliza was under strict instructions not to open the door, to ensure her safety. However, when I opened the shower room door, I heard Eliza say thank you and closing the door.

"What the fuck do you think you're doing!" I yelled at her.

"You were told NOT to open the door, under ANY

124

circumstance!"

I looked at her in despair. She really didn't understand any of it. It had to stop now, she needed to know more. She looked genuinely bewildered.

"I..., I forgot, it was just the lunch we were expecting and you, you were in the shower and...."

A tear formed in her left eye, which she hastily wiped away. She was such a fucking snowflake.

"Okay.   Sit down. I'll put some clothes on. Then we'll talk."

I said as calmly as I could. I noticed her clock my body and she glazed over, obviously using her wave technique to gain control. I hastily covered up and stepped away from her. She recovered quickly and once I was dressed properly we sat down to eat.

"I think you're ready to hear a bit more about what we do, as I feel it'll make you understand why I'm so strict with you and why I take everything so seriously. It might make you take it more seriously too."

I gauged her reaction and though she was still feeling upset, her curiosity was spiked, so I carried on.

"So, apart from working to keep each other safe, we also use our gift to prevent crime in the conventional society. We work as an independent unit, never work for someone or any government. Our gift has to remain secret to everyone, apart from our own people. That's our number one rule. The danger of being detected is our deepest fear, as I mentioned before, it makes us a target for persecution, manipulation, imprisonment, being made to work for criminals, governments, or terrorists." I paused.

I wanted it to sink in.

"We put ourselves in danger when we're trying to prevent crimes or help get people brought to justice. We make many enemies, but we feel it's our obligation and duty as Sensorians to use our gifts to do good, help Dullards. Sorry, ordinary people. It is our destiny or 'raison d'etre' so to speak, and hence our rule number two. Rule number three is that if you do decide to deviate from our rule number one or two, you risk imprisonment or even death, as I have told you before."

I hoped it was making sense to her, helping her understand us more and hopefully seeing herself fit in and thrive in our community.

"Any questions?"

Eliza looked pensive, and for one moment I thought she had nothing to say, but that was, of course, not the case. The little minx always had something to ask or comment.

"I was just wondering what sort of crimes you're preventing and how do you do it, without being noticed? It must be hard not to get involved somehow and get caught up in police matters?"

"Good question. We use our gift to extract the truth. Dullards can't lie to us. We have lots of people scouring the internet and lots of eyes and ears everywhere. It could be robberies, murder, embezzlement, rape, theft, corruption, terrorism, anything really. We try and prevent crimes and plots but we also make sure certain evidence and confessions gets 'found' by the police. And luckily, thanks to our gifts we usually are one step ahead of everyone. But sometimes it goes wrong and we do get caught up in dangerous situations or somehow embroiled in a police investigation. So far our team of lawyers always have managed to outwit the prosecution and got our people off the hook. However, sometimes it gets dangerous in the field and that's where our level of fitness, fighting skills and self defence come in handy.

We very rarely use weapons, especially not our younger members. You have to be at least thirty or have special permission to even get trained in using weapons. That's not what we're about."

I wondered if she grasped what I was trying to say. I could see she was mulling things over.

"So, are you telling me, this is what you're training me up for?"

She looked incredulous.

"I don't think I signed up for this! I'm just here to help you find out what's going on with my father, then I'm out, Zack. I want to go back to my 'conventional' life with my mum and Kas and my friends! Have you considered that?"

Hell, she was fucking stubborn and feisty that girl. I had to keep my cool.

"Yes, you're right Eliza. That's why we contacted you and, don't worry, it's totally up to you what you do with your life after this mission, apart from the fact you have to keep it a secret. However, if we were not to trust you, you would not be allowed to return to your normal life ever again."

She needed to understand at least that, so it had to be said.

"Yes, no of course, I would never betray any of you! You helped me discover my gifts and helped me off my medication and I will forever be grateful for that. You can totally count on that."

I could feel she was completely genuine so accepted her promise. However, she had no idea how difficult it was to keep secrets from loved ones. I wasn't going to challenge her on that now though, that could wait till after the mission. It was better she thought she would just be able to return back to her old life afterwards, just like that.

There was another thing that still had to be said.

"So, to you, our community may seem rigorous and military like with our rules and little patience for attitude, but for us it's how it has to be. You cannot question everything you're asked to do. It wastes time and could compromise people. Sometimes you might not understand why you have to do something, but the person who's telling you does. That's why we need discipline in our community. That's not to say that no one rebels occasionally, it's natural. But it's met with punishment. Disobedience is just not tolerated. In training we are told to do things that seem stupid and useless, but it's part of the training to be accepting of orders. It may save your or someone else's life one day."

I paused and observed her again. I could sense she was struggling with the idea she had to fit into our system for our mission to work, but I could also detect resolve. She was going to do her best to adhere to our rules, I could feel it and I was satisfied with that. I could see she would need a lot of help to work within those rules and I'd support her as best I could.

"Do you understand Eliza?"

I gave her a chance to verbalise what I'd already picked up anyway.

"Yeah, I can see how it would have to be that way Zack, but I will find it really difficult. I've had seventeen years of living a mostly normal life. It just all seems so extreme, but, yes, I can see the necessity of it, to keep people safe. Can't promise I will be a star student though!"

She smiled. She hadn't lost her sense of humour yet.

"Don't worry, you have me on your fucking backside to keep you on the straight and narrow. Having said that, it's 2.15pm now, so you have fifteen minutes to do whatever to be ready for our afternoon session. Finish that soup quickly, I suggest."

I left her to it for a bit whilst I myself finished my Panini. I wondered if the afternoon activities I had in mind would prove too much for her, but decided to carry on with them anyway. It would be a good test to see how far she could be pushed.

CHAPTER 19

My head was still reeling from Zack's revelations about the community and what they (or should I say 'we'?) do, but I was desperately trying to relax before this afternoon's session. I needed to be in control of my senses if we were to do any work with them. I closed my eyes for a bit, but I kept thinking of all the things Zack had said. I felt out of my depth in this world, so different from what I was used to at home with mum. I wondered if I could turn back time, whether I would have chosen the same path, but I knew the answer to that to be honest. Of course I would have, I wouldn't have passed on the opportunity to find out more about my father and myself for that matter.

"Get your coat; we're going for a little walk outside."
It was 2.30pm already

"I want you to get used to normal sounds and noise and practise tuning it out. Not just the sounds, but visual, scents and touch as well. You need all those inputs to be tuned down to a normal level, so you can decide which sense you want to focus on around you. When you get used to it you can let all the senses in or choose which ones you need or don't need. Remember to think of all that background noise around you as a radio that you can turn down. I want to see how you cope, then we can target your learning exactly where you need it most. If it all gets too much, turn to visualising your beach and waves. Let's go."

"You're really throwing me into the deep end here. What about all the people everywhere, what if I jump on someone that I happen to like the smell of too much?"

I was genuinely worried about my own actions in the vicinity of people.

"There may be a little risk, but not the same as being in an enclosed area. We're staying outside, so you should be okay. Anyway I have full trust in your capabilities to focus on your waves when you feel out of control. You're very good at that."

I wished I shared his confidence, but it was reassuring to know he did anyway. I had obviously impressed him with something, which felt quite good.

"We're starting at a fairly quiet place anyway. There's a park, just around the corner. That's where we'll be heading first. Then we'll assess how you are doing."

He walked confidently towards the door that led to the outside world.

"Okay, here goes nothing." I mumbled and followed him out.

The fresh air caressed my face, it felt wonderful. It was good to be outside and it made me realise how well I felt, compared to the last few days. It was like a fog had lifted and for the second time in my life I experienced the world as it should be, just like when I was little. The sun was shining a little and I had to put sunglasses on, but I noticed Zack did too, so that must be quite normal for us then. I braced myself for the onslaught of stimulations, but was surprised to feel recognition rather than panic.

I just started to relax a bit, when a group of teenagers walked towards us. I tensed up and grabbed Zack's hand. To my surprise, he held it firmly. I thought he might have rejected my hand and tell me to get a grip, but he didn't. When the group of rather smelly and loud boys had passed, he let go. Apart from noticing their rather acrid body odours, I did not get any urges to jump on any of them. Maybe Zack hadn't been completely truthful on that point!

"How are you doing?" he asked as he looked me straight in the eyes.

I didn't know how to answer. I felt strangely

liberated, but anxious at the same time. There were a lot of stimuli and my brain was working overtime trying to process it all at the same time.

"I think I need to start tuning out soon. I'm letting it all in at the moment and I'm starting to feel overwhelmed."

My brain ached, it was getting too much. People, water, wind, food, trees, traffic, sun, faces, dogs, birds. They were all competing for my attention.

"Focus, Eliza. Focus now, before you lose it."

I heard Zack's urgency in his voice. I tried my hardest to envisage a volume knob and turn down each individual sense. It took a while but it was working, I was able to think clearly now and I saw Zack visibly relax. He must have thought he was going to have a major melt down on his hands and I was glad I was able to keep it together. Not for long though, I was feeling exhausted after only being out for only about thirty minutes. How on earth was I ever going to cope with living outside my room?

"Brilliant. Well done! I'm really impressed with how you kept control Eliza, it's not easy. We'll go back to our room now and do some more exercises there. Don't worry about how long or short you lasted. It will be second nature to you soon. Don't be too impatient with yourself."

It never ceased to amaze me how well he could read me. I was still so busy with trying to control the inputs so I didn't get overwhelmed, I was wondering when, if ever, I could actually use them to my advantage.

"Can I rest a bit, please, before going into the next exercise?

Zack agreed. He thought it would be good as Zaphire was coming to help later, so I should relax beforehand, to build up my energy to cope with my urges towards her.

I was nervous to see Zaphire again. I was much better at not acting on my impulses but that didn't mean they weren't there. I wanted to look good for her, so after I'd rested a bit I went to put some make-up on. I looked critically at my face for a minute and was disgruntled to conclude that I had dark circles under my eyes and my skin was pale and a bit puffed up.

"What are you doing?" Zack piped up.

He didn't look too happy for some reason.

"Are you ready for our next session? You have five minutes."

"Just putting some foundation on, if you must

know. I'll be ready in a minute."

I heard Zack snort disapprovingly. He could be such a grump about things. Then there was a soft knock on the door, and my heart made a little leap. Zack broke out in a smile and jumped up to open the door.

"Hey sis, right on time!"

He pulled her into the room. She strode in, looking effortlessly amazing. She was wearing black boots, leggings with a tunic and a short leather jacket. I wish I had packed some better clothes now. They all felt boring and plain compared to hers. She came over to me but stopped short a few metres away.

"Hey Eliza! You're looking so much better!" she exclaimed.

"Great thanks Zaphire." I couldn't help sounding sarcastic.

"I must have looked awful before then!"

My heart started pounding faster and the blood rushed to my face. Oh well, at least it would give my cheeks some colour.

"Well yes, sorry, you did! Seen you at your worst then, haven't I."

She laughed out loud. Zack was also sniggering in the back ground. I threw him a cross look.

"Lighten up girl. It's a good thing, isn't it? I'm sure

you'll get a chance to see us at our worst at some point, don't you worry. Get yourself a drink Zaph, you look thirsty. Then we can make a start." Zack suggested.

Zaphire poured herself some soda and offered me one too, which I happily accepted. My mouth had gone horribly dry.

"I had a busy morning, lots of meetings and report writing. So bored of it now, I wanna go back in the field." she sighed.

"Well, I need you here for a bit longer, sis. I'm sorry."

"Yeah right, I can really see you're sorry."

She punched him on the arm, but he was quick and grabbed the arm and twisted it around her back within a second.

"You need to up your game, little sis." he teased, but let her go straight away.

She giggled muttering something rude under her breath.

"Luckily Eliza is here to keep my interest piqued at least. So what have you got planned for us Zack?"

As it turned out, he had planned a lot. Exercise after exercise to tune in and out of my senses, concentrating on different aspects at a time. Zaphire was great, offering new scenarios and stimuli, and showed me how to focus better, giving me little tips and advice.

She also introduced me to shielding, which is basically a stronger version of tuning out. Useful especially for those moments when there are high emotions banded about. They are difficult to tune out as they're hoisted upon you so you have to literally shield yourself. It would take quite some time to get the hang of that, it was an advanced skill. In the mean time, Zack was observing and making lots of notes.

After what felt like hours and hours, Zack finally called it a day. We were all starving hungry and Zack ordered us pizza's to be delivered to our room. Zaphire wanted a beer with it, but Zack wasn't having any of it.

"You know the rules Zaphire. No drinking whilst on a mission. I shouldn't have to remind you of that."

He was annoyed.

"In fact, I can't believe you made me remind you. I could report you for even suggesting it and I don't like to be put in that position."

Zaphire didn't look remotely contrite, but she did

apologise. That didn't placate Zack though, who was obviously in a mood with her. She went over to him, and started massaging his shoulders a bit.

"Come on bro, forget about it and let's enjoy our pizza, hey."

He did relax and a smile formed on his lips. We tucked in and it tasted fantastic.

"The food is delicious here." I said.

It made them laugh.

"You've probably forgotten what food tastes like, having been medicated. Downside is, when something doesn't taste great, it tastes disgusting!" Zaphire pulled a face.

"Tomorrow I'm going to take you to the restaurant. Time to meet some other people." Zack announced, looking happy.

The thought of that made me nearly sick to the stomach, but I decided not to dwell on it. In fact, it might be interesting to see Zack interact with his friends assuming that they were the people he was thinking of introducing me to. I had finished my dinner and after we'd watched a bit of television, Zack sent me to bed. Even though it irritated me and made me feel like a little girl, I didn't complain. I was utterly exhausted.

CHAPTER 20

When Eliza went to bed, Zaphire decided to stay a bit longer. Although my twin (younger by 6 minutes) was a bit of a live wire, had a rebellious streak, and could be extremely annoying, I loved her like nothing else. I relished her company. We didn't get a lot of time together, as Zaphire loved being out in the field, going undercover gathering information and took any opportunity to go. However, she was going to be stuck with me and Eliza for a while, and though she would complain and moan about it, I knew she also loved our time together.

"Hey, how are you bearing up?" she enquired after switching the tv off.

"You seem a bit tense Zack. What's bothering you?"

She looked worried.

I groaned.

"Markus is putting so much time pressure on us, I'm worried he's going to ask too much too soon of Eliza. I thought we'd have a bit more time to prepare her as we know more or less where Rick is now, but I feel Markus is anxious to get her involved. I could tell when I last spoke to him. Do you know anything else that I should know about?"

I observed every muscle of her body and face searching for clues whether she knew anything. Perhaps something she wasn't allowed to tell me, for reasons I could only guess at.

"I think you need to talk to Markus again, Zack." she said gravely.

That told me enough. Something was going on and I needed to find out what. I didn't like being kept in the dark. I didn't understand why either, but I had felt it the last time I spoke to Markus when discussing Eliza's progress.

"Fucking great. I knew something was up." I thumped the table in frustration.

"Eliza's making fantastic progress and she learns quickly, but we haven't really touched upon using her senses to her advantage and we only just started on the fitness! She's nowhere near ready! Ideally she would need months, rather than weeks for her to be operational."

I'll have to make my case with Markus and postpone whatever they had in mind. They would just have to observe the Rick situation from a distance for some time longer.

Zaphire sighed, her eyes seeking mine.

"Yes, you need to see him. But, please take a chill pill before you go! You'll be in trouble if you lose your rag. I've never seen you so protective over any of your trainees before."

She gave me a playful punch on my arm and smiled.

"In all seriousness though, Zack. Don't forget Markus is our leader as well as our carer. I've not known him make the wrong decision yet, so keep that in mind when you think about challenging him. He won't take it kindly." she warned.

"Talking about him not taking things kindly....what was this about you showing your feelings for Eliza a little too openly the other day! I'm sure Markus wouldn't appreciate that either!" I teased Zaphire.

"You fucking like her, don't you?"

I was curious to find out what exactly she felt for Eliza. My sister was a little bit of a heart breaker, both for women and men. They all seem to fall in love with her so easily, but Zaphire got bored very quickly and nothing had lasted any longer than a couple of weeks at the most. She did manage to stay friends with most somehow. In that respect she was so different from me. I've had a few girlfriends, but I was far more intense and invested in my relationships than my sister ever was. Contrary to Zaphire, I didn't want to be friends with my exes. Once we'd broken up, it was done for me.

"Yes, I like her. Does it bother you?" she challenged. But carried on.

"She stirs something inside me. She's feisty and funny, she fascinates me and she has this vulnerability which is so alluring. On top of that she is beautiful. What's not to like!"

As she spoke about Eliza I could hear her pulse rising, and her pupils went huge. Yep, she was definitely falling for Eliza. Super.

"You just make sure you keep your fucking feelings in check, sis. Wouldn't want to compromise the mission now, would we." I said a bit too grumpily.

She jumped on that.

Aha, I see she doesn't leave you cold either then!" She guffawed.

"Don't worry, Z. She just took me by surprise that's all. I'm perfectly in control....for now."

She winked at me, teasing.

"Must be hard for you. Being that close to her all the time," she carried on.

"For fuck sake, I'm fine Zaphire. Don't you worry about me. I'm warning you though, be careful with Eliza. I don't want you to use her and leave her hurt."

I was absolutely serious now.

"Otherwise you'll have me to contend with." I threatened.

"Ah, pfff, Zack. Honestly." She waved my threat away light heartedly.

She never could take anything seriously. Apart from her work of course. I decided to leave it for now and we talked about her last mission which had been quite eventful. It made me long to do work in the field again, the adrenaline rush it afforded was great, but I had to be patient as Eliza had to be ready first. We would be wishing for quiet training days soon enough, once we were in the midst of our mission. It wasn't going to be an easy one.

Far too late, Zaphire decided to go to her room and I went to bed, after checking on Eliza, who was fast asleep.

CHAPTER 21

Sssssh, my little one, sssshh
Darkness around me
I'm moving, but not my legs,
they are suspended in the air,
gently swaying
I want to scream, but my mouth is covered
My head pushed against a warm body.
Then
I remembered.

I woke up with a gasp. *Shit!* I was starting to hyperventilate and could just manage a strangled cry for Zack, who thankfully was there seconds later. He put his hand in my neck and just that little touch calmed me down. I started to talk, but Zack put a finger on my lips and told me to concentrate on my breathing first. He wiped my brow with a soft cloth as I was drenched with sweat all over. I took a deep breath.

"I *am* calm now Zack but I need to talk." I urged him to let me.

His eyes searched my body and he felt my pulse. He seemed satisfied.

"All my life I've had nightmares, especially at stressful times. But tonight I've realised something about them." I paused.

I couldn't quite think how to explain it properly.

"My dreams... they're memories."

I knew for sure now, I remembered what the dreams were about and it scared me.

"Can you tell me about them?" Zack pressed on to keep me talking.

"I was little, maybe three years old. The door opens in my room and the next minute I'm being carried. I feel the cold, I'm being taken outside. I can't scream because my face is held against someone's body. It smelled familiar and now I know why. It was my dad. He told me to be quiet but I was feeling scared. I remember it now. He took me to the beach; I heard the sound of the sea. He told me he missed me. I started crying but he wound his scarf around my face so I could hardly breathe. Next thing I knew he swooped me up and walked back to the house and put me in bed. I must have fallen straight back to sleep and when I woke up he was gone." I sighed.

It made sense now; I could feel this is what had happened. It was never a dream. My dad took me, but he must have thought better of it and brought me back. I can't believe I had forgotten such an important event though. But I was so young and that is what the mind sometimes does I suppose; repressing traumatic experiences.

"Has it made you feel better, understanding what the nightmares have been about?" Zack asked, whilst rubbing my back.

It made me feel safe.

"I don't know. I feel I have more questions. What did he want that night and why did he change his mind? Has he been watching me all these years or was that the last time he laid eyes on me? I need answers. I want to know why he abandoned me, I need to hear it from him."

"Soon you may get the chance to ask him yourself. Put the questions in a box, to be opened when you get the chance. Nothing you can do about it now. Go back to sleep. It's too early to get up." Zack said matter of factly.

"I'll sit here, by your side, if it helps?" he said, a bit more empathetically.

I nodded and tried to take his advice. It was easier said than done though, but I knew Zack was right. I resolutely put the questions to the back of my mind and starting visualising the sea, banishing all other thoughts. It must have worked as the next thing I knew Zack was shaking me gently to wake me and the sunlight was streaming into the bedroom.

It took me a while to stretch out my muscle ache from yesterday and the fitness session was hard. I felt less strong than yesterday and Zack was pushing me hard again. I actually cried doing the push ups as he was making me do them over and over again as I wasn't doing them correctly, according to him. Crying made no difference; he just kept making me carry on until I literally collapsed under my own weight. My arms were trembling and ached so much, I didn't think they would ever recover.

"Embrace the pain, Eliza. It means it's working," he kept reminding me.

If he said that one more time I'd kill him! Finally he uttered the words I did long to hear.

"Let's call it a day. You can do your cool down exercises and grab a shower. Well done. You've worked hard."

He was working with weights himself, his muscles deliciously flexing. *Must stop looking at that body!*

I was ready promptly at one o'clock as requested, eager to have some lunch. Unfortunately, I had forgotten about Zack's plan to take me to the restaurant for lunch today. I could really have done without that. I wasn't mentally prepared to meet other people yet. But I don't think that would stop Zack anyway. He would see it as another great opportunity to test my limits.

"Don't forget your tuning out and shielding exercises. Just let in what you can cope with. Don't worry what other people think; they all know your story."

I think he said that to reassure me, but I couldn't think of anything worse than face all these people, knowing everything about me, but me nothing about them. Although that wasn't quite true as Zack had told me a little bit about the people we would join for lunch. There was Ned, who was Zack's best buddy since childhood and Brody, Zack's sparring partner, always competing against each other in the gym. Then there was Sam, who I thought was a boy but turned out to be a girl, who apparently had history with Zaphire, but they were best of friends now. Zaphire would join us too of course.

They were all sat at the table when Zack and me turned up to join them. The boys and Sam whooped and got up, slapping Zack on the back telling him they'd missed seeing him. Zack had a broad smile on his face and was high fiving them and giving big hugs all around. It was nice to see him care free and happy.

Then the attention turned to me and instantly I felt the heat rise to my cheeks. It didn't help that at that moment I also noticed their scents. Pheromones were given off a plenty, prickling my senses. Zaphire's seductive half open eyes observing my every move just undid me. I was just about to turn around and run, when Zack came to my rescue. He grabbed my hand, probably to stop me from running, but it made me jolt and instantly felt more in control.

"This is, you probably guessed, as you'd be fucking stupid not to, Eliza Mankuzay."

He motioned for me to sit down after everyone shook my hand and introduced themselves.

Sam spoke first.

"So, has *Master* Zack been working you hard, Eliza?"

She got an eye roll from Zack, I guess for calling him Master.

"He certainly has. I've found muscles I never knew I had!" I grimaced.

"Oh, I remember those days!!" Sam laughed sympathetically.

150

"No pain, no gain. Embrace the pain." mimicking Zack's gruff voice, making me giggle.

"I was trained by Zack just last year. Somehow we managed to stay friends. Wonders never cease to exist." she said jokingly whilst Zack was trying to punch her arm past my face.

The waitress came to get our orders and whilst the others were ordering Zack and me quickly decided what we were going to have.

"How are you getting on? Getting used to this crazy life yet?"

That was Ned.

He'd been quietly observing me earlier. I saw Zack throw some warning looks around the table, making sure they weren't going to bombard me with questions. But I felt fine for the moment and confidently answered Ned.

"I wouldn't say I'm used to it yet, but I'm starting to understand it a bit more. I feel less crazy here then I've ever felt though!"

They laughed at that and Zack gave me an encouraging smile. Then his face changed and showed mock horror.

"Ned! Did you just let rip!" he groaned. Ned just laughed and shrugged his shoulders. I giggled but then a god-awful stench hit me like a brick wall. I gagged and looked around mortified. I saw a slow realisation appear on everyone's faces.

"Oh fuck." Zack muttered.

"I think Eliza didn't shield quickly enough." he chuckled, but then noticed I was actually struggling to breathe, and pushed me to the window and opened it for me. Air. Thank God. I gulped deep breaths of lovely fresh air in and recovered.

"What the hell was that!" I exclaimed, but realised instantly when I spotted Ned's sheepish grin.

"Sorry." he spluttered under Zack's warning, but twinkling stare.

"Got to learn to be quick to shield around Ned!" Zaphire laughed out loud.

Soon everyone was having a chat amongst themselves, but not ignoring me. They tried to involve me as much as they could and I was surprised to find myself really enjoying the banter. I was so relieved to find it quite easy to tune out the overwhelming sensations and be able to interact quite normally. Only a few times I needed to take a deep breath and focus on the waves to block out any unwanted stimuli. Zack was relaxed and was visibly energised by the interactions with his friends.

Moments later, I picked up a change of vibe. Zack stiffened and his eyes went dark, eyebrows furrowed. It didn't take long before I located the source of his dismay. A tall red headed girl approached our table. Zaphire worked hard to keep the conversation flowing but it was obvious that everyone was on tenterhooks. Immeasurably small glances kept flying across the table. A normal human being wouldn't have picked up any tension, but to me it was glaringly obvious, and I was only new to this. Everyone in the room must have picked it up.

"Hello Jessica, how are you?" Zack said politely.

His body language was telling. It screamed. What do you want and why are you here?

Jessica ignored Zack and went straight to me. All of my senses were on edge. As she approached, I could smell a rather sharp and acrid scent that I would hazard a guess was associated with jealousy. She bent over to me and viciously whispered in my ear.

"Has that arsehole tried it on with you yet? Don't be flattered, you won't be the first, nor the last."

She threw a pointed stare at Zack. Everyone went silent around the table, like the quiet before the storm. A muscle was twitching in Zack's jaw as he slowly got up from his chair.

153

"Zaphire, watch Eliza for me for a moment. Jessica, outside. Now." he hissed, barely keeping control over his voice.

When she didn't show any inclination to follow his order, as that's what it was, he grabbed her by the arm and pulled her through the restaurant, out the door, with a grim look on his face.

"I wouldn't like to be in her shoes." Sam mumbled as she looked at Zaphire, who grunted.

"Disgruntled ex. Don't worry, he'll deal with it in a way she wished she never even set foot in here." Ned said shrugging his shoulders.

I must have looked alarmed wondering what on earth he would do to the girl. Zaphire jumped in to reassure me.

"Don't worry, nothing physical. He'll give her a verbal dressing down like you wouldn't believe, though. She'll feel about this small when he's finished with her." showing a tiny gap between her fingers.

By the looks on their faces I vowed to myself to try my hardest never to be on the receiving end of one of those. All this was so far removed from how I interacted with my friends at home. It made me feel so out of my depth and made me wonder if I ever would fit into this weird community.

When Zack returned he wasn't in the mood to stay any longer so we said our goodbyes and went back to our room. Zaphire would join us later to do some more work which I was secretly looking forward to. I still wasn't sure at all that she would ever reciprocate my feelings for her, but I was happy to spend time with her whenever I could.

CHAPTER 22

Fucking typical of Jessica to spoil our lunch. I had really enjoyed seeing my friends; I missed them and their light hearted banter. We knew each other so well and we'd always be there for each other. Even Sam, who'd only been a recent addition to our group, would do anything for us, and we would for her. Initially I wasn't sure if it would work, having trained and coached her, but she just got on so well with Zaphire, it felt natural to embrace her into our friendship group. I would've felt totally recharged after meeting up with them, but for Jessica's interruption. Eliza had done so well as well and seemed to fit in quite easily with our group. It would have been a total success, if it hadn't been for that spiteful bitch.

"Are you okay?" Eliza asked after a while.

I hadn't really explained what had happened earlier, but I was sure the others would have filled her in. She was my most recent ex and hadn't taken it well when I finished our relationship. We had only been together for a few months, but it hadn't felt right from the start. I'd fancied her and we did have fun times, but I didn't really like her personality, and that soon became a problem. She couldn't see it though, and she felt I had used her. She was right in a way. I should never have let it go on for that long, but my selfish needs were met as she was amazing in bed (and everywhere else we fancied having it on!). I tried to break up with her gently but she wouldn't accept it. She kept trying to persuade me to stay with her, saying how much she loved me and she would make me happy. I had to be quite harsh with her in the end and she has felt bitter towards me ever since.

"I'll tell you how I feel. Annoyed," I snorted.

"She had no right to talk to you like that. She has an axe to grind with me and tried to use you to get at me. It was a cheap shot, and I can assure you she'll never do that again. I banned her from coming near you for two weeks so she can think about what she did, before ever embarrassing you, and insulting me, like that again. And before you ask, if she breaks the ban she will go in isolation for the remainder of the two weeks and, yes, I do have the power to impose that sanction."

Eliza picked up on my mood and asked what we were going to do this afternoon, to change the subject. I instantly started to feel more positive, focussing on the exercises I had planned for her this afternoon.

She was going to have to do a lot of shielding and masking, so it would become more automatic and natural each time she did it. Then she could start focussing on interpreting other people's signals.

She worked incredibly hard and made good progress in the afternoon. I could see again she really thrived when working with Zaphire, she was an incredible motivator and made it fun at the same time. At one point they were having a bit too much fun, and I had to remind them to focus, which earned me two pairs of eyes throwing daggers at me.

"Let's go and try the Dark Room." I decided.

Eliza looked puzzled, but Zaphire's eyes lit up.

"We've been focussing on controlling your senses, but you also need to start trusting them. The Dark Room is perfect for that. I will set up a few tasks and you will have to rely on all your senses, but your eyesight to complete them." I explained.

"It's really cool," Zaphire added.

"You'll love it."

I wasn't sure if Eliza did love it, in fact I was sure she didn't; she cursed a lot! But she grew in confidence under my watchful eye and Zaphy's encouragement. Her performance confirmed my belief

Eliza was going to be an exceptional Sensorian. She certainly did a hell of a lot better than my first attempts in there, to the frustration of Markus! I used to be scared of going in there, but then Markus was an unforgiving teacher, and I didn't have someone like Zaphy to support me.

Whilst working in the Dark Room I received a rather troubling text from our leader. Apparently, Eliza's mum had informed him of Kasper's efforts to try and contact Eliza. She couldn't put him off any longer and needed some help. He would just not accept her excuses any longer and had insisted on talking to Eliza himself. Markus had tasked me to deal with it, one way or another as he would be out for the rest of the day. That scuppered my request for a meeting but I managed to arrange a time for tomorrow, which would just have to do.

I could either allow Eliza contact time or go and see Kasper myself and put him off once and for all. Eliza wouldn't like what I'd have to do and I had thought it a bit drastic anyway, better if it could be avoided. I would give Eliza one more chance to try and deal with him herself.

"Just what we need," I mumbled to myself and

tried to work out the best time to tell Eliza.

I decided to finish off the exercises this afternoon and deal with it after dinner. Give her brain a little time to relax, before tackling Kas.

I wondered how she would react to this news. It would be interesting to see her deal with Kas. I asked her mum to tell him to expect Eliza to FaceTime at some point this evening, but I also reiterated that the less contact between us all, the safer it would be for Eliza. Phone calls could be tracked if someone was looking.

Later that evening, I confronted Eliza with the news I'd had earlier in the day. I had wanted to wait until Zaphire had gone but then thought better of it. It might help Eliza having Zaphy by her side when I told her. She looked concerned, but I also detected a little glimmer of excitement. She obviously missed Kas and was happy with the opportunity to see and talk to him, even though the message she had to give him, wasn't what he would want to hear. I felt a little sting of jealousy towards Kas, even though I knew the relationship was doomed. It was the affection Eliza clearly felt for him that bothered me, irrational as it was. I should be more jealous of my sister in that case. Eliza's feelings for her were clear to see and far

160

more passionate than whatever she'd ever felt for Kas. Eliza had a little chat with Zaphire, explaining who Kas was and what the story was so far. I noticed Zaphire exuding a little sign of jealousy as well.

"Right Eliza, before you make the call we need to talk about how you are going to convince him not to contact you again." I started before she interrupted.

"I know what to say." she stated irritably.

I ignored her rudeness and carried on regardless, but noticed Zaphire lifting her eyebrows at me.

"I'm sure you do, but as well as what you're saying, it's important how you say it. Your body language needs to be confident and open. No crossing arms. Look him in the eyes, not too much blinking or averting your eyes. You can use your arms to emphasize what you're saying, but not too exaggerated. You need to make sure you convince him that you're absolutely serious and, most importantly, that you believe what you're saying is the truth."

I hoped she was able to deliver the message clearly so he wouldn't bother us again, but I wasn't a hundred percent sure she was up for the task. She looked nervous, and that wasn't a good thing. Whatever happened, it was worth a try and if anything, good practice for Eliza.

"I do have to warn you that if this doesn't work, it's not going to be good news for Kas. I might have to get him arrested and deal with him one way or another. It will mean he'll miss his exams if not worse."

"You can't do that!" she exclaimed.

"It's not fair on him! How can you even think about doing that! You absolute dickhead."

She was outraged. I should have picked her up on shouting and swearing at me, but I thought it wiser to ignore it for now and talk to her later. I didn't want her getting into a strop with me as we needed to work together on this one and she needed to be able to concentrate.

I clocked Zaphire shifting uncomfortably in her chair.

"It's up to you to solve this one then, as I won't hesitate to do the necessary." I said matter of factly, completely ignoring her outburst.

Nothing better than a bit of pressure to sharpen the senses. She glowered at me which I returned with a hard stare. There really wasn't another solution and I hoped she'd step up to the mark and make it work.

Zaphire got up, gave Eliza a reassuring hug and

left, looking slightly bemused at me. I turned my attention back to Eliza, who had calmed down somewhat, and we started to prepare for the call.

CHAPTER 23

I took a deep breath before dialling Kasper's number. I had to steady my nerves before I spoke to him. I felt both apprehensive and excited. I had missed Kas so much and now I was about to talk to him and even though it was just online, it was the closest I would get to actually seeing him.

The message I had to deliver wasn't going to be easy. Kas wouldn't like it at all and wouldn't understand. Though I had been cocky to Zack about knowing what to say, my mind had actually gone blank. I hoped my constant rehearsal of the spiel that I'd rehearsed would help me out when needed.

It didn't help that Zack was there, observing me like a hawk. How could I act naturally under his watchful eye? I had to block him out, pretend he wasn't there, which was double as hard because for some reason Zack's scent was even stronger than normal this evening. If I failed it could have dire consequences for Kas, making me feel angry and anxious. I had to do whatever it would take to prevent that from happening...

Kas answered the call after the first ring. I saw his eyes searching for my picture. We had tampered

164

with it somewhat so it looked like it was a poor
connection, but I could see him clear as day, as if he
was in this room.

"Hey." I said tentatively.

"Hey, Eli!"

His face lit up when he heard my voice.

"I've missed you so much, babe!" his voice rough
with emotion.

"I've missed you too, Kas." I squeaked back.

I couldn't help being excited to see him. All sorts
of mixed feelings flooded me and it must have showed
as I noticed Zack lifting his eyebrows. *Block him out.*

"How are you doing? How is revision going? Do
you feel prepared?" I blurted out.

He looked pained.

"That's not what I want to talk about, babes," he
paused but I waited.

I wanted to find out what exactly he wanted to
know. I hoped, rather naively, it would be something I
could resolve easily.

"How's your father?"

Concern had crept into his voice, but it was mixed
with scepticism.

It was obvious to me he didn't really believe that I
had gone to visit my sick father.

"He's not well at all." I managed to say with some

conviction.

"It has all been very strange, finally meeting him again but in these circumstances. I feel emotionally drained."

I sighed and rubbed my fingers against my temples hoping it looked convincing.

"I just don't get it Eliza," he said, clearly frustrated.

"Why can't we talk? It's not like you not to want to talk about what's happening. It's not good for you."

He sounded desperate and worried now.

"It's the time difference babe, and the internet connection is shite here. It's difficult to find anywhere with a decent connection. I'm just too tired...."

"Cut the crap, Eli." Kas interrupted.

"I don't buy it. You're managing now aren't you. I'm worried about you. Something is off. Even Bella was questioning it the other day. Why can't you tell me the truth?"

His face was determined.

Shit. I really had to try and convince him now. I thought about all the advice Zack had given about body posture, eye contact and such and tried to pull it all together one more time.

"Listen, Kas. I *am* telling you the truth. It's difficult. I just want to deal with it first, without any

166

interruptions. You know what my mind can be like when too much is going on. I thought you, of all people, would understand..."

I looked him straight in the eyes, leaning slightly forward, eyes wide open, my voice steady but trying to convey I was hurt by his distrust at the same time. He was silent for a while, looking me over. Clearly annoyed and bothered by the bad connection. I thought for a moment I had succeeded but unfortunately, that wasn't the case. He wouldn't give up.

"Okay," he said slowly, his West Country accent strong.

"I'm sorry if I've hurt your feelings but I love you and if you need me, I want to be there for you. You don't need to protect me from whatever it is you're hiding from me. Can you promise you will FaceTime me tomorrow, just for a couple of minutes? It would stop me from worrying."

He insisted.

I looked at Zack for permission but he shook his head. Damn. Now I had to come up with something good, otherwise Zack would deal with it and I had to avoid that at all cost. I didn't want Kas to suffer for my cause. I had to tell him a big lie now, but it might work. It just had to.

167

"Oh my sweet Kas." I sighed.

I saw his eyes waiting, hoping.

"I really didn't want you to know, or anyone else..." I paused, letting a tear roll down my cheek.

It wasn't difficult. I felt so sad for him, as I knew what I was about to tell would crush him.

"I had a big setback the other night. The night I went away, I had a breakdown, Kas." I was sobbing now.

"I've been committed to short term closed psychiatric care."

I saw Zack springing into action out of the corner of my eye, phoning someone.

"I can't have contact with people at the moment Kas. My realities are all mixed up, I need to get myself sorted first. I begged to FaceTime you and try and put you off without telling you the truth, after mum had said you kept asking. She wanted to let you know, but I didn't want her to. Please don't tell anyone else. Please Kas..." I cried.

I saw the pain in his eyes. He was hurt, because I hadn't trusted him enough to tell him, and sad for my plight.

"I didn't want you to see me like this Kas, it scares me. It scares me to think you won't be able to see

168

past it in the future."

I put my head in my hands.

"I...I.., I love you Eli."

His eyes welled up and his voice hitched in his throat.

He was saved from saying any more by a nurse that had magically turned up out of nowhere. Zack's work. She gently moved me aside and sat next to me so Kas could see her. She spoke softly to Kas.

"Kasper, it's best we stop this call now. Eliza needs to rest. She needs to take a step back from the real world for a while to heal her mind. You do understand that, don't you? I'm glad she told you, it will help with her recovery, so feel pleased that she eventually opened up to you. It's a big step for her. I'll give you a number you can text for information about progress, but no more approaching Eliza until her psychiatrist deems she's ready for it, okay?"

She spoke kindly but firmly.

Kasper looked distraught but nodded.

"Is she going to be okay?" he managed to utter, all the fight and distrust had left his body.

I felt so mean.

"Yes, we're confident she can beat this. It's a small set back in her treatment plan, but she can recover. We need to get the medication right, but we just don't know how long it will take, that's all. Say your goodbyes now please."

She moved over to let me speak.

"I'm so sorry Kas. I miss you. Goodbye my love."

I studied his handsome face that looked so distraught. I wasn't sure what I felt. I missed him and cared for him deeply but I don't think I could ever again love him the way I did before I had met Zack and Zaphire.

"Don't be sorry babe. Just get better, okay. I love you."

With that we broke the connection.

I sighed a deep breath of relief and looked at Zack, who was observing me with, if I wasn't mistaken, some admiration.

"That was ingenious, Eliza! I thought I was going to have to step in but you managed to save it from the brink. Well done."

He instantly realized I wasn't feeling great about it.

"Don't feel bad. You had to do what you had to do and you did it well. Be proud of yourself. He may feel bad now, but he'll cope. Better than being arrested innocently, remember. It's actually perfect, as there's no time limit now. Absolutely brilliant. You're a

170

natural!"

He looked so pleased, but I felt bad. I hoped I would get used to deceiving people as that is what I, apparently, was a natural at, I thought bitterly.

"You better let my mum know the recent addition to our deception." I whispered flatly.

"Good point, Eliza. I'll do that straight away." he said whilst getting his phone out.

He signalled a thank you to the nurse who had helped us out. She came up to me and rubbed my back.

"Are you alright, love?" she asked kindly, and introduced herself as Nurse Kate.

"I'm glad I could be of help but let me know if you need anything else, love. You look exhausted."

She smiled warmly at me.

I let her give me a hug and I had a good long cry. One that I hadn't allowed myself to do, but was massively overdue.

CHAPTER 24

I gave Eliza some time to get herself together after the nurse had left. Kate had done a brilliant job having been put on the spot like that.
I knew I could rely on her. She was the queen of improvisation, quick to adapt to any situation and incredibly intuitive. Perfect for situations like these.

I was contemplating not pulling up Eliza over her earlier insubordination toward me. She'd done a great job, but she was obviously quite shook up over it. I had a suspicion that she had an extremely heightened sense of morality. Deception was going to take a toll on her, if she didn't learn to turn that sense down somewhat. In our job we were all too often asked to use some form of subterfuge to get our results. She might do better not being out in the field after this mission, but instead doing an office job. That would be a waste of her talents though, as she had a lot of potential.

Even though I knew she was feeling rubbish, I had decided I couldn't ignore her indiscretions from before.
"Eliza?"
She looked up at me questioningly.

"Remember before speaking to Kas, you were extremely rude to me and I can't condone that again. I'm not going to discipline you now, but, if you *ever* speak to me like that again, there *will* be consequences."

I spoke sternly, hoping that would be enough to put her off trying that again in a hurry. I doubted it would be enough though, she felt things too strongly not to react impulsively. That would probably take years of training and discipline to achieve.

She sighed and actually looked remorseful.

"I know; I'm sorry Zack. I know you're only doing your job. I didn't mean to shout at you. I know I'm not a perfect recruit."

She looked down hearted. I couldn't let her feel like that after she'd done such a good job and had to put her boyfriend through misery for our mission.

"Maybe not perfect Eliza, but damn promising! You're one of the most naturally gifted Sensorians I have ever seen. You learn quickly, are able to make on the spot decisions and read people's body language plus manipulate your own so easily, and that with the little training you've had. You will be amazing." I said, hoping she would believe me and start believing in herself.

173

"Thanks for your vote of confidence Zack. I hope I'll deserve it one day."

She smiled a bit. I moved a strand of hair out of her face tenderly.

"You'd better believe it, girl. Off to bed now I think. Self-defence lessons tomorrow, plus we need to factor some time in for your revision as well."

She grunted with the prospect of that.

"I don't know if I can concentrate on that, as well as everything else!" she sighed.

"You'll just have to, Eliza. No grumbling. Bed. Now."

I woke up energised the following day, feeling optimistic about the day ahead. Eliza seemed to be in a good mood too. No residual bad feelings from yesterday by the looks of it. She must have been able to compartmentalise any negative experiences and put them away. That was a promising sign for her to be able to deal with those, building her resilience. It improved my mood even more.

Zaphire and Eliza had the best self-defence session ever, with Eliza putting into practise some skills she learned straight away. I always loved seeing my sister fight, she moved like a leopard, so

174

gracefully. Moreover, the chemistry between the two of them was a sight to behold. Zaphire woke me from my musings and challenged me to attack Eliza.

"Don't hold back Eliza!" Zaphire shouted.

"Remember what I taught you; think about a man's weak spots."

That gave me enough warning to dodge a swift kick between my legs, but I hadn't accounted for Eliza then taking advantage of the imbalance I got myself into and she nearly managed to floor me. She fought dirty. I had to use all my strength to pin her down to the floor, but she was feisty, and kept twisting and turning, digging her fucking fingers and nails in my face and nearly escaping me again. My pride got the better of me and I sat on top of her with my full weight, until she begged for mercy, laughing.

"Wow, Eliza. Yet another thing you seem to take to like a duck to water!" I said admiringly as I let her go from underneath me.

She kept on surprising me as she hadn't stricken me as a physically apt person at all. The way she fought wasn't gainly or fair but certainly effective! My face still burned from her fucking scratches, the cheeky bitch!

"That'll be my amazing teaching I'll have you know." Zaphire boasted proudly.

"In self-defence it's all about being clever and aiming for weak spots. You can floor any man with a well aimed kick or prod!" she laughed.

"Good to know." Eliza said wickedly as she winked at me.

"Don't you get any ideas young lady." I warned her.

She shrugged her shoulders and laughed, giving Zaphire a hug to say thanks for the lesson. I saw her take a deep breath in just before she got close to Zaphy, showing she wasn't quite trusting herself being so close up to her yet.

Our meeting with Markus was looming after lunch, and my mood took a dive. I had a sense of foreboding about this one and the feeling wouldn't go away. It didn't help Zaphire wishing me luck, which only made my suspicion grow stronger that she knew more about what was coming than she was letting on. I decided to forewarn Eliza about my worries about the meeting, so she knew what to expect at least a little bit.

"First of all, Markus will want an update as to how you're getting on so he can work out where you're at. He also may have some information about your father.

Then I expect him to have some plans for you that I get the feeling I may not agree with." I admitted.

"Okay."

She paused a few seconds.

"How come you have that feeling?"

"I'm picking up a vibe from Zaphire. She isn't telling me something that she knows, which worries me. Markus must have ordered her not to say anything, because she would've done otherwise. And it must have been serious as Zaphire doesn't shy away from breaking the rules occasionally. No doubt we will find out soon, whether we like it or not."

CHAPTER 25

I felt nervous about our meeting with the big boss.
I had encountered him several times and he always
seemed perfectly calm and reasonable, but the way
Zack spoke about him made me feel on edge. He
was a big deal in this community and in my previous
meetings I hadn't quite realised his power and
standing, which made me nervous whereas before I
didn't have that burden. However, I was still eager to
find out what had been found out about my father.
Feeling more in control over my gift I had allowed
myself to think about the mission and my father, rather
than just keeping it together.

On our way to Markus' office, I looked sideways at
my coach. He tried to look as relaxed as possible, but
wasn't masking his tenseness very well. I was going
to say something, but thought better of it. Zack
knocked on the door, which was opened immediately.
Markus in a sharp dark blue suit, beckoned us in
whilst he finished off a phone call.

"Take a seat Eliza and Zack."
It somehow made me feel like I was in the
Headmaster's office. Both Zack and I did what he

said and he also made himself comfortable.

"How have you been?"

He addressed me directly, so I couldn't avoid saying something. I wasn't sure if I could keep my voice steady but I had to answer. I quickly glanced at Zack, who gave me an encouraging nod.

"Uh, yes, doing well I think, ehm."

I stumbled over my words embarrassingly. *Get it together for goodness sake.*

"I think the medication is more or less out of my system and I am starting to feel much better within myself now."

"Good, that is great to hear Eliza."

He gave me a heartfelt smile which made me feel instantly more relaxed. Zack, however was still visibly tense. Markus had picked up on that as I saw him assess Zack's body posture. A frown crept on his face, but he just asked Zack to tell him how the training was going.

"She's making good progress in controlling her senses and we're just starting to work on how to manipulate them to her advantage. We did a little work on her interpreting other people's behaviour and signals they give out. She also did very well dealing with Kas, rescuing the situation with good improvisation skills. Her physical stamina isn't great

179

but she is working on that. Her fighting skills are surprisingly good. Quick and clever for someone who has never done anything like that before."

He didn't look at me once when he was giving Markus this report on me, but at the end he threw me a glance. He must have spotted my cheeks going red as he suppressed a little smile. Markus looked impressed and pleased, but Zack's face betrayed his worries creeping to the surface again.

"It sounds like you are doing a great job with her." Markus crooned.

"Not down to me alone, Markus. Zaphire's been a great help but it's mostly Eliza's own determination and natural ability, to be honest."

Zack shrugged his shoulders as if to say he was just lucky to be there to claim the glory.

"Right okay, whatever you're doing to enable that, keep it going. It's obviously working." Markus concluded.

"I suppose now it's my turn. I will bring you up to speed with our mission." Markus began.

He shifted in his seat, just showing a little unease.

"You may not be aware, but we have been able to locate your father, but haven't made contact. We believe that first contact should be with you, Eliza. I have to be honest and say that we are not entirely sure what his situation is. We're currently working under the assumption that he's working for this group of criminals under duress and they have some sort of power over him, but we're not entirely sure. You should know there is a possibility he's doing it for personal gain, but we really don't have any reason to assume that at this moment. I just want to be totally honest with you."

I wasn't sure what to think of this, but a chill went through my body. In the pits of my stomach, an icy clump formed. I thought about what the punishment could be for people who betrayed their gift and the Sensorian community. I didn't allow myself to go there and was relieved to hear Zack speak, so I could concentrate on that instead.

"What criminal organisation are we talking about?" Zack asked, and I could see it was news to him too.

"It's a group totally under the radar of the police. It seems to work on a different level than all the other criminal gangs in the country, and we know there's a lot of money and drugs involved. It seems they're trying, and succeeding, to infiltrate into the police and justice system, and there are political links too. We've been planning the next course of action after the

181

observation stage is over, and we're basically ready for the next step, which is where you come in, Eliza."

He paused to let his words sink in.

I took advantage of the break and put in a question, under the watchful eye of Zack.

"Forgive me for probably being naïve, but now you know where my father is, why don't you just bring him in?"

I had directed the question to Markus, but then looked at Zack's face to see his reaction. His face gave nothing away, and was relying on Markus to answer the question.

"I can understand your question Eliza, but there's a lot at stake. We need to know Rick's situation before we can take any action. We want to tackle the organisation as it looks to be developing fast, and seems to be posing a threat maybe even for the security of the country. We need to know what role Rick is playing in it, as if we just take him out, it may trigger events we have no control over. We want you to make contact in the next few days and figure out what we are dealing with here. Zack you need to make a plan to set it in motion by tomorrow."

Zack looked shocked, I didn't really know what to think, but before I knew it, Zack had jumped up on his feet and paced round the room.

"She's not fucking ready for that!" he roared at Markus.

"It would be far too dangerous!! I'm not having her exposed to that yet! It's way too fucking soon! What are you crazy idiots thinking!"

He was incensed, squaring up to Markus who had also got up from his seat. He stared at Zack, his face giving nothing away, but his eyebrows raised.

"Zacharya, sit yourself down *immediately*." he said with the sternest voice I had ever heard, and Zack complied instantly, looking distressed.

"We will *talk* about how we'll proceed with our mission, but you do not raise your voice. You do not talk to me like that Zack. You forget your place. You're too emotionally involved and not objective. That's why I was reluctant to share our plans any sooner with you."

Zack and Markus' altercation physically hurt me, it was that strong. Markus was resolute.

"I will have to discipline you for that disrespectful attitude and we'll have to resume our meeting after your punishment."

Zack grunted and reluctantly got up when Markus ordered him to stand, trying to say something but was silenced straight away.

"I haven't given you permission to talk. Save it for later. You get to spend the next four hours in isolation. You're lucky we can't afford wasting time, otherwise it would have been at least a week. And as it's only four hours, you won't be allowed to sit down and you can face the wall. You can think of a fitting way to apologise there. The both of you."

Zack looked up at Markus, not understanding and frustrated as he wasn't allowed to speak. But I was, so I did.

"Uh..., Markus. Me? Why? What have I done?" I said indignantly.

I surprised myself by daring to question Markus after having just witnessed Zack being reprimanded so severely.

"Well, Eliza. Even though you're making great progress, I've heard you have, at times, been less than respectful to Zack. He's been remiss not to pick you up on it. I think a little discipline won't go amiss for you as well, young lady. You're not to talk until you get back in to this room and you can apologise to him, in front of me."

I was stunned. I didn't think Zack had said anything about that to him, but by the thunderous look on his face, it hadn't been him that had reported me.

184

"Oh, I..." I started but the incredulous looks on both faces made me shut up instantly.

"Samuel, can you please take them to the cell, both of them on opposite sides, facing the wall and switch the camera on please. Just as a word of warning to both of you, no talking or looking at each other. We may be pressed for time but make no mistake. I take insubordination *very* seriously, so I won't hesitate to prolong your time in isolation."

He turned to attend to a phone call that had just come in and left us in Samuel's hands.

Zack sighed and resigned himself to be led away to the cell. I felt awful, I wasn't sure what felt worse. The fact I was being punished like this, or that, as it had dawned on me, it may have been Zaphire who had told on me and Zack. I also felt bad for Zack who was called out over having been lenient when I've disrespected him. It was all a bit ironic really. I decided to just let it go and get through the next four hours. It wasn't going to be very comfortable, especially as I was hungry too, and I needed the toilet. Pants.

The time couldn't go quickly enough. I wanted to know what the next part of the mission was and how

185

we would be able to find out what my father's roll exactly was in this criminal organisation. It sounded bad. Very bad. However, time did not fly. It felt more like ten hours and the worst thing was that there was no way of telling the time. It was torture and in my previous life, a few weeks ago I may have cried. Not any more though. I just had to endure it.

CHAPTER 26

I could not believe what the fuck just happened.
Why did I shout at Markus! I don't think I had raised
my voice or sworn at him for at least five years, when I
was just hitting puberty. I do believe I had forgotten
my place. Damned Eliza. I feel so protective over her
that I dared challenge Markus, my leader and carer. I
could kick myself, I felt so stupid. I could have just
calmly raised my concerns and Markus would have
listened. We would have sorted something out, I
knew that. But something had just snapped inside me
with the thought of Eliza being thrown into the deep
end, into danger at that.

I was worried about how Eliza would feel about
being punished like this. I've had to endure plenty of it
in the past, so though an inconvenient and humiliating
experience, I was used to it. I wanted to talk it
through with her but we wouldn't have an opportunity
to talk until we were faced with Markus again. I think
Eliza would have worked out by now that it was most
probably Zaphire who'd informed Markus about her
behaviour, and I'm not sure if she'd understand. I was
annoyed with Zaphire, but she probably felt that
Markus should know about Eliza's fiery side and to be

187

honest he would probably have just had a quiet word with me about it, had I not challenged him. Zaphire couldn't have predicted that and I'm sure when she finds out it had landed Eliza in the isolation cell with me, she would feel mortified.

Four hours was a long time to just stand there. The muscles in my back started to ache and I could hear Eliza fidgeting behind me. I didn't risk taking a peak at her and I hoped she resisted as well. I didn't want to spend any longer in here than necessary, it was such a fucking frustrating waste of time as it was. I hoped she remembered the cameras, as we wouldn't get away with anything. I heard her sigh deeply and I wished I could give her a word of encouragement, but unfortunately she would have to battle this one herself. I hoped she was mentally strong enough, but I was encouraged that I couldn't pick up any significant stress signals from her body.

Finally, after what had felt so much longer than four hours, I heard the door unlock. I breathed a sigh of relief and I could hear Eliza do the same.

"Turn around please, and follow me, Eliza first then you behind her." Samuel ordered.

He looked smug, probably enjoying the temporary

188

position of power over me. I only caught a glimpse of Eliza's face, but what I saw, didn't disappoint me. She looked determined, not broken, distraught or angry. That was a good sign. Just before we arrived at Markus' office I managed to grab Eliza's hand and gave it a quick squeeze before letting go again in case Samuel noticed. I didn't want to risk being sent back to the cell. Markus hadn't specifically said anything about holding hands once we were out, but the fact we were told to walk one behind another gave me enough reason to be careful.

We entered the room and Markus was sat behind his desk, looking less than impressed.

"Zack, please step forward. You're allowed to talk now, so what do you have to say for yourself." he said expectantly.

I hoped my words would be enough for him to forgive me and move on. I lifted my face and looked Markus straight in the eyes.

"Sir, I sincerely apologise for my behaviour earlier. It was totally uncalled for and disrespectful and it won't happen again. I hope you can forgive me."

I lowered my eyelids again, not to look defiant.

"Good, I'm glad you have realised your error, but what brought it on? It worries me. Maybe you are too

189

invested in Eliza. Do I need to replace you as her trainer?"

He observed me very closely, and shocked though as I was with the prospect of being relieved from my responsibilities, I answered as calmly as I could. I knew he was testing me. If I lost it now, it would spell the end of this mission for me for sure.

"If Sir feels that's the right course of action, so be it. However, I would ask to get a second chance and continue my task as I think I can bring the best out of her, Sir."

I hardly dared to breathe whilst he was considering his answer.

"Right well, luckily for you I do agree with that Zack. However, you must promise not to let your emotions take over like that again. It will cloud your judgement. Do not disappoint me again."

His eyes fixed on mine, willing me to understand the consequences of another outburst.

"I won't Markus. Thank you. I won't let you down." I said relieved.

"Good, glad we have sorted that Zack. Let's move on to Eliza. Let's hope she has learned something from this too."

Both of us turned towards her, Markus' eyes

boring into hers. She shifted from one foot to another and looked so uncomfortable. I really felt for her. However, I needed to show Markus I could deal with her appropriately, so she just had to do this properly.

"Well? Eliza, is there anything you would like to say to me," I prompted her.

She hardly dared look me in the eyes, but she drew a breath and started to speak.

"Zack..."

I had to interrupt her straight away to correct her.

"You mean, Sir."

I raised my eyebrows to underline I was expecting her to say it. Her eyes widened. She wasn't happy with that at all, but under Markus' stare, she complied.

"Sir, I'm really sorry if you were offended by my earlier outbursts..." she started.

That wasn't going to do. I couldn't believe I had to actually teach her to fucking apologise properly, but I needed to keep calm, reminding myself she was not brought up in our community. So I stopped her again.

"Eliza.... *if* I was offended?"

I looked at her sceptically.

"Please apologize properly. Think carefully how you're going to phrase this now."

Her cheeks went a lovely shade of pink, to her own annoyance. Bless her. I hoped she would hurry

191

up as I wasn't sure how much longer Markus' patience would hold out, though his posture gave nothing away but utter calmness. However, he was a master at cloaking.

Eliza took a deep sigh and looked as if she'd resigned herself to the situation she found herself in.

"Sir, I apologize for my behaviour. I will try my hardest not to treat you like that again." she eventually said, doing her utmost best to avoid eye contact.

I walked up to her and put my face inches away from her.

"Now, say that again and actually look at me, Eliza. I need to see you mean it." I said curtly.

She did, but what I saw in her eyes was annoyance not apology. I turned towards Markus disappointed, shrugging my shoulders.

"I'm sorry Markus, but this is what I meant when I told you she isn't ready yet. She needs to understand our way of life better, before she can be deployed on a mission, even if her skills are good. Her reluctance to accept orders and argumentative disposition can put other people and herself in danger. It's my mistake. You were right; I've been slow to discipline her. It's time to crack it, otherwise she'll be useless to us. We can't have a loose cannon amongst our midst."

I had made up my mind, no more making excuses for her. It's got to be done.

"Hmmm," Markus mused.

"I understand; she needs to be taught more about what we do and the reasons why we operate the way we do. She needs to see what happens when people start going astray and think they know better. It's up to you Zack. Make it happen. I can't stall for much longer. We need to find out what is going on with Rick as soon as possible, before he or the organisation he's possibly forced to work for find out we are on to them."

"How long do I have, Sir?" I asked, looking at Eliza, who I could tell was bursting to say something and it wasn't going to be good. She looked seething. I sighed. This was going to be a hard one to crack. I really liked her, despite her irritating temper and occasional childishness. I wanted her to like me, but she was going to hate me for the next few days. I hoped we could get past it afterwards like I had managed with Sam.

"I'm not sure Zack. We can stretch to five, maybe six days maximum, but the sooner the better. I hope it is enough." Markus said with a sigh. He turned towards Eliza.

"I hope you understand what we're talking about, because we all believe you have massive potential. You're well liked by everyone and your gift promises to be exceptional. But, and there is a big but. If you can't work in a team, show respect and follow orders, it'll be wasted. You will either return to your previous life, feeling frustrated and never really free from us, or you will end up doing an office based job with us, wasting your potential. It's a choice only you can make. Submit to our rules, wholeheartedly or we muddle through this mission and it will be your last one ever."

He grabbed both Eliza's hands and looked her straight in the eyes.

"I hope you make the right choice Eliza."

CHAPTER 27

Markus' words had struck a chord with me. Just before he had spoken to me I was annoyed and cross that they were talking about me like I wasn't there. I nearly had burst out telling them so, but I was glad I hadn't. I hadn't understood what the big deal was, I had apologised, hadn't I? What more did they want! I couldn't believe what Zack had made me do and say. I was so proud of myself for getting through the four hours of isolation; I didn't understand what the importance of the apology was.

After Markus' little speech and Zack's disappointed look, I started to get what they were trying to do, but it was a bit late by then. Zack was going to treat me harshly now, because I let him down and I wasn't sure I could convince him that I resolved to work hard on my temper and try my hardest to show him the respect he expected. I hoped he could feel my mood now, there was no defiance left. How could it all go so horribly wrong in such a short amount of time?

On our way back to our room I glanced sideways to catch Zack's eye, but his face was grim and determined, looking stoically ahead. I had to just put my head down and work hard. Follow every order, however ridiculous it would be, as I was sure he was going to test me severely. I desperately wanted to prove I was up for this mission. I didn't want to be a liability.

I wanted to tell Zack all my resolutions, but I would wait until Zack decided to talk to me about it. He didn't look in a talking sort of mood. I also wanted to know more about the mission as I had so many questions. I was scared there was a chance my father was embroiled in this criminal organisation by choice, with all the consequences that would bring. It all had to wait. I was frustrated with myself. Why did I have to be so stubborn and impulsive! I was dying for a wee by now as well, as we still hadn't had a toilet break. When we got to our room, I dashed towards the bathroom only to be stopped with a heavy hand on my shoulder.

"Where do you think you are going, Miss?" Zack barked at me.

I was afraid this would happen. I turned around and told him I needed the bathroom.

"Fuck it." he started, taking a long hard look at me.

"This is how it's going to be for the next three days. You will have to abide by a very strict disciplinary regime to teach you to follow orders and show respect at all times. You will need to ask permission for anything you want or need to do, including talking. You don't move unless you've asked me, you don't sit unless you've asked me, you don't eat, drink, wash, brush your teeth, or anything without asking permission. When I ask you a question you answer straight away, and you will address me as Sir, until I decide you can use my name again. Do you understand?"

His eyes were cold. He had put his mask on; there was no emotion showing, just expectation of total compliance on my part. *Shit, this was going to be tough. Just grin and bear it. I can do this.*

"Yes Sir. Permission to speak, Sir?"

I tried to look as serious as I could, even though it just felt so stupid calling him Sir. I hoped he could see I was really trying, but I could feel he wasn't satisfied. It was so hard to hide anything from him. I had to take this seriously now.

"I'll give you one more chance to say that, without a smirk on your face this time Eliza." he responded.

I was really dying to go to the loo now and I was going to wet myself, if not careful.

"Sorry, Sir. I understand. Please, may I have permission to speak Sir?" I pleaded now.

No smirk in sight.

"Yes Miss Mankuzay, you may speak." he said more amenable now.

"Can I please go to the bathroom Sir?"

Please just let me now Zack, I am bursting. I was desperate.

"Be more specific. What are you going to do in the bathroom? Have a shower? Do your make-up?"

I had been right; he was going to be an insufferable pig. I sighed before answering, but bloody hell, nothing got past him.

"Is it too much of an effort to answer me Eliza?" he taunted.

"No.., no sorry. I'm desperate for a wee now though. Can I please go to the toilet?"

I looked at him beseechingly, but he just raised his eyebrows.

"Sir." I added quickly. Hitting myself mentally. To my relief he did finally let me go. I was so rubbish at this. The next three days were going to be hell.

When I came out of the bathroom I saw Zaphire sitting on the sofa, next to Zack. They were in a heavy discussion, but stopped immediately when they sensed me. Zaphire's eyes lit up when she noticed me, but they also betrayed guilt. I knew for sure now that it was her who had reported me to Markus. My emotions rose up inside me and I wasn't sure if I could hold them in check. I was truly annoyed with her, but loved the way she had looked at me, all excited to see me. I was struck by her beauty every time I saw her and I couldn't keep the butterflies out of my belly.

I felt embarrassed when I had to ask Zack permission to sit down on the empty chair. I noticed Zaphire throwing Zack a questioning look. He obviously hadn't yet discussed his decision, to teach me a military style crash course on discipline and respect.

"Oh, I see." Zaphire looked me over, which made my hair stand up.

"Can we speak?" she asked Zack uncertainly.

"If she wants to after that stunt you pulled on us, sister." he winked.

"But she will have to ask me for permission first."

He looked at me, his face devoid of any emotion. I felt like sinking into the ground there and then, face burning once again. It was just so humiliating. However, I gritted my teeth and asked for permission to speak with Zaphire, which he allowed. He wasn't going to be a total arse, then. Zaphire took my hand and knelt beside me.

"I am so sorry it turned out the way it did for you,

my sweet. I told Markus out of concern for you, and he said he would just have a word with you and Zack. Had it not been for my annoying dick of a brother blowing his head off at our leader...."

She glared at Zack.

"You wouldn't have had to stay in that damned isolation cell for hours!"

"Not that she learned anything from it." grumbled Zack.

"Hence the predicament she got herself in. I had no choice." he said almost apologetically to Zaphire.

I wished I could tell him I understood, but that wouldn't be enough. I needed to show him I could do this, without having an outburst, be in total control of myself. Instead I focussed on Zaphire. Her hand on mine filled me with intense pleasure and I had already totally forgiven her.

"No worries, Zaphire, I probably deserve this."

I waved my hands around to signify the situation I was in.

"Probably?" Zack interrupted sarcastically, rolling his eyes at Zaphire.

"See what I mean Sis?" he added, annoyed.

He really wasn't happy with me. Everything I said was wrong in his eyes.

"Okay *Sir,* I meant I *totally* deserve this." I

200

couldn't help myself again.

"Sorry Sir, I didn't mean to sound sarcastic. It's a habit. So sorry."

I hoped I had been quick enough to avoid his wrath and luckily it looked like I got away with it as he stood up and poured himself a drink. Zaphire, though, looked at me with naughty twinkly eyes.

"I didn't think I could like you even more, sweets, but you have me hooked."

She gave me a little wink. Zack gave her a withering look as he heard of course despite the whispering. Zaphire couldn't have really thought he wouldn't have heard. But she just smiled at him, and though he wasn't happy, he left her alone, shrugging his shoulders.

"As we haven't done a lot of physical exercise today, we will do a session now. Get it in before dinner. Go and get changed Eliza and I will get you a water bottle. You haven't drunk enough today, so you need to make sure you take sips throughout."

He motioned for Zaphire to leave.

"See you tomorrow Zaphy."

She gave him a tender hug and waved bye to me whilst blowing me a kiss.

"Good luck Eli. You can do this!" she shouted

whilst Zack pushed her out the door, now quite forcefully.

That was the first time she called me Eli, what all my friends call me at home. It felt good.

I thought Zack had put me through my paces before, but that had been nothing compared to what I endured in this last session. I didn't think I could walk, sit or lay down ever again! I bit through it though, determined not to be beaten. I wanted to impress Zack and him to be proud of me again. However, he still didn't show any emotion towards me. He was just the hard task master he had earned his reputation for, which I admired in him, but hated.

I wondered if he'd ever treat me more like a friend again, someone he cared for. I suppose I had to keep showing him I did respect him and that I was capable of following orders without arguing or questioning everything. I knew it wasn't all about me, he also had to prove to himself and Markus that he could handle me and train me so that I would be a useful and trustworthy member to our community, worthy of being a Sensorian.

The rest of the evening panned out as I had feared. Zack still insisted on me asking permission to

202

do anything. And he picked up on every tiny little thing I did. I hoped he would get tired of it himself but, oh boy, was I wrong. He was absolutely relentless. Then he started ordering me to do useless tasks as well, and I have to say I nearly lost it when he asked me to take all my clothes out of the cupboard for the fourth time and put them all back, colour coded. I managed to stay in control and did the task, but he had picked up on my vibes, those damned senses, and made me do it all over again. When I had finally finished, I was so tired and my body was aching all over from the earlier exercise session. He finally gave me permission to go to bed and I barely made it. I didn't even undress. I think I was asleep even before my head hit the pillow.

CHAPTER 28

Fuck, I needed a drink to relax so badly, but I couldn't. It was such bloody hard work being on top of Eliza the whole time plus having to disguise my signals so she couldn't read my emotions. I was absolutely knackered, but I had to persevere. I had picked up on Eliza's mood of determination. I knew she wanted to impress me and she hated me not showing any approval or any emotion. She was desperate for me to see she had learned something from the whole incident at Markus', but I couldn't let her off the hook yet. I had to persist for at least three days with this harsh regime, depending on how it was going. If she managed to keep up her determination for those three days we could probably ease back into the normal routine, which couldn't come quickly enough as far as I was concerned. I already missed having our little relaxed chats over dinner and her sharp sense of humour.

From the moment she got up the next morning, I ordered her around to do the most stupid tasks I could think of and she complied with each and every one of them without complaint or even any other signals of discontent. She had completely submitted to me with no trace of sarcasm. She must have been working overtime to control her senses as it was so against her grain to be this obedient without showing some disdain or irritation. I wondered if she'd last the day without an outburst, having to work this hard. At least she was practising cloaking, which would only benefit her.

"Permission to speak, Sir?" she asked for about the tenth time today.

I hadn't given her permission at all yet. I had just ordered her around, including telling her to eat, drink, wash and go to the toilet.

"Granted," I relented.

"Please may I see Zaphire at all today, Sir?"

For the first time today she showed her feelings as she was anxiously waiting for my reply. She really wanted to meet up with her and hadn't been able to keep quiet about it. I had been planning a self-defence session with Zaphire later this afternoon, but wasn't sure to give in to her request now. I needed her to be tested to her wits end so I decided to deny her the pleasure.

"Not today, Eliza. I will cancel the session with her this afternoon and will do the self-defence session myself with you."

I carefully gauged her reaction. Her shoulders

dropped a bit and a little sigh escaped her mouth.

"Is my answer not to your liking, Miss Mankuzay?"
I pressed.

She looked up at me, steely eyed. She had
recovered her determination.

"No, it's not a problem, Sir." she said, even
managing a little smile.

"I'm glad it's not a problem for you, Eliza." I said
sarcastically.

"Go and get a book now and copy me ten pages.
Make sure I can read your writing."

I was getting bored of thinking of useless tasks
and this would keep her busy for a while. She didn't
bat an eyelid and went straight to the task. I texted
Zaphire to tell her about the cancelled session. I got
one straight back saying "*Arse*!" Guess she wasn't
too happy with me either.

I looked forward to a bit of exercise and hurried
through our lunch. I hated not being active and we
had been cooped up in our room all morning. I gave
Eliza a bollocking for not getting changed quickly
enough, which she accepted and apologised for
straight away. She was getting bloody good at this.
She probably hated my guts now, but she didn't show
any sign of it. She clearly had inherited her father's

cloaking skills, and this training had brought it out of her. I was incredibly impressed with her. Some of my previous trainees had coped far worse and they had grown up in our community so were used to the discipline and our way of life. I wasn't going to let her know that though. Yet.

"No, place your arms here, and here."

I showed Eliza how to get out of a strangle hold, moving her arms in the right position.

"Now jerk both arms in opposite directions."

There wasn't enough venom in her movements.

"Hold me in strangle hold, and I will show you."

I made it look easy, but in fact she had me in a good hold, probably fuelled by her dislike for me at the moment, so I had to put quite some force in. I swung her around so her face was nearly touching mine. She smelled delicious and looked gorgeous with her fiery eyes. I could see my scent and closeness didn't leave her cold either as she closed her eyes, and pushed me away. She was visualising to keep her urges under control. I hadn't realised how much she was still struggling with them. But she let her guard down whilst fighting me and they had gotten on top of her. She was quickly back in control though, glaring at me.

I backed off and turned around, next thing I knew I was on the floor. She had scissor tackled me from behind and taken me completely by surprise. She stood over me with her fingers jabbing at my eyes. *Little minx.* My instinct kicked in and I grabbed her arms and flipped her over. Within seconds I was on top of her and I couldn't help giving off an abundance of pheromones. I wanted her, there and then. The scent must have been overwhelming , but as quickly as I had been on top of her I flew off her again and marched to the far corner of the room. She was left panting on the floor, rosy cheeked and feisty looking. One day, she will be my undoing.

"Let's take a break."

I tried to sound as relaxed as possible and gave her a little smile, momentarily forgetting I was meant to order her around and not show any emotion. I quickly recovered, telling her to get up, putting my guard back up. She had noticed though, but if she thought this was the end of it, she had another thing coming. I wasn't going to do combat with her again anytime soon. Can't lose control like that. She will get her time with Zaph tomorrow. That'll be interesting to watch!

Eliza wasn't going to like what I had in mind for her this evening. I planned to take her to the dining room and have dinner with my friends. She wouldn't be allowed to talk or interact with us though and I would have to make her ask permission to sit, eat and drink. I knew she would really hate me for humiliating her like that, but I've done it with my previous trainees and I needed to show Markus, I wasn't treating her any differently. I wouldn't be popular with Zaphire either, but she'll understand. Not so sure about Eliza though.

CHAPTER 29

We walked into the dining room and I could really kill Zack now. He had made me walk behind him, but I could still see all the questioning looks from Ned, Brody and Sam plus a murderous look from Zaphire, all directed at Zack.

"She's under orders not to speak during dinner." Zack explained, as if it was the most normal thing in the world.

It looked like they all immediately understood what was happening, and they all just carried on with their conversations, apart from Zaphire who was still glaring at Zack. I caught a little sympathetic glance from Sam, but she quickly focussed on Brody when she realised Zack looked at her. She probably had the same treatment from Zack, so would understand how awful I felt. I had only met these people once and I felt comfortable with them and they'd been so kind and had accepted me straight away. Now I just looked stupid and immature.

"Zaphy, please just let it go," Zack pleaded with her softly.

"I have no choice," trying to explain himself.

She shook her shoulders and with one last look at

me, turned towards her friends and joined their conversation. I was still standing and looked uncomfortably at Zack, but he seemed to have forgotten about me.

"Err, Sir, may I sit down please?" I whispered.

Zack turned around; all joyous expression he'd shown to his friends had disappeared in an instant. His face hard.

"Did you ask for permission to speak?" he spoke loudly.

It felt like the dining room fell silent and everyone was looking at me. I wanted to sink into the ground, but answered instead.

"No, I'm sorry Sir." I said lowering my head.

I could kick myself. Stupid mistake.

"I won't grant you permission to talk or to sit at the moment, Eliza. You can wait till I order you to sit down and then I may let you eat, if you don't interrupt me again."

He didn't wait for acknowledgement; he just turned back around again and focussed on his friends. This was going to be a tough evening. He left me standing for another half hour or so and by the time he allowed me to sit and eat my dinner, it had gone cold. I was so hungry though, I had no choice but to eat it. I felt so miserable I could cry. Zack, on the other hand, had a great time, enjoying a laugh with his friends and sister, who all seemed to have completely forgotten about me.

As if it wasn't bad enough already, as soon as I had finished my dinner, Zack ordered me to stand up again and face the wall. I have to admit I may have cried a little at that point. I felt very sorry for myself. I told myself no one had noticed, but I was under no illusion that each and every one of them had felt my despair. There was no hiding emotions from that lot. All I wanted to do was go back to our room and go to bed, but I doubted that was what Zack had in mind for me. I started to wonder if I was cut out to do this any longer and for a moment I thought I was going to run out of the cafe, shouting abuse at Zack. But then all of this would have been for nothing and I would probably be subjected to this treatment for even longer. It's not like I could just go home, so I just had to endure it. I found my resolve again just in time for the next task Zack had dreamed up for me.

"Miss Mankuzay."
I hated it when he addressed me like that as nothing good had ever followed it.

"I've told the waiters you'll clear our table and clean the floor. Use the cleaning equipment from their trolley and make it quick. I want to go back soon. Understood?"

He waited for me to respond.

"Yes Sir, of course." I answered dutifully.

I went to get the plates off the table, starting with Zaphire's. Her hand brushed past mine and the soft touch sent electricity down my arms and made my whole body shiver, resulting in a rather clumsy move which sent Sam's half empty glass flying over the table, splattering all over Sam's legs. She jumped and yelled in surprise.

"Oh Sam, Shit! I'm so sorry!" I blurted out horrified, covering my mouth with my hands in embarrassment.

I quickly grabbed some cloths and started frantically cleaning the mess up.

"Here, let me wipe that off your legs. That was so stupid of me. Shall I get you a new drink?"

I looked up at her face but she was looking at Zack, her eyes warning me to be quiet. I also turned towards Zack, realising my mistake.

"Did I give you permission to speak?" he asked sceptically.

"No Sir, I'm sorry. But it just came out." I tried to

defend myself.

"It just came out. That's your excuse?" his words dripping with sarcasm.

I lowered my eyes and head, hoping he would leave it at that. In vain of course.

"You just earned yourself another day of punishment regime, Eliza." he said shaking his head.

I caught Zaphire rolling her eyes at me.

"But Sir, I just...." I tried to explain, but he cut me off with a brusque, "two days".

I threw my hands up in the air and opened my mouth, but he stepped forward and put a finger on my lips.

"Do *not* make me have to make that three days." he implored, his eyes boring into mine.

I relented, an involuntary shiver running through my body. He was uncompromising and there was nothing I could do but accept two more days on top of the one remaining.

"Now apologise formally to Sam and clean the rest of that mess up and make it quick. I'm getting bored."

He sounded really pissed off, obviously forgetting to cloak and I hurried over to Sam and apologised again, before finishing off the table. When I was done with the floor as well, I walked up to Zack and waited

214

by his side. He didn't even acknowledge me and just walked off, expecting me to follow him like a dog. I was getting fed up with this. Enduring it was much easier said than done, but that was exactly what I had to do. I knew I was being pushed to my limits, but I also knew I was learning a lot about myself and the ways I was able to cope with much more than I would have ever thought.

I hurried after Zack as he was walking at pace, clearly still in a mood. I was fully expecting a heap of tasks to do but he just told me to sit at the table and piled my school books in front of me.

"Time to do some studying. We've neglected them, so you need to catch up. I expect to see notes, spider diagrams or revision cards at the end of the study session."

He retreated to the sofa with a book and left me to study. Whether I was in the mood for studying or not hadn't come into it and once again I found myself pondering what I'd let myself into. Yes, I may have been drugged up in my life before, but I had a lot more freedom to do what I wanted. My mum had never been that overbearing and let me decide most things for myself. However, I loved my newly rediscovered

215

senses and the intense feelings that came with that, but it came with responsibilities I could not avoid. Still, I realised I wouldn't change it for the world.

CHAPTER 30

I was fucking annoyed, to put it mildly, that I had to add the two days as I really wanted to concentrate on preparing Eliza for the mission. I kept reminding myself that it was all part of the process.

After a tedious morning ordering Eliza around, my mood was lifted when Laura came in for a chat and an update from Markus. She was impressed with how Eliza was handling the tough treatment she was receiving and I admitted that apart from talking without permission she really was working incredibly hard to impress me. I could tell Laura was proud of me too, which meant a lot to me. She had clocked my soft spot for Eliza early on and she knew it was a struggle for me to keep up my hard exterior towards Eliza. I was handling it though and actually perversely quite enjoyed it, if only it wasn't 24/7! I doubted Eliza would think the same though, and it pained me to think she might hate me for putting her through this.

Laura informed me that Markus was confident we had eyes on Rick without arousing any suspicion. Yet. It had been difficult monitoring him without anyone around him noticing, so time was still an issue. We were working under pressure. Rick seemed to be working for a highly organised type of syndicate, which didn't bode well. We still hadn't discovered whether he was there by choice, or whether they held something over him which could be used to force him to cooperate. Markus thought Eliza would be instrumental in finding this out, so he asked me to think up a game plan using Eliza's strengths and trying to cover her weaknesses somehow. This is why Markus was such a good leader; he recognised that I'm in a far better position to advise him on Eliza's strengths and weaknesses than he is, and he would delegate accordingly. Though he would always double and triple check as he would never leave anything to chance.

I asked Laura to set up another meeting with Markus and me in a couple of days time and I was hoping he would allow me these few days. I really wanted to stretch it to at least a week, but I knew time was of the essence and I didn't want to be responsible for blowing our cover or losing eyes on Rick. It was a hard act to balance, with Eliza being so inexperienced.

In the back of my mind there were Eliza's exams as well, starting imminently. She wasn't going to be happy missing them and having to sit them after the mission, as it will prolong her time away from her mum and friends. However, I was quite happy to have her here a bit longer, and hopefully in a more relaxed atmosphere with the mission over. Though I knew, annoyingly, it would be Zaphire who would probably benefit the most from that time.

As if she knew I was thinking of her, Zaphire came knocking, ready for the self-defence session I had scheduled for Eliza and her. She was half an hour early so I guess she was keen, especially as she wasn't known for her brilliant time keeping. I had just given Eliza another task to do which she needed to finish, so she plonked herself down on the sofa and observed Eliza wistfully. I prodded her in the neck and told her to snap out of it. She seemed to have it badly for her as she wasn't normally this obvious. Interesting. Not something she would readily admit though.

I could do some exercise myself whilst keeping an eye on Eliza and I was craving it. I needed a good work out and I was particularly looking forward to having a good boxing match with Brody. If anyone could kick my ass, it would be him and I had to work incredibly hard to keep on top of him. Not always successfully, I had to admit. He was a much better boxer technically than me. Like Zaphire, my stealth and speed were the only ways I could win a fight against Brody as our strength was equally matched.

Exercise made me focus and get a clear head, which I needed to devise my strategic plan to present to Markus. We somehow had to make a meet happen between Eliza and Rick without arousing any suspicions. I wasn't quite sure what angle I had to go for to facilitate this. There won't be any hiding the fact Eliza is his daughter as he'll detect the familial scent straight away. He probably knew exactly what she looked like anyway. I still hadn't decided whether to make the meet seem coincidental or arranged.

Whilst distracted by my musings I got drawn back to reality by Brody breaking through my defence and splitting my lip. I winced but wanted to keep going. Brody stopped though, and made me clean up my face before proceeding.

"Mate, I can't fight you if you get distracted like that again. Your face will be a mess and you won't thank me for that later. You'll have to explain yourself to Markus then, and you won't want to say you lost concentration! You'll end up in isolation again." he laughed out loud.

I didn't think I'd live that one down for a long time.

Great. I landed a right hook right on his chin to shut him up and we were soon fully concentrating on the fight again. I felt elated after we called it a day when both of us were feeling a bit bruised and battered. Such an adrenaline rush, I loved it.

I looked over at Eliza and Zaphire, who, by the looks of it were done too. They were sitting together on the floor doing stretches and having a good old chat. It was nice to see Eliza in such good spirits, but I had to put a stop to it. No rest for the wicked as they say.

"Eliza, get your arse over here, please." I shouted across.

I could see the disappointment in her face but she did get up just about quickly enough not to warrant a shouting at.

"Yes Sir, on my way."

As she stood up she whispered something to Zaphire, who looked alarmed as it was directed at me and it wasn't very polite. The silly girl kept forgetting we could hear whispers, even though she had the same ability now.

"Let's start with an apology for your rude comment and then you can give me fifty push-ups, Miss

221

Mankuzay. I'm tempted to take you to the bathroom and wash your mouth with soap, especially when bad language is directed at me." I said sternly.

She looked mortified and stammered out an acceptable apology. She quickly went down to the floor and struggled through her push-ups. Tears were starting to form in her eyes, but she did not give up. She managed out of sheer determination, but when she counted her fiftieth one she collapsed on the floor in a heap. I ordered her to get up, not giving an inch. I didn't want to know what rude names for me went through her head now, but she stayed calm.

"Time for a bath now. You need to give those muscles time to recover."

I pushed her gently to get her moving in the direction of our room. She was absolutely exhausted. Zaphire walked along side her, looking concerned. I could feel she was annoyed with me but was wise enough not to challenge me in front of Eliza. I'm sure I would hear her concerns soon enough and as expected when Eliza was in the bath, Zaphire started on me.

"You push her too hard, brother. You are being a complete dickhead." she challenged.

I let out a deep sigh before answering.

222

"That's my job, Zaphire. I know when things get too much for her, and she hasn't reached that limit yet. Don't worry, she's a tough one. You're letting your feelings for her get in the way. Be careful, Zaph." I warned her.

"How did she get on with her self- defence techniques?"

I changed tack to avoid further criticism.

"She was awesome. Looks like you can do with some more defensive skills though!"

She pointed teasingly at my split lip.

"I gave as good as I got," I said haughtily.

"I think Brody will be wearing a bruise on his cheek too. Serves him right for mocking me!"

CHAPTER 31

The bath was heavenly and Zack had given me, uncharacteristically, quite a long time to soak and pamper myself. I needed it and as usual, Zack knew. My muscles were already sore from the work out and then the annoying punishment push-ups. Why couldn't I just remember to keep my mouth shut! I'd been doing so well, but Zaphire entices the cheeky side out of me. It was particularly harsh of him though, as it wasn't even that rude what I'd whispered. However, I should have known better. This was all about being respectful to him, and that, it hadn't been!

My mind wandered back to Zaphire. She was amazing. Maybe it was curiosity, as I had never felt these feelings for a girl before. It had knocked me sideways. I needed to figure this out, but there was no chance to explore or even talk about it with her. Maybe after the mission we could have a chance, but then I wanted to go back to mum, Kas and my friends too. It was going to be a hard decision and I had to stop myself thinking about it. It wasn't going to help my concentration if I kept worrying about the future.

I glanced over at the clock and to my horror I saw I

only had five minutes to get ready! I had enjoyed the soak a little too much! I quickly threw on some clothes and went out to report to Zack, dripping wet hair, no socks and my top inside out. For the first time in ages a little smile broke through on his face, but it disappeared as quickly as it came.

"Well, it looks like you have to visit the cafe looking like a drowned cat, Miss Mankuzay. Work on your time management!"

Typical of Zack, making me bear the consequences of my actions in the most humiliating way. He was waiting for a reply so I hurriedly did.

"Yes Sir, I'm sorry Sir."

It became easier to address him like that. It almost rolled out of my mouth now and it didn't feel so awkward. I was looking forward to calling him by his name again, though. I missed the supportive and fun side of Zack plus the ease with which we used to get along. I hoped it would return. He seemed to be okay with Sam though, so it must be possible.

Off we went to the cafe and had some food, me looking wet and dishevelled, eliciting a few giggles on the way. However, Zack made sure people went on with their business quickly, no one dared to make any comments. I admired the authority he emanated so

225

naturally. He only had to look a certain way and people would respond. I wanted to find out why people showed him so much respect at such a young age. I was curious to find out how he so quickly earned his reputation of being such an excellent coach. Though I could hazard a guess by the way he was training me, that sort of respect usually came with a lot more experience. Then I remembered Markus' words to my mother telling her how he had saved someone's life, so it was no wonder people were in awe of him.

Time couldn't go fast enough as I was dying to get back to our room, away from the staring eyes. Luckily, Zack wasn't hanging about either and after we finished our food we made our way back, but a young girl called Maisie came up with a note for Zack. She hardly dared make eye contact, but Zack made time to have a little chat with her. She turned out to be Ned's sister and was obviously thrilled with Zack's attention. She can't have been more than thirteen and not very good at cloaking her feelings yet. Zack ignored it and treated her kindly then thanked her for the note she passed him. I was about to ask what the note was about, but narrowly remembered I was to ask for permission to talk first. I couldn't stop my curiosity so I did.

"Yes, you may speak Eliza." Zack said surprisingly.

"I was just wondering what the note was about, Sir?" I tried.

He took a breath and waited a second before answering.

"Markus wants to see us tomorrow afternoon, which is a bit sooner than I would have liked, but so be it."

"Why didn't he just text you or email? A note is a bit old school isn't it?" I wondered out loud. But Zack gave nothing away. He just nodded and said Markus would have his reasons.

"When we get back to our room you are to do two hours of revision and then it's early bed today. You need to have a good night sleep tonight." he said, changing the subject.

I kept forgetting about my impending exams. Didn't look like I would be able to do them until after the mission anyway, which was just as well as I hadn't done nearly enough revision for any of my subjects. School felt like a life time away, even though it had only been a couple of weeks. It didn't seem important any more, but I knew Zack wouldn't have any of that. I was predicted A grades and he was damn well going to make sure I would do my revision. So, when we got back I reluctantly got my Biology books out and immersed myself in the subject I had always loved studying.

CHAPTER 32

Markus wanted to see us tomorrow and that didn't
bode well. I had hoped for a few days more. *Fuck.*
I'd better get a plan together tonight. Luckily Eliza
was studying so I could concentrate on it, without
having to discipline Eliza all the time.

It wasn't going to be easy to orchestrate a meet
between Rick and Eliza. The man was artful in
concealing his daily routine, and it had taken the team
a few weeks of hard work to figure it out. At first
glance it looked like he had no routine, but if you
looked beyond the surface he definitely had one. It
was just not easy to discover as he was clever
enough to have injected some randomness in his daily
routines. Our team had found a certain pattern
though and with patience we would be able to arrange
a 'random' meet.

He always took a morning break, not always at the
same time and not at the same place either.
Sometimes he'd go for a walk, other days he would
stay in the building, having a coffee and a chat or read
a book. Once every so often he would go to a cafe
around the corner, or the one a short walk across the
park. We would have to be patient and stake out at

229

one of the cafes and hope he would go there at some point during the week.

I would have to come up with a plan to get the two of them talking without raising suspicion in Rick. We could have Eliza wanting to find her father and pretending she had tracked him down or randomly bumping into each other and claiming a weird sense of familiarity causing her to address him. The problem with the first one was clear. It would almost be impossible for a normal citizen to track him down without any help from us, so we couldn't really use that as a way in. It would be too suspicious. However, the problem with randomly bumping into him is that he knows she doesn't live here so what the hell would she be doing here on her own. We could spin a story around it, but the problem with back up stories is that they are fallible and all too often discovered to be untrue.

Unless we involved Alice, Eliza's mum. If Rick would spot Alice, he would find it almost impossible to ignore her. His love for her was known to be strong, and the only way he'd been able to resist going back to Alice was by keeping a safe distance between them. That's why he never had returned to her. Plus the genetic bond with Eliza would trigger intense feelings he would find hard to control too. Brilliant idea, if I say so myself!

It would be a risk to use an untrained person, but it would be the most natural way of introducing the two of them, however awkward it may make Alice feel. It would be a great starting point for Eliza to wheedle her way into his life and suss him out. I felt buoyant having found a solution, but now I had to convince Markus of that in our meeting tomorrow. I started writing down my plan in detail to present to him tomorrow, trying to think of all the pitfalls that may occur. I knew Eliza was very good at improvising as she proved during the phone call to Kas, but a plan was much more reliable and I had to have a scenario in place for every eventuality.

When I looked at my phone to check an incoming message I was shocked to find it 10.30pm already. *Fuck!* So much for an early night for Eliza. I glanced over at her and she was still pouring over her books too.

"Time to stop Eliza. You can get yourself a drink and a snack before going to bed. Make me a cup of tea too."

She immediately put her books away and with a

"Yes Sir" made her way to our little kitchen. I wished I could relax with her for a bit before going to bed, but it would have to wait. I could not be slack with her. Word would get out and that would ruin my reputation. However, I longed for tomorrow to be over so we could normalise our relationship again. She would still have to respect me obviously, but I wouldn't have to order her around and monitor her every move. I was fed up with barking orders at her. I loved her being so subservient and I didn't miss her rude attitude, but I did miss her spark, intelligence, sensitivity, her sexy cheeky smile and kind personality. I fancied her, but I knew I wouldn't stand a chance with Zaphire around. Eliza might have feelings for me, but unfortunately, she was totally infatuated with Zaphy.

"Sir?" Eliza gently interrupted my thoughts as she passed my tea.

I hoped she wasn't concentrating on picking up any signals from me as I had let my guard down. I didn't notice any spikes in her signals though. Her heart rate still would rise on approaching me, but that was normal. Nothing to give away she had picked up on my own heightened emotional state. Her eyes were down waiting for me to give her permission to sit down. I nodded in the direction of the chair and she sat herself down to eat her snack. She looked tired

232

and I was cross with myself having forgotten the time. I told her the schedule for tomorrow and waited for her to finish her drink to then send her to bed for some much needed sleep. I followed soon after.

Music awoke me from my slumber. *Bollocks.* My phone alarm was going off, getting louder and louder as I frantically tried to find it. *For fuck sake.* I must have forgotten to put it on charge as it wasn't in its normal place. I found it eventually at the foot of my bed and silenced The Stone Roses, my wake up call. I plugged it in to charge as it was nearly out of juice, before jumping out of bed. I thought a second about taking a shower, but didn't see the point as I would have to take another one after our work out session. I just splashed my face instead in a bid to wake up a bit and slipped on my sports gear. I went to wake Eliza up, only to find her bed empty. Where the fuck was she?

"Eliza!" I shouted through the apartment.

She sheepishly got up from the sofa.

"What the hell are you doing out of your bed! Did I tell you to get up?" I exclaimed, cross for her disobedience and slightly overreacting from the shock of finding her bed empty.

"Well, answer me Eliza!" I now shouted as she stood there silently.

"Uh, yes Sir. It's just that, uh, I don't really know...."

"What the fuck do you mean. You don't know!?" I interrupted, feeling outraged.

She was shuffling her feet and she shook her shoulders helplessly. The slight expression of fear appearing on her face brought me back to my senses and I calmed down somewhat. I took a deep breath.

"Okay. Tell me what happened." I managed to make my voice sound calm, even though I was still seething inside and wanted to punish her for the shock she caused me.

"I.., uh.., woke up here. On the sofa. Just now, when you shouted my name. I'm really sorry Zack, uh, Sir, I mean."

She looked mortified but carried on.

"I'm so sorry Sir, I must've been sleepwalking or something."

Ah, okay. That was a different matter, and I wasn't quite sure how to deal with it straight away. However, I couldn't have that happen again, and I was annoyed with myself for not noticing last night. I would have thought I would've woken up if she'd been wandering around at night. I must have been letting myself relax enough not to be as alert as I normally

234

am. That was no good.

Eliza looked at me waiting for a response.

"Give me fifty push ups for calling me Zack and making me worried. We'll talk about how to deal with the sleepwalking later."

I had to have a think about how to contain that myself first. Eliza's face was thunderous but she did start her push ups straight away. She looked so much stronger already, even after only the few weeks she'd been training.

During breakfast I told her what I had in mind to deal with her little nightly escapades. I would put my bed across her door so she'd have to climb over me to get out. That would wake me, no doubt. She looked a bit dubious at my solution but accepted it, at least for now. I wasn't sure if she would bring it up again later and I wouldn't put it past her to be honest. I could tell she didn't think it was necessary and she thought I was overreacting, but she wasn't going to tell me that today. She had learned something alright; picking the right time to broach a topic and choosing your battles wisely.

CHAPTER 33

I knew Zack thought that I thought he was overreacting with the whole sleepwalking thing. He wasn't cloaking his feelings as well this morning as he has been doing the past days. He was preoccupied with this afternoon's meeting with Markus and so was I. I let Zack's ridiculous solution slide and would bring it up later. I really didn't need babysitting like that. The worst that would happen is that I would fall asleep on the sofa or on a chair.

I might try and creep in his bed though, I thought, mortified. Probably even more likely if he parks his bed right by my door! *Grrr*. Why did I have to start sleep walking again. So annoying. Usually, it was a sign that I was worried about something, just like my nightmares used to happen at stressful times. So, not really that surprising, as I was definitely stressed and worried about the upcoming meeting with my father.

How on earth I would pull off what they wanted me to do was a mystery to me. To get the information out of him without raising any suspicion would be nigh on impossible with my father's skills of using his gift. I doubted he wouldn't see straight through my intentions and just run. If he was doing things

236

because people were controlling him, he probably would want to keep me away from them to keep me safe. If, on the other hand, he was choosing to work for these people he won't want me to know about it, and would vanish as well. In both cases I would have failed my mission and I wasn't looking forward to that one single bit. I would've let everyone down and I'm not sure if I could face Zack, Markus or any one of our community ever again. Failing was just not an option.

The exercises Zack made me do were a welcome distraction. I never thought I would actually enjoy exercise and being pushed to my limits, but I'd absolutely grown to love it. Every ache I felt in my body I attributed to becoming stronger, and that felt good. Zack was really pushing me again this morning, barking orders at me constantly and making me work insanely hard.

I spotted Zaphire out of the corner of my eye, sweat pouring past my eyes. I did not imagine myself making a pretty picture, but Zaphire clearly thought differently. Her pheromones penetrated every pore in my body. Right up until I saw Zack looking admonishingly at her. He had noticed too. And as if by magic, anything I felt, smelled or thought I saw had dissipated into thin air. She was still there but she had obviously been made aware what she was emanating and she had instantly turned off the tap.

"Is there any time to do some self-defence?" she asked Zack.

He looked reluctant. Probably annoyed at her obvious feelings for me that she had failed to hide.

"If there was, would I be wise to give her to you Zaphire?" he asked icily, not expecting an answer back from her.

She didn't give up without a fight though.

"Very wise indeed, brother," ignoring his alluding to her temporary lack of self control.

"She needs practise and we don't exactly have a lot of time left before she might have to put any of it to use."

She knew she had won him over already. She knew his worry about the lack of time and she tapped into it unashamedly. I so admired her, I had never met anyone like her.

So Zaphire got her way and we practised some more techniques for an hour or so. No further sign of her earlier lapse in cloaking unfortunately. She was just intent on teaching me and that was it. She probably felt she had to prove something as Zack was watching us like a hawk whilst he was doing his cool down exercises. His muscles were flexing and a fine sheen of perspiration covered his arms and face. The sight of it made my legs go weak and Zaphire instantly took advantage of my lack of concentration.

"Keep your eyes on the ball, girl!" she whispered viciously in my ear as I was floored.

I couldn't detect any jealousy in her scent, but that sure as hell sounded like it. Hawk eye called her out on it too.

"Zaphire. Enough. End the session. Now." he growled as he stared her down.

Nothing ever got past the bloke.

We started our cooling down and Zaphire complimented me on my progress. She didn't want to leave on a sour note, I suspected.

We all desperately needed a shower so Zack ushered us back to our rooms to get cleaned up, promising Zaphire to give her a text to join us for lunch.

Both Zack and Zaphire had to encourage me to eat as I felt too nervous to eat. Well, Zaphire was encouraging, Zack ordered me. As if that would work. My stomach was knotted and I felt positively sick with the thought of meeting Markus again, as our last meeting wasn't exactly a resounding success. Also, even though I was curious and looking forward to meeting my father, I still felt wholly unequipped and inexperienced to actually do anything I was supposed to do, and it was going to happen a lot sooner than I'd thought.

"Don't worry so much, Eliza. Whatever is decided, you have all of us to back you up. You'll be fine, babe."

Zaphire was trying to make me feel better, but failed. Zack was less subtle as usual.

"Zaphire is right. Stop thinking ahead so much. Eat your lunch. Now." he insisted.

I sighed and did my best to struggle through some of it. After about twenty minutes of pushing the rest around my plate, Zack actually gave up.

"Let's go." he sighed.

He told me to take the plates back to the kitchen and clean up, which I happily did. I was so looking forward to tomorrow when my punishment would end. I didn't mind doing useful things like clearing the plates, but the mindless tasks, just to prove I would obey, were getting very tedious indeed. I started to feel a bit like a robot, not having to think for myself and just mindlessly following orders, even to the point of being told when to go to the toilet. I would try my damned hardest never to have to do this again.

Markus was ready for us when we arrived at his office. He was joined by Laura, two other men and a woman that I had not met, which did nothing to sooth my nerves. Zack had made me stand behind him and Zaphire, which was quite handy because it gave me the chance to observe everyone without being too brazen. The only problem was that I couldn't see Zack and Zaphire's faces to read their expressions. I could smell their anticipation though, and Zack was emanating a calmness which surprised me considering his earlier tenseness.

"Zack, can you please introduce your trainee to your leaders."

Markus stepped aside to let us past. Zack beckoned me to come and stand next to him.

"Mr Michael Jones, Mr Frank Van der Veldt and Ms Lois Langfield, this is Miss Eliza Mankuzay, daughter of Rick." Zack nodded at me.

"You're allowed to speak and make acquaintances now."

I stepped forward and gave them a hand.

"Pleased to meet you all, Sirs, Ma'am."

I managed to be polite, but didn't really know what else to talk about. Luckily Frank asked me how I was doing with my training and we were soon talking about techniques and what worked best for me so far, with Lois and Michael listening intently. Zaphire was by my side but Laura, Zack and Markus were having their own little private conversation, until Markus called us to sit down at the table.

I waited for Zack to give me permission to sit, also to see where I was expected to go. Not surprisingly he put me right next to him with Laura sitting next to me. It was intimidating to sit across from Markus with his henchmen and woman beside him, but I didn't detect any signs of nervousness from Zack. He either was fully cloaking or he was just that confident. Whichever it was, I was in awe of him.

Markus addressed Zack to present his plan, who proceeded to explain in detail how his thought processes had let him to decide to enlist my mum in the whole operation. *My mum! What the hell.*

I wanted to shout at all of them to leave my mum well out of it, but was wise enough not to interrupt or criticise. The consequences would be unbearable.

There was a lot of discussion about it, as none of the leaders were keen to bring in an untrained person to work with me, myself barely trained. However, unbelievably, they all agreed that it was the best option they had and unanimously agreed to the plan. No one seemed to want to ask my opinion, even though I must have emanated all sorts of emotions. I didn't even want to try and hide them. I couldn't bear it any longer and I had to ask Zack for permission to speak. He granted it but there lay a deep warning in his eyes to tread carefully.

"With all due respect." I started, though was immediately interrupted by Michael muttering with a little smile playing across his mouth.

"That statement is usually followed by something generally lacking in respect."

The others sniggered a little, except for Zack who was staring at me icily. Markus however, asked me to speak.

"It would be incredibly difficult for my mum to face the man who left us without any explanation and without ever trying to contact us again. Have you even considered that?! Or worse, it could put my mum in danger and I just won't have that happen." I said defiantly (though not shouting), avoiding Zack's eyes but not being able to ignore his surge of agitation. Markus answered.

"Zack, please have a word with her as to how to voice her worries without the attitude. Eliza, I would have loved for you to have learned something from your previous stint in isolation. You're always allowed to say what you think, but respectfully please and be under no illusion that you can stop any decision that is made by us. What we decide is what happens, whether you or your mum like it or not."

Zack nodded but Markus hadn't finished yet.

"However, you made a fair point. Of course we'll protect your mum from harm. Her involvement will stop as soon as we have introduced you into the life of your father."

I considered his answer for a minute before answering, starting with an apology.

"I'm sorry about the way I worded my concerns. I'm fully aware that I cannot stop you from doing anything, but feel my frustration. It's my mum you're talking about. The woman who has always been there for me and has supported me through everything life has thrown at me. She won't be fully safe, as you won't be able to control what my father will do. What if he decides he wants her back in his life? What if she wants to be back in his life? Stranger things have happened! What if the organisation my father works for gets wind of her existence. She could become a pawn for them, something to use in controlling him. You cannot cover every angle as to how this will end, surely? So I'm asking, no, begging you not to involve her. Please?"

I tried to keep the emotion and desperation out of my voice, but failed miserably. I dared to glance at Zack and even though his face looked like thunder, I did detect something else. His scent and demeanour had changed, it wasn't just anger I could smell. It was admiration.

"She has a point, Markus." Zaphire piped up.

"We can do our utmost best to keep Alice safe and in 99% of cases that's enough, but we cannot *guarantee* her safety."

I was grateful for her support, but I knew the decision had been made already and Markus confirmed my fear.

"I do take your point Eliza and Zaphire, but it's the best and probably only option we have. We don't compromise on that. As always, the mission comes first. But as I said, we will make sure your mum is safe as best we can. You'll just have to accept that and move on now."

There was no budging him and as he said, I had to put it aside and concentrate on making sure I would carry out this task as safely and efficiently as possible and get my mum back home as soon as possible. Out of harm's way.

CHAPTER 34

I felt happy the leaders had agreed my plan. It was the only way in, without arousing suspicion and they had realised that too. I had hoped the careful discussion about it between the leaders, where every angle was explored in front of Eliza, would have convinced her. That's why I hadn't mentioned it to her before, to avoid an argument. It was a risk, and feeling her frustration and fear, I was surprised she handled it pretty calmly. For her. Remembering how I lost my cool when I thought she would be in danger, which resulted in our detainment, I felt proud of her and the way she managed to stay in control of her emotions. Just about.

"I know that was difficult for you in there Eliza, but you are going to have to work on how you phrase your concerns without sounding disrespectful or defiant, so I am going to give you some exercises to work on now."

She nodded her head.

I sensed her relief about just receiving some work to do. I think she was scared I was going to add more days on her punishment, but I remember having to do the exercises myself and it did teach me an awful lot.

Some things don't come naturally, and have to be learned.

   She worked hard all afternoon and evening and before she went to bed I decided to tell her that from tomorrow she could stand down. She could call me by my name again and she didn't have to ask permission to do everything any more. I did give her a stern warning though, that if I detected any disrespect towards me or in fact towards anyone else, I wouldn't hesitate to reinstate the punishment again.   Soon after she went to bed I received a text from Markus. D-Day was going to be the day after tomorrow. Alice was already booked on a plane to join us.

   Eliza's emotions went through the roof when she set eyes on her mum the following day. She ran up to her and threw herself in her arms and the warmth and love was felt by everyone in the room. I thought they were never going to let go of each other, so intense was their reunion. I felt a little stab of envy as although I knew Markus and Laura loved me, there was no closeness and warmth like I witnessed here before me. Zaphy and I loved each other and had an incredibly strong bond, but to feel so secure and safe in someone's arms was something both of us had missed out on growing up.

"I have missed you so much, sweetheart. How are you doing? Here. Let me look at you." Alice said when Eliza's grip loosened a bit.

"You look so strong!"

Admiration trickling through in her voice, though quickly replaced by a worried tone.

"But also exhausted! Are you feeling okay?" still looking Eliza up and down.

"I'm fine, mum. In fact, better than ever!" Eliza tried to allay her mother's worries.

She sounded upbeat and confident and her positive demeanour certainly comforted her mum. I could see her physically relax.

"Remember Zack, my trainer and coach, mainly responsible for my increased fitness."

I stepped forward to shake Alice's hand, who instantly stiffened. She was still wary of me, not trusting me to look after her daughter. She worked hard not to show her reservations.

"Yes, of course. Pleased to see you again, Zack."

She tried to sound pleased but was failing miserably. I knew I had a lot to prove to her, before she would genuinely shake my hand and be happy to see me. Eliza picked up on it too of course, and was about to confront Alice, but I shook my head slightly to signal her to just leave it. She took the hint this time which I was grateful for.

"Let's get you settled in your room, then we can meet in an hour to discuss our plan, though I assume Markus has filled you in somewhat?" I asked.

"Yes, I know the idea, but we need to discuss the finer details of course. Can Eliza come with me to my room?"

I was afraid she would ask that. I couldn't trust them to be on their own together as I didn't know Alice well enough, and my responsibility for Eliza was still a hundred percent 24/7.

I thought for a moment.

"She can, but Zaphire will have to accompany her."

Eliza looked surprised and elated. She hadn't expected me to let her out of my sight and was visibly grateful. Once found, Zaphire was pleased to be asked and took them both to Alice's room, but not after I had impressed on Zaphire the absolute necessity to stay with Eliza at all times and to contact me if she noticed anything out of the ordinary.

I should've prepared for our meeting later, but I couldn't resist having a little catch up with Ned and Brody. I hadn't been able to relax for the last few weeks on my own at all, so I took my chance. I was lucky they happened to both be in the building and on a break.

"Hey Zack, nice to see you mate!" Ned shouted across the room.

"And without your trainee?" Brody questioned.

"Just for an hour. Zaphire is on watch, and her mum is there."

I defended my cheeky hour off.

"Ah, well. I guess Zaphy is not complaining." Ned laughed, shooting a knowing look to Brody.

"But how do *you* feel about that, Zack? Was that a wise decision?"

Brody was moving onto thin ice there. How the fuck did they know about my feelings for Eliza. I surely had been carefully cloaking.

"Shut the fuck up, Brody." I grumbled but the looks they exchanged did not escape my attention.

I wasn't going to rise to it today, though.

"How's your mission going Ned?" I asked to try and drag the attention away from me.

As Rick was located some of us were released to be back on normal duties for the time being.

"Have to go out in the field tomorrow and gather some evidence against a woman. We know she's supplied drugs to kids but the police can't find any concrete evidence. No one seems to be willing to talk.

We're going to try and manipulate one of her friends to divulge what they know to the police, or at least tell us where we can find evidence. It'll take a bit of convincing so we need to play it smart. The cops don't know anything of our involvement and we need to keep it that way. It's going to be hard work keeping under the radar, as she is under surveillance."

Ned loved these challenges; I could feel he was in his element.

"We so need a night out soon. When's this 24/7 babysitting Eliza going to finish?" Brody asked.

"We miss you mate." Ned added.

"Not nearly finished." I sighed.

I didn't mind too much, though, as I was spending time with Eliza, but I did miss a good knees up and a beer or two with my mates. The guys groaned.

"All work and no play...you know how the saying goes!" Ned joked.

"Ha ha, yes well. Not much I can do about it. 'Mission comes' first and all that!" I groaned, mimicking Markus' voice, which made them snigger an appreciative 'suppose so'.

The hour was nearly up and I left them to it, preparing myself for the meeting with Alice and Eliza. I was hyped up for it now. I thought my plan was good

251

and, though apprehensive to work with such inexperienced people, I couldn't wait to put it in action and get the mission started.

CHAPTER 35

It was amazing hanging out with mum. I'd missed her more than I'd realised. She was getting on with Zaphire like a house on fire too, which I loved. I could feel Zaphire's nerves to meet my mum dissipate quickly, being replaced by a sense of ease. She worked hard to make my mum feel settled and appreciated and she was succeeding. Unlike the reservations my mum held towards Zack, she seemed to trust Zaphire almost from the start. That was a bit funny, because out of everyone, I knew Zack was the most trustworthy person ever.

Zaphy helped me explain a bit more about the gift we shared and how being off the medication had brought it all back to me. I could tell mum was feeling guilty about drugging me, but I managed to reassure her that she had only done her best. She couldn't have known better as no one had told her anything about the gift. If it was anyone's fault, it would be my father's. And anyhow, I'd functioned well enough in the normal society, thanks to those drugs.

After exactly one hour we heard the knock on my door, quickly followed by Zack coming in. He radiated focus and authority, ready to lead the meeting. He talked us through the plan and to be fair, it all sounded sensible with little risk to my mum. We went through a few scenarios and what to do when things weren't quite going to plan and with a firm warning to abort if any suspicious vibes were picked up. I didn't tell Zack I wasn't quite sure if I would recognise 'suspicious vibes' as I hadn't really encountered them before, but I hoped I would naturally pick them up.

"Are you both clear as to what is expected from you?" he asked looking us both over, trying to detect any lack of confidence or insecurities.

We both nodded in unison.

"It could be a waiting game as we don't know if and when he'll turn up to the desired location. But we must be prepared as he might turn up on our first try and we must be ready to deal with that." he warned.

I felt my nerves go up a notch with that statement. Zack was right. I could be seeing my father tomorrow morning and I must be ready to face him and play my role. Part of me didn't believe it yet and I had to make myself stop pushing the reality away. But I felt I was ready for it and having mum there was an unexpected bonus. It definitely made it feel a less daunting task.

My mum, however, was also nervous about meeting Rick. I suppose she had unfinished business with him and the feelings of abandonment and rejection she must have felt were brought to the fore again. She was doing this for me, but part of her also wanted answers. Whether she was going to get any directly from him was another matter. He wasn't aware of her knowledge of our community and she wasn't to let him know either. It was going to be tricky.

A relatively new member of our community, Claude, was going to be in the coffee shop with us. On a separate table, and in contact with Zack. It had to be Claude as it was one of the few members that Rick wouldn't recognise the scent of, him being of new blood, not part of any of the known families. He was born with the gift without either parent having it.

Amazingly, Claude had managed to grow up with his family and able to find a partner to start a family of his own, disguising his gift to everyone all his life and not been caught out. His family always thought he was peculiar, but never sought any professional help. How he managed to deal with his gift in this way was extraordinary and he was held in high esteem in our community.

Without training or guidance he had managed to control all the overwhelming feelings and experiences of the world around him and somehow stayed sane, making me feel slightly inadequate to be honest. Now his wife knows and they live within our community with two children who both possess the gift. It was rare, but it did happen occasionally. I suppose it was good for the survival of our kind, having an injection of new blood to keep the gene pool varied.

"I've noticed when you talk about the people here, you refer to them as being from *our* community. Do you see yourself as part of them now?" mum asked a little hesitantly.

Now she had mentioned it I realised she was right, even though I hadn't made that choice consciously. I hesitated for a moment and decided to answer truthfully.

"I guess I am, mum. I'm definitely part of their world and I'm beginning to feel it as my own. I haven't really thought about it, but now you're asking, I think I do. I am a Sensorian."

I saw a flicker of disappointment and unease in her eyes, fearing she might lose me to this world.

"Don't worry mum, I'll always be part of your life too. In fact my plan is to return home after this mission." I tried to reassure her, but her demeanour was unsure.

She didn't seem to like me reading her emotions so

well. She would just have to get used to that and
given time, I'm sure she would.

Zack signalled for me to follow him and I excused
myself from my mum, who had started busying herself
with rearranging the furniture in the room.

"Is she okay do you think?" he asked, looking
slightly concerned.

"Yeah, but it's just a lot to contend with. Meeting
Rick again and on top of that she feels she's losing
me." I confided.

Zack nodded indicating he understood. I could
feel he was worried about my mum putting the
mission in danger, but he didn't need to. She would
put all her worries aside and deal with what was in
hand, like she'd always done.

Morning came much too quickly, after a fitful night
full of talking in my sleep and sleepwalking on my part.
Zack managed to relocate me back to bed several
times during the night, so he didn't have much sleep
either. However, adrenaline soon kicked in making
me feel wide awake, but also making my senses
function even more acutely. I was in danger of being
overloaded with sensations. I made myself focus on
the waves of the sea in my mind combined with some

breathing exercises to calm myself down. I was getting very adept in using those techniques and soon I felt in control again.

Mum joined me, Zack and Zaphire for breakfast. Zack was monitoring my breakfast intake and I forced myself to eat something. My stomach was somersaulting so really didn't feel like anything at all. My mother tried to get away with just having a cup of coffee for breakfast but Zack wasn't having any of it. It made me giggle seeing my mum cope with being told what to do, and by a nineteen year old at that. She hadn't been one for taking orders ever in her adult life and she definitely resisted today.

"No Alice, you *can't* just have a cup of coffee. I'm tired of having to repeat myself. We're not leaving until you've had something to eat and you wouldn't want to be responsible for having to cancel the mission today, would you?"

Zack's expression was non-negotiable, and my mum finally relented, rolling her eyes like a ticked off teenager, helping herself to a croissant.

"Please don't roll your eyes at me. If you were my trainee, there would've been consequences." Zack growled.

I glanced at Zaphire who suppressed a smile witnessing the encounter, and when she caught my eye she broke into laughter. Mum looked at me in despair.

"How on earth do you put up with him!" she whispered furtively, forgetting Zack could of course hear everything.

He wisely chose to ignore the remark and tucked into his breakfast.

"With difficulty." I dared say, smiling, earning a warning stare from Zack.

I wondered what my mum would have thought of the regime I was under before. She would have been shocked to see her daughter treated like that, but probably more amazed by the way I had dealt with it. I had learned from it though and knew not to push Zack any further by being too disrespectful, even if it was just joking around.

When we'd finished eating we all gathered everything we needed to take on our mission. Zack gave Claude some last minute instructions and orders not to let us out of his sight, under any circumstance. Claude did his best to reassure him, but I could see Zack had difficulties accepting not being the one on the ground. He would not be far away though, monitoring everything. Markus and Laura came by to check everything was ready and prepared and gave us the green light to go ahead.

So this was it. Time to prove I could do this. It felt oddly liberating, stepping outside with my mum, as if we were going out on a shopping trip together, like we had done so many times in the past. I realised this was the first time in weeks where I wasn't under the watchful eye of Zack. Well, not directly anyway. It felt good, but also a bit scary. Zack had been like a big security blanket I'd started to take for granted. I briefly felt panic rise within my chest, but managed to keep it at bay. I focused on my mum instead. I had to work hard tuning out all the impressions hoisted upon me when we were in the outside world. It took me a little while to feel confident enough to deal with them without being overwhelmed.

"Remember Rick can hear everything, so don't whisper or say anything that could compromise our plan. We might not see him, but he could be near enough to hear us." I quickly reminded mum, before we got near to the coffee shop we would use as our base. In the next couple of days he'd be sure to show up, if not today. I could feel the tension rising in my mum as we entered the cafe and I quickly started to make some small talk to distract her. There was no sign of him inside, as we expected. Surveillance had been in place since 7am in the morning and there had been no news from them.

We found ourselves a little table and settled down. Claude, dressed in a smart business suit, installed himself near us with his laptop, nicely blending in with the clientele. I ordered myself a hot chocolate and a latte for mum and made myself comfortable in a soft leather chair. Then, out of the corner of my eye I spotted something that none of us had predicted. My heart sank. Panic started to engulf me. How was this possible! He shouldn't be here. He should be safely at home revising for his exams. There was no avoiding this encounter. Kas was here, and he had clocked us. Surprisingly, I also felt excited to see him. I clearly still had feelings for him, though nothing like what I felt for Zaphire or even Zack.

Claude had picked up on my body tensing and raised pulse and scanned around on high alert. His phone pinged. I knew that was Zack informing him of Kas' arrival. I could just imagine Zack's mood taking a dive with this curveball.

"Hey babe!"

Kas came bustling over, making my heart beat a little faster. So familiar his voice and mannerisms it almost made me long for those simpler times, when Kas had been my rock.

"What....how...what are you doing here?" I managed to squeak.

"Mum? Did you...?"

She shook her head vigorously, looking as dumbfounded as I was. Kas enveloped me in his strong arms and again I was thrown back to a time before I was asked to help find my father. Kas' gorgeously recognisable smell stirred feelings of nostalgia and for a second time I felt myself almost wishing I'd made a different choice.

"I'm so sorry to surprise you like this Eli. I know you weren't meant to meet with anyone and I really don't want to hinder your road to recovery, but I couldn't help myself. As soon as I had an inkling about your mum's plan to visit you I made up my mind. I had to see you. I've missed you so much..."

He stumbled over his words to explain, but I needed to know more. How on earth did he find out about my mum coming here, but I only had to look at my mum's face which was changing expression when realisation dawned on her.

"Mum? How did he know? Kas, how did you find out about the visit?" I urged them.

"Oh sweetheart, it must have been when I got the phone call. When I hung up, Kas was by the door, I hadn't heard him come in. Did you hear Kas?"

My mum threw Kas a hurt look, realising he'd been eaves dropping. He didn't need to say anything; it was plain to see that was exactly what had happened. Well, no disaster yet. We would just have to play along and pretend I was on day release with mum, and get rid of him as fast as possible.

"Well, I sort of heard the end and put two and two together. I followed you to the airport and checked where you were going and then drove through the night to get here. I was just going to get myself some breakfast and ring you, Alice, and plead to come and see Eliza with you, when I spotted you both in here!"

"Bloody hell Kas, you're crazy! But it's good to see you!"

I gave him another hug before I gently pushed away from him.

"You look absolutely amazing Eli, whatever you're doing, it's working!"

His eyes looked me over in awe.

263

I was just about to explain to him he couldn't stay long as I really wasn't allowed to see anyone but my mum according to my treatment plan, and that he should make his way home as soon as possible, when events took another unexpected turn.

CHAPTER 36

I couldn't believe my fucking eyes. What the fuck was that fucking twat of a Dullard doing here! Someone, and that would be me, was going to get a bollocking over this lapse of security afterwards. That was fucking guaranteed. I knew I should have trusted my senses as I thought I'd picked a slither of his scent earlier, but I had dismissed it, until I saw him making his way into the cafe. I texted Claude straight away to alert him.

I let Eliza and Alice deal with him as I trusted Eliza to improvise and get rid of him as fast as possible. However, just when I relaxed a little as I saw Eliza taking control over the situation, you couldn't make it up; I received the text I did not want to see at this moment in time. Rick was on his way. *Fuck.* I had to act quickly or else the whole operation could be blown. Kas was too much of an unknown factor and could say something to make Rick suspicious. I could not let that happen. It was too much of a risk. I texted Claude to be prepared and I rushed over to the cafe. In less than ten minutes Rick would arrive.

I burst into the cafe, flashed my card which on quick inspection was just like police identification. The

shocked faces of Eliza and Alice didn't deter me but I
had to focus as I could feel the stress levels rising
around me.

"Kasper Mahony, please come with me. Do not
make a scene or I will have to arrest you."

I acted as authoritatively as I could, but I knew I
was going to have a struggle as he instantly
recognised me.

"Zack? What the hell?" he exclaimed indignantly.

Kas looked around to Eliza, totally confused, but
also determined not to be pushed around. Eliza came
to the rescue though.

"Please, just go with him. He's not joking. He will
arrest you, don't let it come to that. I'll explain it all
later." she pleaded quietly, and successfully, as I
could feel Kas' resolve to resist diminishing.

I took advantage of that by taking him by the arm
and encouraging him to move. We literally had
minutes as I was also worried about the scent I might
leave behind, even though I sprayed myself with a
neutraliser before I went in. It wouldn't mask for that
long and the more time in between me leaving, and
Rick arriving, the better.

Kas reluctantly got up and walked along with me,
dragging his feet and staring bemusedly at Eliza
imploring an explanation. She nodded encouragingly,

to keep him moving. I signalled to Claude to clarify
the situation about Rick's imminent arrival to Eliza and
Alice, whilst ushering Kas through the door. I ignored
the staring eyes of the other customers and hoped
they wouldn't be still talking about it by the time Rick
arrived.

I didn't really have time for Kas and as annoying
as it would be for him, he would just have to be
collected and taken to our compound for now. I hoped
I could palm this off to Michael or Frank, or even
Zaphire, but I didn't think they were going to humour
me. I'd have to deal with him myself later. Kas
spluttered profanities all the way to my hide out post,
but at heart Kas was no rebel and I knew he would
comply.

"Just sit there and be quiet. I'll arrange for
someone to collect you."

I pushed him into a chair and looked at him sternly,
making sure he wouldn't get stupid plans in his head.

"Zack, I just don't get it. What's going on? Please.
Is Eliza in danger? What has she got herself into?"

Kas sounded desperate and insisted on answers.
He wouldn't let this lie.

"She's not in danger, but you got to let me do my
fucking job and just shut up for now. As Eliza said,

we'll explain later."

I was busily texting for back up. Zaphire was on her way and Kas would be no match for her. He'll be under her spell in no time and be putty in her hands.

Rick was about to enter the cafe and my gut reacted. This was the moment of truth. Would our plan work? I sincerely hoped it would. Even though I felt confident, there were so many unknowns we couldn't plan for.

I could just about see the scene from my vantage point with my binoculars. I fucking wished I was nearer, but I just had to rely on Claude keeping me informed as best he could. I hated not being in total control of the situation.

In the mean time, I still had Kas annoying the hell out of me asking questions, blatantly ignoring my 'request' for him to shut it.

"Tell me why I shouldn't just walk away now. You have no jurisdiction over me? You can't keep me against my will." he challenged.

I looked at him menacingly and raised my eyebrows, looking directly into his eyes, tensing my muscles.

"Well, you could try..... But you'll fucking regret it,

that's for sure."

I really didn't have time for this fucking shit. Thank God Zaph was near and would relieve me of him.

Trying to concentrate on the scene again, I noticed Rick changed posture the instant he had opened the door of the cafe. He must have caught Alice and Eliza's scent immediately (not my scent I hoped) and he was scanning the place to find them. This could go one of two ways. He could turn around and avoid them all together, or, and this is what I was counting on, he would want to see the love of his life, not to mention take the opportunity to meet his daughter, the family bond too strong to ignore. Rick had clocked them almost at once and, after just the tiniest of hesitation, moved towards them.

I heard Zaphire approach and told Kas to get ready to go with her, without taking my eyes off the developments in the cafe. He started to protest but I cut him off.

"Just fucking do as you're told!" I roared.

"Hi to you too, brother." Zaphy joked when she entered at that exact moment, but I didn't have the patience for it.

"Get that fucking Dullard out of here. I need to

269

concentrate. Just fuck off." I grumbled rudely.

"No worries Zack." At least she didn't sound pissed off.

I had missed how Alice and Eliza reacted initially, but I saw Rick and Alice talking and it looked like she was making some space at their table for him. That was a good sign. I hoped they would keep to the script as closely as possible, which basically meant for them to try and divulge as little information as possible, so that they would minimise the risk of raising any suspicion. All I could do for now was wait and observe.

CHAPTER 37

The moment the door of the cafe opened, his scent penetrated me, taking over all other surrounding smells. It was so familiar and brought me back to my childhood instantly. How could I have forgotten this scent? It overpowered my whole being and part of me wanted to jump up and run into his arms. But I couldn't. Under no circumstance should I show any hint of recognition and I had to work extremely hard to cloak any signal that was going to give it away.

Even though Zack had warned me, I hadn't been prepared for the intense feeling his scent evoked. The draw of the familial bond so strong I could hardly resist it. The incident with Kas hadn't helped. It was hard to concentrate and I was doubly glad my mum was here to centre me. Her eyes willing me to calm down as Rick approached us. I was visualising the sea with as much energy as I could muster and fought the urge to just out myself to him. I couldn't let everyone down at the first hurdle.

"Alice?" Rick spoke softly as he touched her arm.

I could almost see the sparks flying, it was that charged. Mum looked up acting surprised and shocked in the most natural way. She was brilliant.

271

Rick was an incredibly handsome and charismatic man. I could see why mum had fallen for him those many years ago.

"Rick?!" Her two hands covered her mouth.

He was going to be able to read all the mixed emotions going through her head, as I could. She didn't need to hide any of them as they were all the ones he would expect. Anger, happiness, confusion, sadness, surprise, regret, all rolling off her like tumultuous waves. I did detect a tiny bit of guilt too, but nothing that would give anything away.

"I'm sorry to interrupt you here so unexpectedly Alice, but once I spotted you, I couldn't ignore you and walk away," he said with the most charming voice and a serious look on his face.

I could feel his nerves, but to the naked eye he was as calm and collected as anything. Poor mum was struggling.

"I....I don't know what to say..."

She looked at me and then back at Rick and she turned a bright shade of red. He picked up on the inference straight away, thinking mum didn't know what to say to me to explain who he was. He didn't hesitate and extended his hand out to me.

"Hi, I'm Rick. You probably worked it out by now, so

there is no point beating around the bush..."

He paused for a moment, gauging my mood. I tried to look apprehensive and curious at the same time.

"Me and your mum go back a long way. In fact just over eighteen years ago we met and fell in love and Alice fell pregnant soon after. So there you have it; I am your elusive father."

He looked at me with concern. He was obviously trying to read my reaction and I had to let some feelings out otherwise he would be suspicious. I went with the most obvious one and that was shock. The shock for me was to see how much attraction there still was between the two of them so I focussed on that.

"Uh... what? What is this? Mum?"

I looked at him and mum with what I hoped looked like confusion, shock and some scepticism thrown in too. Mum cleared some space on our table and got him a chair.

"Please sit with us if you have time. We could talk." mum suggested.

"Yes of course, I'll get myself a coffee."

As he walked to the counter, I noticed him checking the place out. Claude was working on his laptop, seemingly not paying attention to anything

273

around him. My feelings were still all over the place, a strong sense of loyalty to my family overwhelmed me. If my dad was in some kind of trouble, I was determined to get him out, even though he had been an arse and left my mum without any explanation all those years ago. I would confront him over that when the time was right.

"So, what brings you here? It's miles from your house and not your type of scene at all?" he started, directing his speech to Alice.

"The same could be said for you, Rick. Except I have no clue where you live now." mum deflected.

"I'm working in an office nearby at the moment. Contracting, so only temporarily. I move all over the place, renting or staying in hotels."

He looked away for a moment before resting his gaze on me.

"How about yourselves? Isn't Eliza in her final year with exams approaching? Have you moved house?" he inquired, clearly not forgotten that we hadn't explained our presence.

"It's a delicate matter, Rick. Eliza's having a bit of a break from her studies at the moment, but it's only temporary." mum said, still being evasive.

"We could maybe talk about it, if we decided to

keep contact." she suggested tentatively.

She sounded a tad defensive. I could see Rick mulling it over and deciding to leave it for now. He once again directed his attention on me.

"Look Lizzy, I'm sure this is really awkward for you and you must be feeling confused and have millions of questions for me. I would really like to get to know you better and I hope we can meet up soon? I haven't got long today, so I really hope you'll consider it."

He wrote his contact details down and gave them to me. I nodded but looked bemused.

"Why now? What has stopped you from contacting me in the past? I don't understand how you can just walk in here and drop this on me, and on mum? I really don't know what to think."

I looked at him accusingly and he lowered his eyelids. I picked up a glimmer of guilt.

"Oh honey, nothing in life is straight forward and simple, but I would like to get a chance to explain, if you let me. Just not now. It's too complicated." he sighed.

"Please phone me in the next couple of days so we can arrange to meet up. And Alice, I would like you to be there too, if you want."

I looked at mum and her face was showing a kaleidoscope of emotions, each fighting to be the dominant one. But she answered coolly.

"I'll think about it. Eliza and I will have a talk about it. I'm not sure she's ready for this, or me for that matter, but we'll try and work something out."

He looked satisfied with that answer, clearly anticipating that our curiosity will win over any apprehension we might feel. He gathered his coat and picked up his coffee to leave.

"Hope to see you soon." he whispered in mum's ear when he hugged her.

"I would love to see more of you, Eliza. You have grown up into the beautiful young lady I always knew you would."

Then he left, without looking back.

Mum looked pensive but I breathed a sigh of relief. I'd been waiting for the chance to meet my father since the moment he'd left us, albeit subconsciously. It was weird it had come under these circumstances and I couldn't fully work out what I felt. I didn't really allow myself too much time to think about it. The fact it was part of the mission had pushed my own feelings to the background and I wasn't ready to let them all out, so I focussed on the assignment.

It had gone rather well I thought. He didn't seem suspicious at all at the moment. He had genuinely been surprised to see us there and he clearly had to improvise to arrange another meeting, but left the ball in our court. That was great as we could arrange something on our terms and there would be fewer unknowns. I couldn't wait to tell Zack the good news. Though, looking at Claude texting away, he must be fully up to date already. We finished our drinks and gathered up our belongings, preparing to leave. Claude would follow shortly afterwards and we were not to make contact until everything was clear and checked, just in case Rick had us followed or anything. We left to do a bit of window shopping, waiting for the all clear signal which came after about twenty minutes.

CHAPTER 38

Back at our compound, Eliza walked up to me, her face excited and relieved, her eyes still shimmering with adrenaline. She looked beautiful, a fact not missed by Zaphire, who was standing by my side. She ran up to Eliza and embraced her lovingly. My heart felt the stab of jealousy all too much, but I pushed it away instantly.

"Well done, my sweet. You held it together brilliantly." I heard my sister whisper in Eliza's ear tenderly. I was selfishly pleased to see Eliza's eyes searching for me, whilst still in Zaphy's embrace. My sister must have felt it, as she let go and looked away trying to hide her disappointment. It was clear to me, but Eliza wasn't tuned into her at the moment, still brimming with excitement from the successful start of her first assignment.

"Zack! That couldn't have gone any better! Mum was brilliant! I was so lucky to have her there. Without her I would have given myself away, for sure."

She looked around, still quite bewildered and suddenly remembering the Kas situation.

"Apart from the Kas debacle." she said a little dejected.

"Where is he?"

"He's safe and under my care at the moment." Zaphire interjected.

"Don't worry about him. He'll be fine, though we're not sure what to do with him as Zack still needs to decide what action to take."

That was low. She knew that Eliza would hate what I'll have to do with Kas, and she's not going to forgive me easily. My sister was feeling a little stung by jealousy too.

"I'll deal with that later, sister." I said poignantly.

"First, Eliza and Alice will need to tell me exactly what happened and then we'll devise a plan for the next step. After that, I will talk to Markus about what to do with Kas. In the mean time, you can look after him, Zaphire. You seem to have him eating out of your hand already." I countered. Effectively, if I say so myself, as Zaphy looked guiltily away from Eliza, who did notice this time. She'd picked up on us trying to have a dig at each other, but chose to ignore it. For now at least. I could feel her discomfort with it and I promised myself not to let myself do it again. Zaphire could be so annoying, though.

"Can I see him at least?" Eliza asked.

I knew she had guessed the answer to that

already by the way she hung her shoulders.

"Maybe later. Let's get some lunch and talk about the next stage now." I said decisively and walked towards the meeting room purposefully.

"I'll get a selection of sandwiches to be delivered to us in the meeting room and there are drinks here already." I told Alice and Eliza as we entered the room urging them to take a seat around the table. I was keen to work out what we'd do next to get the information we needed out of Rick. The quicker we found out whether he was in on it, or forced, the better. The whole next stage hinged on the fact he was either an innocent pawn in this or, something far more disturbing, part of the organisation. We needed to find out what their plan was as the movements we had seen are worrying to say the least, with them infiltrating into the courts, police and government. It didn't spell much good to be honest.

"So, do you think I should meet him alone or should mum come with me?" Eliza started.

"What do you think yourself, Eliza?"

She took a moment to answer, nervously glancing over to her mum. She wasn't sure how her mum would feel about her opinion.

"I think..." she nodded as if to encourage herself.

"I think I should go on my own. Pretend mum wasn't quite ready to meet him, needing some more time to think about it, but that I'm keen to find out more about him. What do you think Zack? Mum?"

Alice looked unsure but I agreed. I was relieved the suggestion was Eliza's, as I it meant I didn't have to fight over it with her, which would make the arrangements so much easier.

"That's exactly what I was thinking. He'll be more likely to open up to you when you're on your own. He might even tell you about your gift and see what you have to say. Claude said emotions were highly charged in the room with a huge spike when he spotted you next to your mum. He's definitely very keen to get to know you. The bond is strong. Even stronger than his love for Alice, which was also duly noted by Claude. He said he was surprised he ever managed to leave you, Alice. The love was still there and forceful."

"I noticed that when he touched your arm, mum. You must have felt the electricity, it was so powerful."

Eliza looked at her mum, wondering if she would accept her feelings for Rick were still as strong as ever. Though, she might not have even admitted that to herself yet.

"I don't know." Alice started hesitantly; clearly not ready to let her daughter launch herself into this alone, without looking at the alternatives.

"Could I not come along but go home after a while? When I know she's safe?" she tried.

"How will you leave without raising any questions or suspicions? Eliza is right in thinking he'll accept your reservations to meeting him again. After all, he left you without any clues as to why or where he went. He'll understand if you needed more time to decide. It's quite a natural reaction. It's also natural for Eliza to want to find out more about her dad, so again, nothing out of the ordinary, which is exactly what we need."

I hoped she would see it was the best way forward and not be difficult about it. We needed to be on one level with this. It would make deciding so much easier. I noticed a shift in Alice's attitude which was encouraging.

"Also, we did promise Eliza to withdraw you from the operation when first contact was made. We don't want to draw you in further than we need to, for your own safety." I added.

It wasn't just the safety of Alice we were worried about. Alice was still an unknown quantity to us, we didn't know if we could trust her not to warn her ex, if they were to rekindle their relationship. Love could make you do all sorts of unexpected things. It was not a risk I was willing to take.

"Well, if you both think that's the best way forward, then so be it." Alice relented.

"Will there be anyone on site with me? Can we use Claude again?" Eliza asked.

I was considering the same question.

"It's too much of a risk to use him again, because Rick will have logged the scents of each individual who was in that cafe; maybe not consciously but definitely subconsciously and if he was to notice the same scent he might be alerted and not proceed. He's a very clever and ultra cautious man so he'll try and minimise each risk. However, I haven't worked out an alternative yet."

"Would we be able to use a young Sensorian, pretending to be out on a date or something?" Eliza suggested.

I ran through all the options in our community and there were some suitable kids who could do it, but the problem was that the place suitable to meet for Rick and Eliza would not be a hangout for young kids on a date, so I shelved that plan. No, we probably needed to get technical and have a listening device so we could stay at a safe distance.

"Let me have a think about it and I will come up with something workable." I concluded.

We decided to stick to the cover story of Eliza recovering from a setback in her mental health and had deferred her exams to autumn. Best to keep to the story we spun to Kas before as too many lies would just confuse matters. We were lucky to have one of the best specialist mental hospitals in the country here in town, so we could easily use it as an alibi.

Next, I had to turn my attention to the Kas situation, which was delicate. I couldn't do this in front of Eliza, it would be too upsetting and it wouldn't do the mission any good to have her all emotional. Markus agreed and let Zaphire look after Eliza whilst I dealt with Kas. I wasn't looking forward to this. We had hugely underestimated Kas' love and loyalty for Eliza and his resolve to find out what was going on with her.

I enlisted the help of Brody to get Kas to our small interview room to add some gravitas. I had drawn up a contract which I had to get him to sign somehow or the other. We couldn't risk him talking about our actions, location or involvement with Eliza. Our safety and mission depended on it. I wasn't hopeful it would be resolved today, but I'd give it a go.

"Take a seat Kas." I ordered.

I pulled out the chair for him and proceeded to sit myself down on the other side of the table, putting the papers right in front of him. He reluctantly sat himself down and looked at me and Brody curiously.

"I'll be straight with you Kasper. You have two choices.   You can fully cooperate with me, sign these confidentiality papers, get your driving licence back and be on your way home by tomorrow, so you don't miss your first exam. If you sign the papers you're legally bound to never speak of what you have seen, heard or experienced here, with the promise of prison if you break the terms and conditions of the contract." I looked at him intensely.

He emanated strong scepticism, which didn't fill me with great confidence for a swift resolution.

"What's my second option?" he asked defiantly.

I glanced over at Brody, who shifted his weight uncomfortably from one foot to the other. I leaned back in my chair and crossed my arms, stared at Kas and sighed.

"Your second choice is to refuse to sign these

papers. This will have severe consequences for you. We'll set you up to take the blame for a crime committed which will land you in prison and a lifelong registration on the sex offenders register. You'll never get to see Eliza again and I doubt your friends and family will want to associate with you."

Kas leant back in his chair emitting a sigh, shaking his head, looking down in his lap. But not for long. He steeled himself and got ready for his reply.

"I may only just be eighteen years old, but I'm an adult and I'm not stupid! You can't do this! I'll go to the police and tell them everything. I know my rights and what you're doing is totally illegal! I'm sure Eliza will back me up. I've done nothing wrong! Let me go home. Now!"

He threw his chair back and got up, but Brody was there already, twisting his arm and bending him over the table. Kas squirmed in pain and shouted at Brody to stop and leave him alone.

"Calm yourself down, man. Pick up that chair and sit your arse back on it." Brody ordered.

I knew he'd come in handy. Kas complied, shaking Brody's hands off him.

"Kas, fucking listen to me. I'll give you one more chance to read through the papers and sign them. It won't do you any harm to commit to them. We're being extremely reasonable to even give you this chance to get off so lightly, and that's only because you're Eliza's friend." I urged him to reconsider.

"Boyfriend." he retorted angrily.

"She'll never forgive you if you frame me for a crime I didn't commit."

"You're probably right, Kas. But that's not going to stop us, trust me. She'll get over it. She knows when things are necessary to guarantee our safety, plus the success of our mission is paramount. Even if she doesn't forgive me, Eliza won't come to your rescue either. Make no mistake about that."

I hoped sincerely that he would give up his fight and see sense, but it was in vain. It wasn't the end of the world to be sworn to secrecy, but the other option would be disastrous for him. However, it was clear to me he wasn't convinced we would follow through with our threat and he chose to challenge me.

"I take option two. I'm not signing any of your damned papers. You won't get rid of me that easily. I want to find out if Eliza is okay." he answered stubbornly.

It left me with no option to get Brody to handcuff him and make him stand in front of me. I studied his face for a while, his eyes growing more worried by the minute, but still showing nothing but defiance.

"Eliza is fine. I'm putting *you* in isolation for now. Use that time to make the right choice, or ruin not only your own life, but also that of your family. You should thank me on your hands and knees for the patience I'm showing you, Kas. You've no fucking idea what you're dealing with."

He flinched but was determined.

"Brody. Take him away."

Fuck me, this guy was stubborn. I hoped he would break in the isolation cell. I may even have to get Eliza to talk to him before I see him again. If he refused to sign, his fate would be sealed. I couldn't give him more leeway than I already had. The leaders wouldn't be happy with me as it was, but I had to try and make him see sense, for Eliza's sake.

CHAPTER 39

Marching back into our room, Zack's face looked thunderous. Zaphire, mum and me were cuddled up on the sofa watching a rerun of Gilmore Girls. I loved that series, but Zack snatched the remote, switched off the TV and beckoned me over.

"A word, please." he ordered.

I reluctantly left my warm and snugly place next to Zaphire, obviously not quickly enough.

"Now!" he thundered.

He definitely was not in a good mood, telling me whatever he had to do with Kas hadn't gone the way he'd wanted it to go.

"That dickhead of a boyfriend of yours is causing me a fucking headache." he snarled.

"Boyfriend?"

I hadn't really thought about Kas as my boyfriend for a while but it dawned on me I hadn't let him know that. In his opinion we were clearly still an item.

"Yes, Eliza. He referred to himself as your boyfriend. I suggest you sort that out as I can clearly see that you don't regard yourself as his girlfriend any more. It's irrelevant anyway. He won't comply. The fucking idiot is risking being falsely accused of a crime and ending up in prison with a tarred reputation for life,

289

to try and help you. He doesn't think we will carry out our threat and he is naïve enough to think he can just go to the police and report us."

Zack rolled his eyes in annoyance, but I understood where Kas was coming from. He had no idea what the Sensorians were and that they'd do anything to save a mission or prevent any one of our community being compromised in any way shape of form. I was shocked to find myself so easily accepting the threats Zack had made to Kas. I didn't like it and would resent Zack if he had to go through with them, but I did understand why he had to be so severe. A few days ago I would probably have screamed at him with the thought of him ruining Kas' life. How quickly perceptions could change.

"Where's he now?" I enquired.

"I could have a word with him, plead with him to just take the deal." I offered.

"He's in isolation for a while. Maybe leave him there for a few days and see if he gets the picture. I'm so fucking fed up of pussy footing around that fucking Dullard, all for your sake Eliza. Realise that, if it wasn't for you, he would have been on his way to prison now. I just haven't got time for this!" he exclaimed in frustration.

290

"The leaders will be on my case for this as well. They aren't as fucking patient as me."

That made me snort. *Zack. Patient! Hah!* However, he had given Kas a chance to reconsider, albeit in an isolation cell. Poor Kas. He won't have a clue what's happening to him. He was more loyal to me than I ever would have expected and I felt guilty I'd left him none the wiser about my feelings for him. Having said that, I still loved Kas and didn't want him in trouble.

"Please let me speak to him, Zack. I'm sure I can convince him to do the right thing." I offered again.

"The exams haven't started yet, I can still talk to him without any repercussions for me." I added to help me convince Zack to let me see him.

"Tomorrow. Let him stew a bit in the cell. It'll do him good. Bloody fucking idiot." Zack relented, still visibly annoyed with the whole situation.

The rest of the day was filled mostly with more exercise. Zack was really going for it and I came away rather bruised after our boxing session. Zaphire wasn't happy with her brother, but was wise enough not to mention anything to him. She handed me an ice pack for my emerging bruise on my arm, where I had just about managed to fend off a vicious right hook.

"He should have given you pads if he wanted to let off steam," she muttered whilst tending to some other scrapes I had sustained.

"It's okay, Zaph. I gave him a decent fight too! It felt good in a way. I've never been in a situation where I thought I could genuinely get hurt and it felt liberating to see I coped with it."

I saw Zack approaching with a slightly concerned look on his face. He must have heard me talk to Zaphy.

"Were you scared of me going too far?"

He looked bemused and a little hurt.

"I knew you were coping. Your adrenaline was keeping you safe, your reactions were incredible today. I would've pulled back, if I thought you couldn't handle it. A little pain is just part of the course."

That last comment was more directed at Zaphire than me, I noticed by the way he glanced at her rather accusingly, annoyed she was making a big deal out of it.

"Can I please go and have a shower now?" I was sweating like a pig and I could feel my body cooling down too much.

"Stretches first." Zack said decisively and I didn't object.

Surprisingly, I slept like a baby and I felt refreshed, though slightly aching, the following morning. The feeling didn't last long however, as I was hit with a wave of nervousness almost immediately thinking about the two tasks ahead for today. Firstly, I had to talk some sense into Kas and then I had to make contact with my father and arrange a meet. I was apprehensive to do either, though strangely excited at the same time. I heard Zack waking up too, his bed still situated across the door so I couldn't get past him if I were to sleepwalk, without him noticing. A ridiculous arrangement that I deemed totally unnecessary, but Zack wouldn't budge on. I still feared I was going to creep into his bed one night and embarrass myself totally. I promised myself to have another word with him about it soon.

After breakfast and another pep talk by Zack, we headed over to Kas. I caught a glimpse of him in the camera. He was sat on the floor with his head in his hands, looking thoroughly dejected and dishevelled. I noticed Zack hadn't even afforded him the luxury of a bed or a toilet. I felt engulfed with sympathy for Kas and anger for Zack. He could be so harsh on people without any qualms. Zack felt my anger and put a

293

hand on my arm to try and calm me down and be in control of my emotions.

"Do you need a minute?" he asked, looking slightly worried.

"It's important you keep focussed on getting the message across to Kas so he can go home. I had to be harsh with him to convince him of the seriousness of the situation. Don't let your feelings distract you."

"God no, not your *feelings*. Wouldn't let *those* get in the way." I muttered sarcastically under my breath, to which Zack threw me a warning scowl.

"Get it together, Mankuzay. We need to work as a team on this." he grumbled.

I shrugged the bad feelings off and concentrated on Kas instead.

"Yeah. You're right. I'm sorry." I relented and Zack notably relaxed.

Kas lifted his head when he heard the door and his eyes lit up briefly when he realised it was me. The light in his eyes dimmed instantly when he spotted Zack and his face crumpled. I felt his anger like fierce stabbing pains in my stomach and head, but it was mixed with another emotion, a deep fear which materialised in me like my legs had turned to jelly. And it stank. I hadn't encountered this combination of sensations before and it threw me off momentarily. Zack noticed me struggling and took charge.

"Get up." he barked at Kas, looking as imposing as he could muster.

I detected a strain in Zack that I'd not noticed before. He really had to work hard to be authoritative with Kas, who didn't know his reputation and therefore did not hold the automatic respect Zack enjoyed in the Sensorian community. He still pulled it off beautifully, with Kas complying immediately, probably more motivated by fear than respect though. Zack didn't care what motivated him, as long as he did what he was told.

By the time Kas had scrambled to his feet, I had composed myself and was dealing with my initial sensory overload.

"Hey, babes." I started.

"We need to talk. Come, we'll find somewhere more comfortable."

He looked at me and I saw my sympathy reflected in his eyes, but it was met with shame. He turned his head, avoiding my gaze.

"I need the loo. Pretty promptly or it'll be more than just me that has to be scraped off the floor." he tried to joke a little, but he wasn't smiling.

"Yeah, sure. Of course." I said hastily, beseeching

Zack to take him, willing him to give him that dignity.

To my relief Zack allowed it, escorting Kas to the toilets. I used the break to collect my thoughts. I was shocked to see Kas in the state we found him. He looked broken, scared and angry. No one should have to feel like that, and I felt guilty for having caused this for Kas. If only he had listened to me and not come after me to find out more. Everything would have been fine. But how could I blame him for caring for me? That wasn't fair. I had to fix this for him, but the experience won't go away. He will feel humiliated for the fear he'd shown, and the anger and feelings of dread will stay with him for the rest of his life.

When they returned we walked in an awkward silence towards a little cosy looking private room with some chairs and a sofa in it. We sat ourselves down, I placed myself next to Kas and Zack chose a chair a little away from us, trying to create the illusion we had a bit of privacy. I knew better of course. There was no privacy.

"Does the dick have to be here?" Kas whispered.

I nodded. I could feel Zack's heart rate go up, really trying to keep his cool, but seething on the inside.

"Are you safe?"

He looked so worried and I felt awful.

"Kas, I'm in the best of hands here." I tried to reassure him, glancing over to Zack, to the annoyance of Kas.

"I'm working for these people temporarily, on a special job. Mum knows, but it's a covert operation. I can't divulge any details for obvious reasons, but I can let you know it has to do with my father. That's why I'm involved. After this job I'll be back, and all will be back to normal."

I detected a little stir in Zack, but he should pick up that I was saying this mainly to placate Kas. I hadn't made my mind up at all yet.

"Back to normal? What the hell does that mean Eli? You lied to me! Several times! I was worried sick. You shamelessly tapped into my worries about your mental state. And for what? 'These people'? It's sounds dodgy and illegal to me and I want you out!"

Kas was getting agitated, his voice rising.

"Keep it down, mate." Zack warned.

Kas flew up to his feet and strode towards Zack who immediately jumped up and squared up to him.

"Sit the fuck down. Now." Zack hissed threateningly, his muscles flexing.

Kas' temporary bravery dissipated. He knew he couldn't match Zack and wisely retreated to the sofa.

297

I took his hands, squeezing them gently.

"Kas, listen to me. I'm fine. It's a straight forward job. It just has to stay secret. That's all they are interested in. Just sign the contract they offered you. They'll leave you in peace after that, as long as you abide by it. Please. Don't risk your future for me. I don't need protecting or saving. Do you think my mum would let me get involved in anything dodgy? She would be first in line to haul me out of here!" I pleaded and reasoned, hoping it would sink in and that he'd give in.

Kas sat in silence for a while, staring at our interlocking hands. Then he finally spoke, looking me straight in the eyes.

"And what about us?"

I looked away for just an instant, but Kas retracted his hands from mine.

"Right." His face hardened.

"Get me the damned papers. I'll sign them and I'll be out of your hair."

"Kas?" I started, but his reply was icy.

"Don't, Eliza. I don't want to hear it. We'll talk when you're back. If that ever happens."

He turned to Zack.

"Please, give me the contracts and please let me drive home. No one will ever hear of any of this, I swear."

Zack phoned for Zaphire to take care of it and moments later she appeared and took Kas. He threw me one last look, but made no effort to come over and say goodbye. I moved towards him, but Zack stopped me and gently pushed me towards the door.

"Leave it." he whispered.

"You've done your job here."

Before I left I glanced over to Kas once more, but he'd turned away from me. I felt a mixture of sadness, relief and shame. I hated having to lie to him. He'd always been my rock and I had deceived him. But I was relieved he had chosen to sign the contract so he could carry on with his life. I resolved to somehow make it up with him after the mission, though I would never be his girlfriend again. I knew that much.

CHAPTER 40

I felt Eliza's despondency as if it were my own.
She emitted such strong signals they were hard to
shield. She wasn't making any effort to mask her
feelings as she'd probably forgotten what impact they
had on all of us. We'd learned from a young age to
cloak our feelings or at least take the edge off them,
as we knew how debilitating it could be if everybody
had to feel everyone's else's emotions all the time.
We can tune out and shield of course but sometimes
the feelings are so intense it's hard to, or they take
you by surprise.

"Let's go. I want to show you something you
haven't seen yet, one of our little hidden treasures."

I suddenly felt quite excited, pleased with myself to
have come up with something which might help Eliza
feel better. Her curiosity was piqued.

"What little treasure would that be, then?"

She glanced sideways at my face, her eyes still
showing the hurt from what happened just minutes
before.

"Just follow me." I smiled and took her hand.

"See if you can control your curiosity!"

We had to walk for a few minutes to a part of the building I hadn't shown Eliza yet. I was taking her to our Room of Tranquillity. It was a simply beautiful space, full of plants, flowers and butterflies. Spread around were some gorgeously ornate fountains trickling water at a steady pace, giving the whole room an air of serenity. It opened out into a large balcony, full of colourful flowers and luscious plants. Tucked away in several places were some benches where you could just chill out, on your own or with company. The room was a sight to behold, and one of my favourite places to go whenever I was feeling overwhelmed.

I absolutely loved the look on Eliza's face when we entered the room. She was enthralled and her eyes shone with wonder. It stirred up my feelings for her again, which I found harder and harder to ignore and stow away.

We strolled around for a bit before Eliza decided to pick a little bench to sit on. I could feel her relaxing and in better control of her emotions. Slowly but surely I could only detect a little spilling over. She hadn't put it behind her, but she was working on cloaking it better.

"Wow, this is an amazing place," she whispered,

still in awe.

"I would like to show my mum later."

She noticed me stiffen a little at her request.

"If I may?" she added hastily.

"I'm not sure if that's possible, Eliza. I like your mum, but she's still regarded as an outsider in our community. I don't want to antagonise those who weren't totally convinced she should even be involved."

I tried to say it tactfully, but I knew what I said was right. Markus already had had to defend his decision several times and stamp out some dissent as some of the Sensorians had been quite vocal about their disapproval. I didn't want to give them another excuse to stir up trouble again.

"Shame." she conceded reluctantly.

She sank back into a state of contemplation and I let her be.

We spent another half hour or so just enjoying the atmosphere and sounds of the room, before we headed back for some lunch where we met up with Zaphire. She'd seen to Kas and made his arrangements. She organised a driver to take Kas home as she didn't trust him to be in the right state of mind to drive the long distance on his own. He would then also help explain his 'disappearance' to his

302

parents. Zaphire came over and gave Eliza a big hug, something I wished I could have done. She stroked Eliza's face tenderly and looked her deeply in the eyes.

"That must have been hard for you, my sweet," she whispered softly.

A tear rolled silently down Eliza's face, which Zapire gently wiped away. Seeing them being so intimate gave me the acrid burning sensation of jealousy. I had to do something quickly before it showed.

"I will get us some baguettes." I said, gruffly marching away to the food counter.

To my relief, when I returned they were sitting opposite of each other, leaving a space for me between them. Zaphire had managed to make Eliza smile somehow and the mood was much lighter now.

"Really? I leave you two alone for two minutes and you are giggling like two naughty school girls!" I jokingly admonished them.

They both looked at me, then back at each other and promptly burst out laughing again. I raised my eyebrows at them, but decided to ignore it. There was to be more serious business to be done after lunch, so a little light-heartedness was a good thing.

A little later we were back in our room discussing

our plan to set up a meet with Rick, when a knock on the door surprised us. I opened the door to find Markus immediately striding into our room.

"Sir?" I stood aside to let him pass, wondering what he wanted.

"When are you planning to make contact?"

There was no beating about the bush with Markus. If he needed to know something he would ask straight up. I was a little put out as he would normally just check with a text, so there must be something going on.

"We're contacting him this afternoon to set something up as soon as possible, as discussed."

I emphasised the latter, to hint that everything was under control.

"Good. We noticed some unusual activity and we're getting worried they're about to relocate. Even if Rick didn't want to, I doubt he would have much say over whether they are leaving or not, so we must make sure this meet happens ASAP."

"Yes Sir, understood." I reassured him.

"Anything else, Markus?" I prompted, though I knew he would come out with it anyway.

"Yes." He shot a sideways glance to Eliza and I knew instantly what was coming.

"Alice." I pre-empted.

He nodded.

"What do you reckon, Zack? How long do we need her here for?"

I felt Eliza's temperature shoot up in agitation.

"She needs to go home. We don't need her here anymore." I decided.

I knew that wouldn't go down well with Eliza, but it was exactly what Markus wanted to hear and it was the right thing to do at that moment.

"What do you mean?" she piped up.

"Now, you used her you will just kick her out? Is that how..."

I cut her off.

"Not now, Eliza. We'll discuss this later." I said sternly.

To her credit, she did stop but she could not hide her anger. Markus moved towards the door satisfied nonetheless.

"I'll get Laura to make arrangements. She'll be gone by this evening."

He glanced over to Eliza.

"Be assured that we are enormously grateful to your mum and that you two can meet again as soon as the mission is over. We just have to be practical now and minimise risk factors. Nothing personal."

He went, leaving me to deal with the

305

consequences. Probably not the best timing just before we had to make contact with Rick. I needed Eliza to focus so I had to talk to her straight away. She was about to burst anyway.

"Before you blow your top off at me Eliza, I'm sorry we had to do this in front of you."

She took a breath to start her reply but I carried on quickly.

"She'll be looked after by Laura and she can always contact us. We need to concentrate on the mission so we have to minimise any distractions. Mission first, remember. We did agree to pull her out after first contact was made. That was actually one of the things you made us promise."

I studied her face and posture and although she was still cross and disappointed, I could see she understood. She knew it was the right thing to do. It was just as well I could tell what she really felt because she wasn't ready to admit that to me at all.

"But we hadn't agreed to just throw her out and send her packing! It's just such bollocks." she hissed.

"I suppose I do get to say goodbye to her at least."

"That depends on whether you can talk to me in a respectful manner, Mankuzay." I reminded her of her place.

She didn't need much reminding, the punishment regime still fresh in her memory.

"Can I please say goodbye to her, Sir?" she tried again.

"We'll do so straight after we set up the meet." I agreed.

CHAPTER 41

Even though I understood why my mum had to go home, I couldn't help feeling angry with Zack and Markus. They talked about her as if she was nothing but a cog in the machine and I hated that. This mission comes first bullshit didn't come naturally to me. I was just not trained to think that way.

I knew Zack was pleased I didn't accost Markus and that I had stopped when he'd cut me off, but I still hadn't been able to stop myself from being rude to him. I was lucky we had to arrange the meet I think, or Zack may have made more of it and I would have found myself being punished again, and not been able to see my mum off. Anyhow, it was decided now and there was nothing I could do about it so I needed to concentrate on my task ahead.

I sent my father a text asking when it would be convenient to ring. I wanted to be the one to phone him so I was mentally prepared, and not be caught on the hop. It wasn't quite to happen like that because, as soon as I had sent the message, he rang me back straight away. My heart skipped a beat and I could hardly breathe.

"No time like the present." he said on the other

end of the phone.

"I'm so pleased you have contacted me. Does this mean you would like to meet up with me?"

He sounded rather hopeful and I felt a bit guilty. Though, it had to be like this because if he needed to be extracted from a tricky situation he had got himself into, the less he knew, the better. However, my gut kept niggling at me, questioning the amount of freedom he seemed to have, making it difficult to believe he was acting under duress. We had no idea though, so we had to keep an open mind.

"I would like that." I said a little hesitantly.

"When would you be free to have a cup of coffee or something?" I suggested.

"Let's do dinner." he said decisively.

"I can do tonight at 8pm, at The Bellevue. Is your mum coming?"

The Bellevue was a high end restaurant and I had to steer him away from that place, it was too formal.

"She wasn't sure it was a good idea. I think she needs a bit of time, but she was okay with me meeting you. She told me to pick a place I was going to be comfortable, so can we meet at The King's Arms?"

It was a much better place to be kept an eye on by the Sensorians as you did not have to book a table and people were constantly dropping in and out. I held my breath a bit as he seemed to hesitate at my suggestion.

"Okay." he finally agreed.

"Your mum always was a wise lady. Is there no way you can persuade her to come along?"

I breathed out slowly, relieved. I was lucky he could attribute all these signals to nerves about seeing him.

"She wants to take it slowly, see how it goes between us first." I made up.

"Okay, fair enough."

He sounded disappointed.

I decided to ignore it and focus on our meet.

"Good. We'll see each other there then, 8pm?" I asked him to confirm.

I called off and checked with Zack, who seemed more than satisfied.

"Good work, Eli."

He looked at me appreciatively.

My heart flurried hearing him call me Eli and it felt great to have pleased him. Though, I'm sure his appreciation only lasted minutes as not long after, I pissed him off by sighing at him when he ordered me to do some revision after saying my goodbyes to mum.

"Don't annoy me, Mankuzay. You don't want me in a bad mood for boxercise later." he warned.

I certainly didn't. I was still nursing some of the bruises I sustained the last time he was in a foul mood.

It felt horrible waving off my mum. She was so sad to go and worried about me. I had to be strong and show her I believed it was for the best and that I was fine. It was difficult to pull off and by the looks of the Sensorians around me I wasn't convincing them. But then, my mum was no Sensorian and she seemed to relax a little, so I must have seemed confident enough to convince her at least. Zaphire did her best too, making sure mum was feeling positive about the whole thing.

"Alice, she's being looked after by the best people to keep her safe. Time will fly."

She gave her a big reassuring hug and then stepped back to let us do the same. My body was consumed with all the feelings flying around. It felt like little waves of electricity coursing through my body. It was almost too much, but I stayed strong. Then I felt the soft touch of Zaphire on my back, encouraging me to let go. Mum quickly wiped away a tear, which nearly broke my heart. I could feel myself welling up too, but I resisted, using all the techniques I had learned. Mum may not be a Sensorian, but she was my mum and noticed I was struggling. Now it was her turn to put a positive spin on the situation.

"Look at us silly people. We will both be fine and see each other in no time! Promise me one thing though my baby. Please be careful. Listen to Zack and don't try and be a hero."

I nodded and she smiled gingerly, and with that she picked up her bag and was escorted out of the building by Laura. A heavy feeling enveloped me and my heart felt like it was going to implode. I could hardly breathe and I had to swallow back my tears again, not helped by the fact I could feel every single crushing emotion my mum felt as she walked out, leaving me almost falling apart.

Walking back to our room, me still in a complete daze, Zack suddenly called over one of the little boys, he must have been about eight or nine years old. Zack looked at him seriously and asked him if he could do an important job for him, to which the boy eagerly nodded his head. He gave him a little note and told him to find Ned as soon as possible and deliver it to him. The boy ran off immediately to do his task.

"Remember you asked before why we send the kids on these little errands? Have you worked out why yet?"

"I guess it is to get them used to following orders?"

I assumed something like that last time I witnessed the, in my opinion, rather pointless exercise. I'm sure Zack was just trying to distract me from my misery, but he answered quite seriously.

"There is that to it, but more importantly we do it to get them involved in our community from a very young age. It gives us the opportunity to praise them lots for helping and make them feel important and valued."

Zack paused a moment.

"It makes them *want* to follow orders."

He threw me a questioning glance.

"Something you seem to find quite hard to grasp, especially when you first got here."

I agreed. It did not come naturally to me but I did understand the importance and had worked hard to get over my instinct to question everything and thought I had been doing rather well lately.

"That makes sense. It's a way of life for you all. I just dropped in and have to adjust to this rapidly."

I looked him straight in the eyes.

"Something that some of you forget sometimes."

"No one has forgotten that. We just don't want to constantly make allowances for you. It wouldn't help you. You're strong, you can cope. It's a compliment. I was too fucking soft on you at the start." he said

313

resolutely.

I wasn't so sure, but I wasn't going to say anything. It would be pointless, the way he and I were raised was so different, we might as well have lived on different planets.

Back in my room I dutifully did my revision for an hour and a half or so before Zack told me to get changed for boxing. Zaphire was also coming, which lifted my spirits immediately. It still surprised me how much she affected me. I wish we had the freedom to explore what these feelings meant. I was confused and needed to find out what this was. Had I really fallen in love with her? And why did I then still have feelings for Zack as well? Or was it all just pure lust? I didn't really know what to do with it all and it didn't help that any sexual relationship at the moment was completely off the cards. I knew that Zack and Zaphire were both cloaking their feelings for me most of the time, but by now I had seen enough glimpses to see the attraction was definitely mutual, for both of them. It could become very tricky.

I was starting to get nervous about meeting my father later and the exercise did me the world of good, as always. I loved sparring with Zaphy and fighting with Zack left me no time to worry about anything else but the moves he was making. If I slacked, I would end up hurt. Simple as that. My head was much clearer now and able to focus on what I had to do this evening. I was ready for it.

CHAPTER 42

I loved seeing Eliza blossom when she exercised. She was so focused and totally tuned in to whatever move I made. It was sexy as hell. I had to concentrate very hard on fighting and cloaking at the same time as I found it increasingly hard not to let any of my feelings seep through.

I could see the tension run off Eliza and her face looked like the sun emerging from behind the dark clouds. She clearly needed to let off some steam to enable her to regain her focus and positivity. It felt good to have a bit of a laugh with her as well, she was so sharp witted with her retorts. I was glad the disciplining hadn't squashed that side of her.

When Eliza and Zaphire were sparring together I got a chance to catch up with Ned, Brody and Sam, who were in the gym as well. They were working the equipment like mad and I remembered it must be coming up for our monthly fitness test that Markus had imposed on all of us, even the kids. That explained how busy it was in the gym and sports hall. Everyone was having a panic about not passing it and training obsessively.

It always happened around test time. It was a real

pain if you didn't pass the test because Markus would run sessions at 6am every morning that you had to attend until the next monthly test. Understandably high on the list to avoid, even for those who loved exercising. Once you had passed the basic level, you would be given a target you had to achieve by the next test, so you were always working towards becoming even fitter. A great idea but, when you were busy running a mission, not always achievable and therefore always a slight concern in the back of your head. Fit as I was, I hadn't been working on improving, so was in danger of failing this month's test. A real pain in the arse.

Eliza would have her first test, but it would be the basic one, which I was confident she would pass. I would have to talk to her about it to prepare her, though I was going to wait till after the dinner with her father. The test wasn't until a couple of days later anyway.

My friends were having the same problem as me as all of us had been so busy with work, that even though we kept ourselves in shape, it wasn't a priority to improve ourselves. It was one of the rules I had argued with Markus over before, with the ultimate backing of almost everyone, I have to say. I urged

317

him to give people a bit of leeway in certain busy times, but he wouldn't have any of it. He was convinced it was imperative to always work on one's fitness, whatever the circumstances. He could be so fucking annoying and stubborn at times. Anyway, I wasn't going to stress over it. I would just have to do the extra training in the mornings if I failed. I don't think Eliza would be very happy about it though, as she would have to come with me. Oh well, it'll do her good I reasoned. I shoved it to the back of my head, did a few exercises with Brody and then summoned Eliza to do cool down and get a shower.

After we both freshened up, we went through our plan for this evening again. Eliza looked stunning in the dress she had chosen to wear, one from Zaphy's wardrobe. Perfect for the occasion in its simplicity. Rick would be amazed by her maturity.

She seemed tense but in control and confident. I told her that it wouldn't be the end of the world if her cover was blown or if he suspected anything. I advised her to keep going with the flow as at some point he will pick up on something, it was almost unavoidable. We were not blinkered enough to assume we would be able to deceive him for long. He had been one of our best Sensorians after all. All we needed is for him to open up to her somehow, then we'd know what action to take.

I didn't tell Eliza that I was a little worried about the unexpected movements of the syndicate that Markus had alluded to. We did have back up with some of our most experienced weapon carriers if it all went tits up, but I really did not want it to come to that. I also didn't want Eliza to know how wrong it all could go. I wanted her to just focus on her father, get the information we needed and stay safe.

I felt it necessary to reiterate the importance of following orders and how things could go horrible wrong if you thought you knew better than your mission leader. I decided to tell her the story of Ned, who had learned the hard way. It was rare for a Sensorian to disobey orders, especially for those who have been in the community all their life. But it did happen occasionally, usually with no immediate harm done. However, in Ned's case it probably could not have gone any more wrong with consequences he's still having to deal with now.

It happened when Ned was barely sixteen years old, which in our community is the age of becoming operational. It meant you were expected to help in missions. Ned was raring to be involved, and one day he was asked to be part of a mission, though not in the way he hoped for. He was tasked to keep safe a couple of the children, including his own sister whilst their parents were involved in a risky mission involving some serious criminals. There had been a breach of security and the children were deemed to be at risk, as one of the identities of the parents had been inadvertently exposed to one of the targets. Ned, however, failed to see the importance of his role and thought it was a bit naff. Our community was incredibly well secured, there would be no way the children were at risk. He thought the leaders were over reacting and he ignored their orders. He left the children, having put a film on for them, and went to catch up with me and a couple of others for a bit. We all told him to get back to his duty, but he just laughed it off.

Then, all hell broke loose, as two of the children, including Ned's eleven year old sister, managed to sneak out of our compound, completely unaware of the danger they had put themselves in. Everyone was called to start the search for them, including me. Ned was frantic, but managed to get himself together to join in the search, but it was in vain.

The perpetrators we were after sent us a message to call off the pursuit or else we wouldn't see the

320

children again. They were held for 24 hours in a secret location, which gave the offenders time to disappear. Then the children's location was revealed. We found them safe but traumatised, and the whole operation failed. We never caught them and we had to move to a different location and erase all our traces. It was a logistical nightmare.

Ned was severely punished and spent 3 months in isolation, and then spent about a year just doing menial tasks, but the worst thing for him was that his parents would not forgive him and never have as yet. In their eyes he had brought shame to the family by compromising the mission and had put the lives of his sister and the other kids in danger.

Ned worked incredibly hard to prove he could be trusted again. Markus eventually started giving him some responsibilities, and slowly but surely he was able to work where his abilities were most needed. Now he's back on track again, but he's had to endure the isolation of his family which was still ongoing. It's been a harsh lesson to learn.

I thought the story had the desired effect on Eliza. She looked at me with dark eyes, digesting what I had just told her.

"Poor Ned." she eventually said.

"Three months in isolation? Wouldn't that send anyone over the edge? He was so young still! His parents were harsh on him. Do you think they'll ever welcome him back in their family?" she asked with so much compassion for his plight, I wondered if she had actually gotten the point of the story.

"Don't know. Ned's accepted it. It was his responsibility and rather than being bitter about the consequences, he's put in practice what we're taught; to move forward and accept our lot. He has approached it the only way we know how to; with a determination to do better next time and not to blame anyone. We're responsible for our own actions. That's just how it is."

I wasn't sure if the moral of the story had sunk in, but then she reassured me by her next comment, probably having picked up on my doubts.

"Don't get me wrong, I understand why you told me this story. We must follow orders otherwise there could be disastrous consequences. I get it. It was pretty stupid of him."

"It fucking was. I don't think we'll ever forget it. Not to mention the two weeks of isolation I got for not marching Ned back to his duties." I remembered grumpily.

Markus had been particularly hard on me. I'm

322

slightly younger than Ned and hadn't been given the responsibility for him, but somehow I was meant to have assumed that responsibility. That had been my lesson to learn. My other mates seemed to have gotten away with just a lecture, but I had learned early on in life that having Markus as my carer may have given me some advantages, but there were definitely disadvantages. Harsh punishments always seemed to come my way, and Zaphire didn't fare much better with that either. But we learned to just take it and not gripe about it.

"By the way, when we spend time in isolation, it doesn't mean we're put in some sort of dungeon with no contact whatsoever. It just means prison with a strict regime of exercise, limited outside time and minimal contact with people. It's not going to send anyone 'over the edge', as you called it."

I had to smile a bit thinking of the pictures I had evoked in Eliza's mind as I noticed the obvious relief washing over Eliza's face.

My team had gathered in the meeting room. Frank van der Veldt was there as well to oversee it and keep Markus informed. I'd already sent someone to pay one of the waiters to drop a bug near where Eliza and Rick were going to sit. Bar and restaurant staff usually were willing accomplices as they were always in need of some extra cash. We had sussed out beforehand who would be reliable and suitable people and done a few practice runs, which all were carried out successfully. Everyone knew what their task was, but best case scenario we wouldn't have to do much, but observe. I sincerely hoped that would be the case, but my gut feeling told me not to be complacent.

I gave Eliza the tracker.

"Swallow this." I ordered.

She looked apprehensive but looked for some water to swallow it down with. It wasn't going to be the most pleasant feeling, but it had to be done this way.

"It's the most secure way. The only drawback is that it obviously has a time limit as it will pass through your system."

She nodded with comprehension.

"Tell me your signal in case you want to bail out." I checked.

"If I say I need the Ladies, you will start the emergency extradition procedure immediately, no matter what." she answered dutifully.

I grabbed Eliza's chin and made her look straight into my eyes, clearly giving her the chills.

"If you feel at *any* time things are going out of control or you notice anything suspicious, or feel in danger, you *must* use that signal. Do you understand? That's an order." urging her to understand the importance.

"Yes Sir." she said determinedly, but I knew she would do anything to avoid that from happening. She wanted to succeed this evening and I fucking well hoped she wouldn't be reckless enough to put herself in danger.

CHAPTER 43

On our way to The King's Arms, I could still feel
the tracker making its way down my gullet and gave
myself a little rub. It was larger than a normal capsule
so it had been quite difficult to swallow, and nearly
made me gag. Just as well I was used to taking lots
of pills. Though, the sick feeling could also be down
to nerves, as I was nervous as hell.

I could still feel Zack's hand on my chin, his eyes
only inches away from mine, issuing a stern warning.
It had given me goose bumps all over. I hoped,
undoubtedly in vain, that he hadn't noticed but now
was not the time to ponder over these things. I had
got to focus on the task in hand.

The plan was to ease into the conversation, suss
out his vibes and then hit him straight out with the
question about his involvement, to catch him off guard,
then gauge his reaction. It had sounded straight
forward when we discussed it, but I could see all sorts
of pitfalls. What if he wasn't relaxed and was
suspicious already? I knew we had discussed several
scenarios, but none of them were ideal. Zack also
relied on my improvisation skills a little too much in my
opinion, but he seemed super confident in them. I just
hoped it was going to go as planned so those skills

weren't going to be tested.

I took a taxi as it was safer not to be seen with any of the Sensorians, who'd all made their own way to their stations. I walked over to the entrance, taking a few deep breaths to steady myself. I was a little early, but decided to go in anyway. Rick may be there already. I was totally bricking it, but trusted Zack to have thought through any scenario to ensure my safety. I just hoped I could get the information out of Rick and that I wasn't putting him in danger. I was worried the organisation my father was working for, whether it be voluntarily or not, had got wind of my existence and that would be bad news. They could in theory use me as extra leverage to make Rick do what they wanted even more.

I glanced over to the bar and spotted Rick immediately. His head turned instantly towards the door when I opened it and he lifted his hand to attract my attention. I walked over, having to work on tuning out my senses very hard. I still wasn't used to all the sensory signals that people in public spaces emitted, especially in crowded places. Rick must have sensed my struggle as he walked up to me and gave me a hug. I hoped he just put it down to nerves.

"How are you doing Eliza?" he asked as he looked me over.

"You look..." he seemed to be looking for the right words. "...so grown up!"

I sensed pride and sadness at the same time. I was hit by the intensity of his scent once again. The bond was evident and hard to ignore. It made me want to snuggle into his hug, but instead I pushed him slightly away. I had to stay focussed and not get befuddled with emotions.

"Okay. Thank you."

I smiled a little.

"Have you been here long?" I asked awkwardly.

He shook his head and smiled too.

"This is weird, isn't it?" he admitted.

He felt uneasy too, which I hadn't expected.

"Shall we find somewhere to sit? What would you like to drink?" he asked, taking the initiative.

"May I have a coke, please." I answered politely.

I wasn't going to have any alcohol tonight, although I could really do with some Dutch courage. It was against the rules, however. No drinking whilst on a mission. I was still under age anyway.

I went to find a suitable table whilst Rick fetched the drinks. I observed him whilst he walked back with a beer and a coke in his hand. I noticed again how handsome and charismatic this man was. I had already spotted four women's interest spike when he walked past.

I tried to detect any resemblance to me, but it was hard to see. The colour of my eyes, was the same, a steely grey. Our eyebrows looked similar, just less hairy, luckily. I giggled inwardly. That of course didn't get past him and he asked me what amused me so much. I tried to look a little surprised with his astuteness.

"Nothing really, I was just trying to spot any similarities between the two of us." I said light heartedly.

"It's the eyes." he said resolutely as he placed the drinks carefully on the table and sat himself down opposite me.

"So...how do you feel about meeting me? Do you remember me at all?"

He locked his eyes on me and I knew exactly what he was doing. He was looking for any subconscious feelings I was emitting, but I was doing my best to keep my feelings difficult to decipher.

"Wow, straight to the point then?" I deflected.

"Well, yes. Why dance around the handbag for ages. We know what we're here for, don't we?" he

329

countered.

At that moment a waiter came past and asked if we wanted something to eat. He put the holder with the menus on the table when we answered affirmatively, and I guessed that is where the listening device was hidden. We both took a menu out to peruse.

"I do have a memory I'd like to ask you about, although I used to think it was a dream. After meeting you the other day I'm pretty sure it's not."

Rick's interest piqued.

"Oh? What was it about?" he prompted.

"It's about the night you came and carried me out of the house..."

"Ah. That." he interrupted.

"I had hoped you'd actually been asleep and not noticed, but I see I hoped in vain."

"It gave me nightmares for years." I said accusingly.

"What the hell were you thinking, taking me like that!"

"I missed you. I wanted to introduce you to my community and raise you. I felt I had made a terrible mistake leaving you to deal with..." he hesitated.

"...your perceived mental issues. It wasn't fair on

330

you. However, I couldn't do it to Alice. Not having you around would have broken her, and I didn't want the life I was leading for her either. I could have brought your mum into my community but it would have stifled her and would've killed her spirit. I just couldn't do it to either of you. So I changed my mind and put you back in bed. Alice hadn't noticed a thing, and I always assumed you hadn't either."

I absorbed this for a moment. It was more or less what I'd thought had happened, and it did explain a few things. I couldn't agree more with him that mum would've hated life in the Sensorian community. She could hardly cope with being there a few days, let alone her whole life. I couldn't let on to that to him though, although the feeling would have been hard to mask. As I feared, he picked up on it.

"You don't seem surprised or angry?" he queried.

"Well, I know that mum would have found it difficult to give up her freedom for anything, so I understand where you're coming from. Are you part of a sect or something?" I asked quickly, remembering I wasn't meant to know anything about the Sensorians.

He stifled a smirk before answering.

"I suppose you could say that I was in the past. But I managed to break free from all of that, not so

331

long ago. I have a new life now and I would really like you and your mum to be part of that. I think we would make a great team together."

"Team?" I questioned.

"I thought we would make a family first, if we were to be part of your life again." I said a bit prickly.

Tiny little beads of sweat appeared on Rick's brow, not at all noticeable to a normal person, but glaringly obvious to me, indicating a slight rise in levels of stress.

"Of course. Bad choice of words. Don't be too harsh on me; this has all come out of the blue for me too. Until I stepped into the cafe the other day, I never thought I would get a chance to have you or Alice back in my life ever again."

He paused for a minute, looking pensive.

"But the bond was so strong, I could not let the chance go by. Can you feel it?" he asked a bit hesitantly.

Boy did I want to shout '*yes*'! My body was screaming it. I wanted to be part of his life so badly again, I'd never encountered a feeling of connectivity this strong. I belonged with my dad. However, I had to wait and find out more about his intentions first, so I fought the urge to just fess up and go with him whatever the consequences, and answered measuredly instead.

"I don't know what I'm feeling at the moment, Rick. I definitely want to get to know you better, but I am not sure *you* will want to know me after this meeting."

I could see his body shift uncomfortably. I had aroused a trickle of suspicion, but he wasn't quite ready to let the suspicion take over. He very much wanted to believe I didn't know anything and that it was pure chance we met the other day. The conflict going on inside his head was obvious for me to detect, so he wasn't cloaking at all. I had to act soon before he would start putting his defences up.

"What do you mean, Lizzy? You're worrying me."

He looked at me intensely. No one really calls me Lizzy apart from mum, very occasionally. But I instantly remembered that that was what he'd always called me. Never my full name. A surge of love engulfed me and hindered me from thinking clearly. It was so overwhelming I nearly drowned in it. I actually gasped, before I spoke again, having gathered myself together.

"No, nothing really. It's just that I've always wondered why you left us. You obviously still love mum, so was it me?" I tried to get the conversation back on course.

"Oh no, Lizzy. You mustn't think that..."

"But how was I *not* to think that? What else could have been the reason. You just left!" I interrupted as I lost slight control of my emotions.

"No listen. It had to be like that. I left *because* I loved you both. I didn't have a lot of choice. I had to return at some point to my community and I didn't want either of you to be too attached to me so you felt you had to follow me in."

Rick sighed.

"It made sense at the time."

He sounded regretful.

"But you left us no choice. *You* decided this. Mum was distraught."

I couldn't help digging the knife in a bit further. I had years of resentment built up in me bursting to come out. I could just about keep the lid on it to avoid a major outburst. It wouldn't have helped. I didn't wait for an answer. I had decided to go for the killer question. He was vulnerable at the moment so might not be as alert and guarded.

"I need to ask you something important before we go any further. Don't jump to conclusions but I'm worried. Are you involved in some sort of criminal organisation... dad?"

I hesitated calling him that, but thought it would please him and keep him on my side. He didn't respond, a completely blank face stared at me for a couple of seconds. Then he regained control.

"What on earth has made you think that? Why would you think that Lizzy?"

He tried to sound incredulous and laugh it off, but as soon as he spoke, his worries and his guilt trickled through. I didn't give up and carried on quickly hoping he would open up to me.

"It's just the way you left mum and totally disappeared. She knew nothing about your past and even though she looked for you, you disappeared off the face of the earth. I just thought...."

He interrupted me with a sigh hiding some relief, though still on edge.

"No sweetheart. I wasn't involved in a criminal organisation. Don't worry. I wished Alice had decided to come tonight, we could've talked about it and cleared everything up."

He looked at me with such passion again, it was hard to concentrate. I had to keep prodding though as I wasn't getting anywhere. I decided to go in a bit harder.

"But what about now, dad? I know you're involved in something bad. Have they got a hold over you somehow? Please tell me if they are, we can get you out. Whatever you have done so far, it won't matter."

335

I was talking fast, and it all came out a bit wrong but I wanted him to say yes, because the alternatives were unbearable for me.

"Lizzy, you're not making any sense. Who can get me out? What are you talking about?"

He was still confused, not wanting his dream of reuniting us a family be shattered. Then I dropped the bomb.

"Markus."

Rick was rattled for just a few seconds. His face changed and all I could read was bitter disappointment. Realisation had dawned on him instantly that I was in contact with the Sensorians, and that I had hidden it from him. He immediately put his guard up, trying to close down all emotions he was emitting.

"Is that what they're thinking?" he asked icily.

I still saw a flicker of something, maybe hope, but I couldn't tell for sure. However, if there was even the tiniest bit of a chance to convince Rick to go and see Markus willingly, I was going to grab it.

"They've been trying to locate you with the aim to extract you. But the organisation you're involved with looks dangerous and complex and the Sensorians wanted a way to contact you without alerting them and

336

think of a safe strategy together with you. They don't know what they have over you and didn't want to put anyone in danger. "

I hoped he would understand our actions.

"Except for you." he said bitterly.

"They used you, my own flesh and blood, to trap me."

He started to get very agitated, forgetting to cloak again, and almost spat the words out.

"They didn't hesitate to use you and put you in danger, the fucking bastards. Didn't think they could sink as low as that."

"I'm not in danger. I'm fine." I said calmly, trying to sound as confident as I could.

Rick's dark expression told a different story, and for the first time I felt a smidgen of fear entering my conscious. I told myself sternly to ignore it. I was safe. Zack wouldn't let anything happen to me. I contemplated using our signal to get me out, but I wanted to hear more of what my father had to say. I didn't want to abort the mission yet. There was still a chance I could talk my dad round.

"Are *you* in danger?" I asked boldly.

"Yes, but not from the people you think. It's the lot that sank their teeth into you that I fear."

He looked around furtively.

"I assume they're listening to this conversation right now? I can't detect any of them in here so there must be a listening device somewhere."

He looked at me as if he could look straight through me to scan for it.

"You haven't got one on you. I can tell. If you want to talk to me, you have to follow me to a safe place. Don't even think about intervening Markus, or whoever is listening. I'm not completely stupid and have people in this establishment looking out for me. Don't tempt me to use them. It won't end well."

"Why are you scared of what the Sensorians will do to you? If you aren't doing anything wrong you'll be safe there."

I ignored his threat and I tried again, not moving from my seat, although he had gotten up.

"In their opinion I will have broken the rules, Lizzy. They must have told you the consequences of that? They have their own justice system and it's not known for its leniency."

He was talking fast now, urging me to get up and go with him. I didn't get much time to think as he had me by the arm and was practically pushing me towards the door. This wasn't working out the way I wanted to and a sick feeling got hold of me again. It was clear to me that my father was more than just a pawn in this organisation. He was with them of his own volition. It made me feel scared. I didn't know what to do. I could make a break for it, using my self-defence techniques, knowing that within minutes Zack would be there to help me or use the signal and ask to go to the ladies. But doing that could risk people's lives. Rick had warned us he had people to protect him here.

I was convinced he wouldn't harm me, but I wasn't so sure he wouldn't harm another Sensorian. So I decided to stick with my father and hear him out. Moreover, if I bailed out now, we would lose him. He would go underground and our chance to get to him would vanish. I had made my decision, and crossed my fingers it was one that Zack would endorse. Though, his order not to put myself in danger at any time still rang in my ears.

CHAPTER 44

The damned stubborn girl hadn't used the signal
and I was heading Rick's warning not to intervene.
Eliza hadn't given up yet so she must have thought
there was still a chance that this could end peacefully.
Maybe Rick had given off signs as he'd find it difficult
to hide them from Eliza completely, her being his
daughter. She'd better be right as I'd given her the
order to withdraw if it looked like she was in any
danger, and it seemed like she was. Whatever the
outcome of this mission, she would have to bear the
consequences for violating that order.

We were in full swing, following the car that had
appeared, as if by magic, to pick Rick and Eliza up
from the pub. The tracker worked beautifully so we
could keep a good distance. I hadn't been happy with
the way Rick manhandled her into the car and nearly
made the call to extract her. However, maybe against
better judgement, I relied on Eliza being sensible.
She must have thought it was safe and that there was
a chance she could find out more about the
organisation her father worked for. As our cover was
blown we needed everything we could get now. Rick
wasn't going to help us voluntarily, that much was
clear. It certainly looked like he'd put himself in

danger of our severest punishment, which was something I had desperately wanted to avoid, for Eliza's sake.

It was frustrating not being able to hear what they were talking about and not knowing when to go in and get Eliza out. We had plenty of people available to charge and take her but I'd already clocked that Rick was also not travelling on his own. There were at least two other people in the car with them and I'd also noticed three vehicles in the vicinity of them. They were keeping their distance but definitely were part of their gang. I really didn't want an out and out fire fight, there would be too many casualties. I decided to give her an hour, before undertaking any action, unless something else cropped up that would warrant a quicker response.

I double checked with Frank and he agreed with my decision, though he looked worried. It was an understatement to say that Frank wasn't happy to be confronted with the fact that Rick was part of the organisation willingly rather than being coerced . Even though we had seriously considered that eventuality, it was still hard to come to terms with. Rick was one of us, and had been a tremendous

Sensorian, part of the leadership team. Frank was probably already contemplating what had gone wrong and how to prevent something like that from ever happening again.

"Frank, you know Rick better than me. How far do you think he's willing to go to protect himself?"

I had an inkling, but wanted to know from someone who knew him, even though I feared the answer.

"I don't think there's much he wouldn't do, to be honest. The family bond might stop him from seriously harming Eliza, but if he feels there's no way out for him, he'll be pretty ruthless." Frank sighed.

"Sir, if Eliza's in any danger of being harmed I will issue a shoot to kill order." I said grimly.

I didn't care about the looks everyone shot each other. The stench of heightened stress and worry penetrated my nostrils but, fuck it, I wasn't letting any harm come to my girl. Even though it would mean she'd hate me forever, if it did come to that.

I wondered where Rick was taking Eliza, or whether he was just driving around. I hoped Eliza would stay strong and not be swayed by whatever Rick was telling her. He could be extremely charismatic and persuasive, but I knew Eliza had a

healthy dose of scepticism and wasn't easily
influenced. She was always questioning and critically
thinking about things, which would come in handy now.
I had tried to curb it in training to make her more
compliant, but I was absolutely sure it was so
ingrained, it would come to her when needed.

The car led us to the industrial part of town, an
area not known for its welcoming atmosphere. I
hoped they weren't going to stop here as it was too
deserted for my liking. It made me wonder what
Rick's intentions were. It didn't look favourable.

CHAPTER 45

"Who are they?" I asked nodding towards the two rather intimidating looking men in the front seat. I was just about recovering from the rather hasty retreat from the pub and being pushed into the back of this car that had suddenly appeared.

"Put your belt on first." Rick grumbled, to which I tutted but obeyed.

"So?" I prompted.

"Who are the suit monkeys? Are they..."

"No, they're not Sensorians. They work for me. Keeping me safe. I take it you know all about the Sensorian community?" he sighed.

"Don't bother answering that. Just tell me, how long have you been with them?"

"Not long. Just over a month."

I didn't see the point in lying about that. Rick looked a little surprised and if I read it correctly, a little pleased. But if he was, he didn't say so.

"Are you totally off your medication? You smell clean. I wondered about that when we first met, but now I understand."

He practically answered his own question but I replied anyway, affirmatively.

"Good. How are you finding it? Are you coping

with the return of all your senses?"

Direct as ever. Very similar to Markus and Zack in fact. I liked it.

"Yes. It feels good. I'll be eternally grateful to the people who helped me rediscover myself and gain control over my senses." I said pointedly, hoping to hurt him.

I hadn't forgiven him for abandoning me and my mum. It had the desired effect. Rick looked uncomfortable and guilty. I smelled it too, it wasn't a good scent. I was surprised Rick wasn't disguising his emotions and signals he was emitting more, unless he wasn't able to in front of me. Zack had said it was very difficult to cloak from your direct family, especially if someone was in a highly emotive state. He didn't respond to my jibe directly though.

"Who trained you?" his eyes wary now.

"Zack." I simply said.

He wasn't happy with that, I could tell immediately.

"I see," he said bitterly.

"Clearly, Markus knew exactly what he was doing, as always. He's a clever, clever man. The king of manipulation."

"What has Markus done to you that makes you so bitter about him." I dared ask.

"He made sure my best friend was sentenced to death. That's what he did. Tom only wanted a different life. One not bound by the stifling rules that our rulers have engineered. Yes, he went off the rails for a bit, but I could have saved him, brought him back to us. But Markus wouldn't give me or him the chance. He got Valentino, our then leader involved. That's when I left the first time and that is when I met your mum...and here you are."

He looked at me with admiration and love. I swallowed heavily, feeling emotional. I had to push through though, trying to find out more information.

"But you went back to be with the Sensorians after a few years, leaving me and mum. And you were with them for years! You seemed to have settled in the community and were even part of the leadership That's why they thought you were forced to work for this criminal organisation when you disappeared. What happened? Why now?"

I sought out his eyes and tried to make contact, but he was avoiding me, looking out the window instead. He put his head in his hands and said nothing for a while. Finally, he lifted his head and then looked at me, his eyes shining with defiance.

"I was living a lie, Lizzy." he said vehemently.

I could feel his passion burst into my conscious so powerfully, it hurt.

"I just couldn't do it anymore, towing the line but not believing it any more, was soul destroying. I needed to get out to be able to reach my full potential. We have enormous potential as Sensorians but we are curbed by our leaders."

He stopped to gauge my reaction. I could see where he was coming from but I was apprehensive as to where this thinking was leading.

"Rick," I started still undecided as to what I should be calling him.

"I also find the regimented lifestyle difficult to adjust to, but I believe Markus is right in thinking it has to be like this, to protect our own kind. If people knew about our abilities, we could be abused and forced to work for people and organisations who might not have the best intentions. Don't you agree with that?"

He thought for a moment before answering.

"But how about if it was *us* that ruled. Can you imagine that? I think that's the reason we exist, not hiding in the background trying to help this Dullard civilisation struggle on. No, we're meant to lead it. We are better equipped to lead than ordinary people. Dullards will follow us if they can see what we can do. The world would become a better place. No need for money grabbing lawyers, getting criminals off just because they can afford the best. We can tell when someone lies, there would be no need. No more injustices. No more lying politicians or corruption. All we need to do is make people aware of what we can do but that may not happen smoothly or without violence or illegal actions. People resist change, even if it is for the better."

I interrupted him there.

"What do you mean 'it might not happen without violence or illegal actions. It's a slippery slope to start defending violence and crime!"

I couldn't keep the indignation out of my voice, but he ignored it and his eyes steeled.

"It's a revolution Eliza. That's the stage we're at, so it may look like I'm a subversive criminal but it will all be worth it in the end. A more just world for everyone, where there will be peace and prosperity. Do you get it Lizzy? Are you with me? We would be a force to be reckoned with, us together!"

His eyes were pleading.

Shit. I didn't know what to say or feel, so I kept quiet and waited to see what else he had to say. I needed him to think there was a chance I would choose to join him so I tried not to think too much about what he was saying to stop any strong feelings being emitted.

"I know it all must sound insane to you." he said much more calmly.

"But it makes sense. There are people out there who believe in me already, and recognise our potential as Sensorians. I know that in the Sensorian community there are like-minded people, fed up at being so tightly controlled and always feeling frustrated. Our country would be so much better organised with us leading it, and we wouldn't have to be hiding all the time, scared to be discovered. All we need to do is work together and free ourselves from Markus and the leadership."

I felt I could chip in here.

"But how do you propose to do that? It doesn't sound particularly democratic. You can't expect our fellow Sensorians to just jump ship and follow you. Most of them actually really believe that the way it is, is the best and only way. They believe they do matter; that they make a difference to the world by fighting crime and helping achieve justice. Most Sensorians I've seen seem perfectly satisfied and fulfilled with the lives they are leading within the community, not frustrated and angry."

I was trying to stay calm, but I didn't like the sound of it one bit. However, he was my father and his intentions were seemingly for the good of everyone. Though, I feared the way he was going about trying to achieve his goal were sinister at best.

"Democracy is overrated." he sighed, shrugging his shoulders dismissively.

"Sensorians are better evolved human beings and therefore should be leaders. Trust me Lizzy, slowly but surely we'll win over most of the Sensorian community. Who wouldn't want the chance to make the world we live in a fairer place? We have that power, we must use it. It would be a crime not to."

Rick's idea of a just society was tempting, but I didn't like his belief that Sensorians were somehow superior human beings. We had a gift, but as any human; we weren't infallible nor perfect.

I was acutely aware, if Zack and Markus got to hear about his rather despotic ideas, and the fact he'd already told several people outside of our community about our existence, that my father's fate would be sealed. It would mean the most severe punishment for him. Having only just met him I didn't want to lose him already, and I was racking my brain as to how to prevent the worst outcome. I was lost for ideas though, but I tried a last ditch attempt to somehow change my father's mind. I was going to try and reason him out of it.

"I see what you're trying to achieve, dad. But there must be a different way of going about it. How is using illegal methods a solid start for a new society? Do you have to be involved in these criminal activities and maybe even resort to violence to bring about the change you want?"

I watched his reactions carefully to tune into his mood. He hadn't shut the door yet. He was still willing to discuss things.

"I'm only bending the rules at the moment because I need the money. When we overthrow the current system, there's bound to be violence as they won't want to give up their power. There will be resistance but once everything is in place, we won't need that anymore. I have people in some very instrumental places already, to help it go as smooth as possible. It won't be long. This is just a phase, Lizzy."

"So, am I right in thinking you are actually running this whole thing? Is that it?" I asked, maybe a bit too incredulously as I saw his mood and demeanour change instantly to a much more guarded one.

"Yes."

He looked out the window, avoiding eye contact.

"You don't approve."

It was a statement, not a question and I struggled to keep this conversation going the way I wanted.

"I don't think Mum would. Especially using the money from drug dealing and the violence. It goes against everything she stands for." I tried again, from a different angle.

I could see he was trying hard not to show that it bothered him, justifying his actions once again.

"Lizzy," he sighed, still looking out the window.

"Even your mum knows that sometimes the goal justifies the actions. Once we've established our rule, all these things will become a thing of the past. I can atone for my sins then."

It almost sounded like he was trying to convince himself, rather than me.

"Dad?"

I touched his face and tried to get him to look at me, with limited success. He half turned, but wouldn't look me fully in the eyes.

"Is there really no other way? You could try and reform the Sensorian Community from the inside, without resorting to violence and criminal activities. Maybe there is a way to live within the community and still fulfil your potential"

I tried to sound as confident as I could to portray

that as a viable option, but my father was tuned into me too.

"Lizzy, it doesn't even sound like you believe yourself that's an option anymore." he said shaking his head.

"You're going to have to make a choice, baby. You're either with me or choose them."

I didn't have to answer. He knew what I had chosen, though my choice was full of pain. The familial bond was strong and pulling at me, trying to change my mind, but it failed. My loyalty to Zack, Zaphire and the whole Sensorian community was strong too. They'd helped me to become me again, a stronger and more confident version at that. Rick's face changed as if a mask had been pulled across it.

"I'm sorry, Eliza."

I grabbed his hand and I jolted. Just for a fleeting second I saw myself as if through Rick's eyes, a look of disbelief covering my face. Then it disappeared as I felt my hand being pushed away. I shivered and shook my head slightly. Rick looked at me very oddly for a second but then concentrated on a bag he'd opened up. The content shocked me. I couldn't believe he had even thought about bringing that to our meeting. I felt shit scared.

CHAPTER 46

The black BMW that contained Eliza and her
father had been stopped for about five minutes in a
dark spot near one of the factory buildings and I was
getting tense. It had nearly been an hour since they
took Eliza, and I wanted to go in and retrieve her. I
didn't like the fact that they had stopped one fucking
bit and neither did Frank. I could see him nervously
twitching and I knew I had to act soon, before the
tension became too much and we would be in danger
of making stupid mistakes.

"Teams, be on standby. We're about to commence
extraction." I radioed.

I had clocked the two other cars belonging to Rick,
pulling up just a little bit up the road from our target
vehicle and I ordered our cars to come closer too.
They must have noticed us tracking them by now and
I was under no illusion we were here without them
realising. I looked at Frank and he nodded, then gave
the signal to commence extraction.

All five of our cars screeched forward and
surrounded the vehicles, the guys jumped out and
positioned themselves behind their cars for cover,
guns pointing at the three targets. A tense couple of
seconds followed where nothing seemed to happen.

It felt like a fucking eternity.

I got out of our van, Frank covering me with his weapon. Then I spotted a flicker of a movement inside the BMW with Eliza in it. A door clicked and I heard Eliza's voice shouting out.

"Don't shoot! It's me, just me! I have a message! Please don't do anything! I'm in danger if you do!"

"Hold fire!" I shouted as loud as I could, to make sure Rick's men could hear too. I didn't know if they were Dullards or Sensorians.

The car door moved slowly further open to reveal Eliza. She stumbled out of the car, and I immediately noticed there was something strapped onto her leg. Her hands were bound behind her back and she was blind folded. The smell of her fear hit me like a brick of tonnes. *What the fuck had the bastard done?*

"Zack!" she shouted to me, her voice trembling.

"Rick strapped a device on my leg, can you see?"

"Yes, Eliza, I'm just here, only a few metres away from you. Use your other senses, relax." I said as calmly as possible, which was hard as I suspected the device was an explosive.

"What does Rick want?" I asked.

I heard her take a deep breath, to steady herself.

"He wants you to let them all drive off, without

355

anyone following or shots being fired. He wants you to take me and drive away. All of us. The release button on my strap will be activated after one hour and the device will be deactivated. If we fail to follow his instructions, he'll explode the device."

The last words came out like a sob filled with indignation and anger. But before I could say anything she carried on.

"Zack, listen to me." she pleaded desperately.

"I know the mission comes first and he's dangerous. Do what you have to do Zack. I will live, the device is tiny. It will only affect my legs. Don't let him go! Please!"

My brave, sweet lioness. Willing to lose her legs for the sake of the mission. She was extraordinary. I sighed. Indeed, my mission did come first, before anything else. I sought out Frank, and he nodded. He knew.

"I'm sorry Eliza."

She lowered her head and her shoulders slumped. Fear running off her in waves that crashed into me, almost physically knocking me back, making me feel sick to the stomach. I turned around and gave the command.

"Stand down teams. Get back to your cars and

drive back to our compound. We'll meet there."

I ran up to Eliza, grabbed her by the arm and led her into our van. She hesitated, clearly confused, muttering to herself.

"I don't understand, I thought..."

"Sshh, I will explain in a second." I whispered, untying her blindfold and cutting loose the strap that had bound her hands.

As soon as we had Eliza in the van, and our other cars had started driving away, Rick and the two other cars sped off into the distance. We would get him another day, I vowed.

Eliza was sat straight up in her seat, eyes as wide as plates, her heart racing, still not sure about what just had happened. Her eyes moved to me, questioning.

"I'm sorry I had to ignore your plea to capture your father but do you remember what I promised your mum, all those weeks ago? I would protect you, with my life if I had to. *You* are my mission, my first responsibility is you. I will never let you get harmed, if I can help it. Understand?"

I held her hands and looked at her beautiful face relaxing. Her mouth slightly open, so tempting, so kissable. Her heartbeat slightly rose again and her cheeks went bright pink. I realised I hadn't been

357

cloaking, and everyone else in the car had noticed, awkward glances being thrown around. I decided to brazen this one out. It hadn't happened.

"How are you feeling, Eliza?" I said, trying to direct the attention away from me.

"I won't lie, I have felt better!" she joked to lighten the mood somewhat.

I noticed from the little flashing red light that the device was still emitting a signal, so it wasn't deactivated yet, which meant we were all still in a very vulnerable position. We only had Rick's word he wouldn't activate it, but I was almost 100% sure he wouldn't harm his own daughter if he could at all avoid it. Still, the quicker we were back at base, the better. The threat could be minimised there, and we could even try to get the device off, before the hour was up, enabling us to try and track them down sooner. We were about five minutes away now, and I couldn't wait to get her out and hopefully neutralise the danger.

"I need to tell you what I know about Rick's plans...." she started, but I cut her off.

"Just hang in there for a bit longer, Eliza. I want everyone to be there when you tell us what you know. Nothing will get lost in translation then. We'll make sure you are safe first, then we'll go to the conference room and discuss what we'll do next."

When we got back to our compound, a team of explosives experts, one of them being Sam, was ready to dive onto Eliza's leg. I had to order them to give her a bit of space and when she'd sat down in a comfortable chair I let them do their job. It took them a little while to work out the intricacies of the device, claiming it was one they hadn't encountered before. A tense few moments went by and we were all suffering from the barrage of emotions Eliza was pouring out. Finally, the all clear command came and I sighed a huge sigh of relief. They were bloody good at their job.

Eliza visibly relaxed instantly, and the air around smelled a lot better too. Too much tension and fear made for a rank atmosphere!

I signalled to Frank to get the cars back out, to see if they could locate Rick and his accomplices. I didn't really think we would find them now, but it was worth an attempt.

I noticed Eliza perked up somewhat and seconds later I saw the cause of that. Zaphire strode straight past me, aiming directly for Eliza, and if looks could kill, I would be dead. I guess she blamed me for the whole situation somehow and I let her. For now.

She took Eliza tenderly in her arms, who had stood up to greet her. She sank into Zaphire's body and the tears started to flow freely, with Zaphy gently stroking Eliza's hair and back, whispering softly in her ear reassuring and comforting her. The tears came from relief mostly, but I could also sense some anger and disappointment. It dawned on me that part of her felt she had failed her task and felt guilty. She so shouldn't. She'd done amazingly well to come out of it unharmed, not to mention any information she might have gathered. We needed to get the ball rolling on that, and rather perversely I enjoyed putting an end to Zaphire and Eliza's intimate hug.

"Right girls; let's move to the conference room now. People are waiting to hear what Eliza found out. We need to get on top of this."

They looked at me but Zaphire wasn't budging.

"Give her a break, brother." she said pointedly, her eyes still throwing daggers at me.

I had to be firm. We needed to find out what the story was as soon as possible.

"We have to go now, Eliza. That's an order. Zaphire, comply or you can wait outside the room.

Don't fucking disrespect me again."

That worked, although it probably earned me days of the silent treatment. She hated being called to order by me. However, they both got up and followed me to the conference room. Eliza actually keen, eager to tell everyone her findings. Whatever Rick told her had worried her deeply. Enough to tell me to let him blow her legs off, so we could catch him. It was disconcerting to say the least.

CHAPTER 47

It felt like I was in a whirl wind. My emotions were still all over the place and my senses were hyper sensitive. I had to try and lock it all away over the next few hours, otherwise I would not be able to face the people in the conference room and make sense to them.

After my dad had realised I wasn't going to team up with him, the warmth and love he felt for me hadn't disappeared but he had started to cloak it, harder to receive for me. He did keep apologising, and reminding me, and himself I think, that I had made this choice myself. That the end goal was bigger than us, and that he hoped I would see it like him one day. He kept telling me that if I ever wanted to join him I could, he would never close the door on me.

Then he strapped the device to my leg. It was small, but could still inflict serious, life changing damage to me. He had sighed and grumbled.

"Let's hope to God he'll listen to you when you give my message. If I know Zack at all, he'll abide by my rules. He won't want to you to get hurt."

The message I'd gotten from his subconscious was a very different one. Rick hadn't been at all sure.

He knew all too well how seriously the Sensorians took their missions. His fingers had trembled ever so slightly when he'd programmed the device. I'd felt dead scared and bitterness crept through my system. If this man was willing to put his own daughter at risk, what else would he be capable off? He was ruthless and dangerous and as I realised that, my heart went cold. That was the moment I had made up my mind.

I would tell Zack not to let him go, whatever the consequences. I would remind him of our motto 'mission comes first' and bear whatever would happen to me. Rick must be captured before it's too late, before he would damage our community beyond saving. It had felt like a little part of my soul died when the reality of the situation and my decision really hit me. I was going to condemn my own father to the death sentence, before I'd even had the chance to get to know him. Sadness had engulfed me and nearly crippled me, but I had gritted my teeth and resolved to do what had to be done.

.

However, it hadn't worked out that way, my father had escaped as Zack had done exactly what Rick had tentatively predicted and here we were, facing our leaders and having to report back my findings. I was so glad Zaphire was there for me earlier. I needed to let some of my emotions out as I felt I was going to implode, and Zaphire knew exactly what to do to make that happen. Her soft hands felt glorious in my hair and I felt safe within her embrace. I let myself go. I didn't care what anyone else thought about it. It felt good.

Now, I had to focus and put my feelings aside. I didn't mind too much that Zack had pulled Zaphire and me apart, though Zaphy was visibly annoyed, which actually made me feel pretty good. She cared and that felt amazing.

We entered the conference room where Marcus, Frank, Laura and some of the leaders I'd forgotten the name of, stood ready to hear me out. It was tense in there and my senses picked up several vibes that I couldn't all quite place. There was excitement, suspense, worry, eagerness, impatience, all to be predicted, but I also detected something else. It felt like suspicion, distrust, but I couldn't be sure as I didn't recognise it and I wondered why there would be any suspicion there. I didn't have time to ponder about it for too long as Zack urged me to speak and tell them what I knew.

I tried to tell them what had happened and everything Rick had told me in as much detail I could, including his new world view. How he thought we should utilise our gifts to rule the world and make it a fairer place. I tried to highlight the noble intentions Rick had, with hopes they may punish him less severely, but I knew it would be in vain. I couldn't hide the fact he was planning to use violence to overthrow the existing establishment. When I'd finished talking I caught a glimpse of Markus' face, which looked grim. Zack's hand sought mine and he gave me a reassuring squeeze.

Frank was the first to question me.
"Did he mention any places where he might go next, or where they might base themselves?"
I thought hard, but couldn't recall anything of the sort so I shook my head in disappointment.
Then Markus chipped in.
"Did he mention any names of the people who work for him or who he plans to recruit?"
I had to answer negatively again. He'd mentioned no names whatsoever. Markus scratched his head and I could feel his frustration building. I started to feel uneasy. For the first time it dawned on me where the suspicion came from. They didn't quite trust me. They thought I was holding something back. Markus continued his questioning.

"Has he told anyone about our existence?"

My insides churned with this question. I knew my answer would doom my father, but I had to answer it truthfully.

"I believe he has. He talked about people who believed in him and his abilities and were ready to follow him."

Markus glanced over to Zack ominously.

"Were you able to work out who the other people in the car were, or give us a description of them?" Laura asked.

But again my answer was less than satisfying.

"Well, they weren't Sensorians. But I couldn't really see them as their backs were turned towards us. They were of medium height and one a bit larger than the other. They had brownish hair, cut very short. That's about it."

"That narrows it down then." said one of the other leaders (was it Michael?) sarcastically, rolling his eyes.

"Don't worry, Eliza. You're doing great." Laura said picking up my frustrations.

"I have one more question though. And it's important, so think carefully." Laura continued. I nodded gravely.

"Does he think there is a chance you may eventually turn to him?" she asked her eyes firmly

366

fixed on me.

I had to think carefully how to answer this as I didn't want to implicate myself. If Rick thought there was a chance then I must have given off some sort of signal, infinitesimal maybe but I wasn't sure what the leaders would think of that. I didn't want to fuel their distrust. But I couldn't lie.

"He said the door would always be open to me if I decided to join him." I sighed.

Laura looked at Markus and nodded.

"Okay, thanks for letting us know Eliza. Something completely different but, when did you say he put the device on your leg? Was it straight away when you got in the car or later?" Markus carried on.

"He did it when we were parked up at the industrial site, as soon as he understood I wasn't going to join him." I answered dutifully, though I felt that familiar feeling of annoyance raising its ugly head inside me.

I had told them everything I knew. What were they angling for? I sought Zack's eyes for reassurance, but he was looking questioningly at Laura, raising one of his eyebrows. Suddenly he stepped forward.

"Eliza's told you everything she knows now. She's not cloaking, I can tell. She needs a bit of time to relax and recover so may I respectfully ask to let us go to our room."

Furtive glances took place between the leaders but Markus finally agreed.

"Yes, of course." he said begrudgingly.

"But we will get together again and discuss some more details tomorrow first thing. You're dismissed."

"Before we go, there is one more thing that happened whilst I was in the car." I suddenly remembered.

All eyes were on me instantly, including Zack's clearly questioning whether I had gone insane.

"It's nothing to do with Rick, I told you everything I know. This is about me. It's probably nothing but I had the weirdest experience. I grabbed Rick's hand and it felt like something had hit me. Then I saw myself as if through his eyes. Really bizarre and it lasted probably less than a second."

I stopped talking as the room was instantly hit by all sorts of scents and vibes. Zack looked gob smacked for want of a different word.

"She's a bloody VH!" Zack finally shouted excitedly.

"Sounds like it." Markus agreed in a more measured tone.

"What the hell is that?" I managed to throw in, completely confused.

368

"You're a Vision Hacker. You can tap into other people's vision. That's fucking amazing!"

Zack still looked as if he had just won the lottery.

"Not many of us have that gift. It's latent in you as you have no control over it just yet, but it's intriguing." Markus added.

"Did Rick notice?" he asked, suddenly concerned.

"That wouldn't be good. He'll be even more fixated on persuading you to join him." Frank remarked pessimistically.

"I wouldn't worry about it for now, Eliza. Get some rest and we'll explore this more later." Markus decided.

We walked in silence to our room, leaving everyone behind, even Zaphire, who still had the hump with Zack. Once we got in I threw myself on the sofa with a deep sigh. Zack placed himself carefully beside me, his gorgeous scent once again nearly overwhelming me.

"Wow, you're so fucking lucky! Being a VH is amazing. Looking forward to developing that skill."

I wasn't so sure. It had felt weird and unsettling when it had happened and I wasn't that keen to experience it again and ignored Zack's enthusiasm. I just didn't want to think about it. Uncharacteristically,

369

he respected my silence and didn't mention it again.

I felt exhausted and had to work hard to control my impulses. I was on the brink of a meltdown. Zack turned towards me and gently moved a stray strand of hair out of my face. His touch nearly sent me over the edge. Every hair on my body stood up by the sight of his gorgeous dark blue eyes gazing into mine.

My barriers were down and I guessed his were too as the next thing I knew he had moved his lips tantalisingly close to mine and after a split second of hesitation he'd given in to his desire, which I couldn't fail to detect, was ever so strong. His lips touched mine and his kiss was literally electrifying.

My whole body quivered with anticipation and desire. I kissed him back with so much passion, it shocked me. It didn't stop me though, and then I found my hands on his fuzzy short hair. Gently stroking at first, but soon they seemed to have gained a life of their own, frantically touching his head and face, even digging my nails in. My hands wandered over to his neck and back and I felt every muscle tensing under my touch. I was losing myself in all the sensations that engulfed me. I'd never experienced this feeling of ecstasy before, not even close. My experiences with Kas annihilated and paled in comparison. It was both wonderful and daunting.

Zack reciprocated my kisses fervently and he had found a way inside my top, his hands grabbing me forcefully, lifting me onto his lap. He looked me in the eyes with so much yearning and voracity, my insides seemed to liquefy. He looked absolutely ravenous. A groan escaped his mouth and that turned me on even more, but then I felt his mood change. He was shutting down his senses.

"No Zack, please. I need this. I want you. Please. Don't shut it out. It's a good thing." I managed to pant, still completely overwhelmed by all the emotions and sensations I felt.

I tried to kiss him again, and the fire momentarily returned to his eyes, but his body went rigid again, slowly moving me off his body, which, I noticed, definitely wanted the opposite to happen.

"We can't, Eliza." he simply stated.

"This is unforgivable. I am so sorry." he mumbled fiercely apologetically.

He sat up and put his head in his hands, shaking slightly. I sat up too, the heat still raging inside my body, I didn't have it under control at all. I tried to touch his face, but his hand grabbed mine and returned it to my lap.

"No. Stop. Get yourself in the shower and freshen up. We'll talk later."

He turned around, visibly still fighting his urges. It wasn't coming easy to him either. I begrudgingly got up and obeyed his request.

Moments later I felt the relaxing water of the shower pouring down my exhausted body, and tried to think of anything but Zack's divine face and body. A slight feeling of guilt crept in as I came to my senses. I thought about Zaphire. What had I done? The moment I had an opportunity with Zack, I had jumped on him like a hussy. What had that been all about? I started to feel uncomfortable with the prospect of facing Zack in a minute, let alone looking Zaphy in the eye again. I would definitely find it hard to cloak what had happened. She would sense it straight away. My feelings of ecstasy I'd experienced just moments ago had melted like the proverbial snow. I let out a deep sigh, which hadn't gone unnoticed by Zack, even though he was on the other side of the door.

"Come on Eli, come and face the music." he said, not unkindly.

"We have to talk about this."

"Do we have to?" I squeakily whined, preferring to just ignore it all.

"Yes, come out. Now." he answered less friendly, more like his normal authoritative self.

I took a deep breath and showed myself, to find a determined looking Zack, clearly ready to talk.

CHAPTER 48

Eliza stood sheepishly by the bathroom door, still looking sexy as hell. I had to work so fucking hard to control my feelings for her. My insides were churning, my dick still twitching. However, I was fairly certain my exterior showed a different story; one where I was in full control and having had come to my senses, now set on resolving the matter. In reality I was far from being in control and was pissed at myself for letting it get this far. Eliza deserved better. I knew she was vulnerable and still I'd given in to my basic instincts.

I should let someone else take over training Eliza as I knew if Markus somehow got to know about this, that's exactly what would be happening. But I couldn't give her up, I didn't want to. I felt an intrinsic bond with her that I could not, would not ignore. We had to sort something out to make it work, and that was behind my resolve.

"Come, sit down."

I beckoned her over to the table and when she sat down I placed myself on a chair opposite her.

"Look. We had a moment of insanity, fuelled by the adrenaline and relief. You were feeling vulnerable and I took advantage of that, and for that I'm incredibly sorry. Please forgive me. I'll understand if you want someone else to train you, though I'm hoping we can forget about our, or actually my, momentary lapse of control. It won't happen again. I promise."

I looked her in the eyes and tried to gauge her reaction. It was full of contradiction, quite hard to decipher and her silence didn't help. I could see she was trying to gather her thoughts and gave her time to reply so I sat back and waited for her to say something. After a few minutes she spoke.

"Oh Zack...." she sighed deeply with frustration.

"It's so typical of you to try and take the blame for it all, but I was there too. I jumped on you the minute your lips touched mine! At least you managed to regain control pretty quickly, otherwise our clothes would have been strewn across the floor by now and I would've gone all the way before realising what we were doing."

She blushed whilst she looked at me through her eyelashes, killing me once again. I had to breathe deeply and focus as she carried on.

"So, I want to thank you rather than forgive you and no, I don't want to forget about it, because it happened. It's life."

She paused but I knew she hadn't finished so I

waited, feeling nervous.

"I would like to keep it between us. No one else needs to know. It'll be hard to conceal when asked, but why would anyone ask? I want you to carry on with my training and I promise to work hard at controlling my urges. What do you think?"

I felt relief flooding over me, she was just amazing; so wild and yet so sensible and I felt privileged to be able to carry on working with her. That made me much happier than it should have, once again reminding me my feelings for her were running far deeper than they should ideally be. However, I could deal with that. I would just have to. Besides, I knew she was having feelings for Zaphire anyway, and I detected her guilt, talking about keeping our little adventure quiet.

"I can work with that. However, I must warn you I have to be as strict with you as I have been. That's not going to change. There are a couple of things we have to talk about tomorrow involving some of your actions and their consequences and you're not going to like it. Can you cope with that? I don't want you to think you can give me attitude or use my transgression against me, as the moment that happens we will be done. I would have to resign as your trainer. Understood?"

"Of course, Sir" she answered a bit too eagerly, trying to show me she wouldn't have a problem respecting me.

She smiled her beautiful smile and just as I thought we had more or less resolved things, there was a soft knock on the door.

For a moment I thought about refusing whoever it was entry especially as I suspected it was Zaphire. But it was too late, it was her alright and she had already opened the door. She came in with a beaming smile on her face meant for Eliza, which instantly disappeared as she entered.

"What the fuck is this?" she hissed threateningly.

"The smell of pheromones is so thick you could build a wall out of it!" she exclaimed, waving her hands around agitatedly.

"What the hell have you done, brother. Where the fuck is your honour!"

She paced around the room, absolutely fuming. I moved towards the door to make sure she wouldn't run off before we could talk to her. The last thing we needed was a raging Zaphire stomping straight to Markus. Still cross from having been told off by me earlier, that was a clear possibility.

"Sshh, shhh, calm down sis. Nothing happened.

377

Don't worry." I tried to temper her fury.

"Don't lie to me." Her voice low, eyes glowering.

"You can't hide it. I can smell it all around you." she accused, as she sniffed demonstratively around, glancing at Eliza, trying to work out how involved she had been.

"Eliza, what happened? What did he do?" she asked more empathetically, but still on edge.

She was trying to work out Eliza's feelings and I could start smelling the scent of jealousy creeping in, and anxiousness. She was feeling betrayed and she was trying to work out how mutual the incident had been, clearly hoping it had been my lust, rather than Eliza's desire.

"I..., I don't know what to say Zaphire. I am so sorry. I was overwhelmed by my senses and Zack happened to be the person I unleashed them on." Eliza whispered, barely audible.

The pain on Zaphire's face was excruciating. I felt it in every bone of my body and soul. It was crushing to experience. Eliza felt it too, and was barely able to cope. The intensity of all these emotions were just too much for her and she fled back into the bathroom.

"We stopped it Zaphy. We came to our senses. Nothing happened apart from a kiss. We knew it was wrong. I'm so sorry." I pleaded hurriedly.

378

"You're just such an arsehole! You just couldn't help yourself, could you!" she sneered, her voice breaking.

"You are not fit to be her trainer if you can't control yourself! I can understand it from Eliza, she's not used to the intensity of the urges, but *you*, of all people, you should."

Tears welled up in her dark eyes, something I hadn't seen for quite some time. I felt bitterly ashamed as she clearly was right. I should have known better; been in control. I hated myself for letting everyone down, having given in to my yearnings. I had been weak.

"I don't know what to say. You're right."

I paused and looked at Zaphire who barely could look me in the eyes.

"But I swear, on my life, that it won't happen again. We talked about it; we know it wasn't meant to have happened. It was a mistake. I offered Eliza to resign as her trainer, but we both agreed it felt right to continue. Please Zaphire, can you accept that? Please?" I begged.

I knew if she didn't accept it, it would be over. There's absolutely no way that Markus would let us carry on once he was told. Zaphire was silent, but the hostility had ebbed away the slightest bit, which I grabbed hold on.

"Please, trust..." But she didn't let me finish.

"Don't say another word." she barked.

"Let me think."

In the mean time Eliza had appeared back out of the bathroom, her eyes red from crying, but appearing much calmer now. I signalled to her to keep her distance for now and she crept onto the sofa, waiting for Zaphire to speak. Slowly but surely I sensed Zaphy's attitude change from downright hostile to one which was more conciliatory, though far from calm. She was fighting her initial urge to run to Markus and I could feel, to my relief, she was succeeding.

"Zack. You're a dickhead. But even I can see that you bring the best out of Eliza, though you have the potential to elicit the worst from her too, and from yourself as well. I'll give you one more chance before I report you to Markus. Don't give me an excuse to do so, because that will be it. I will not take any prisoners next time, even a whiff of it. No pun intended."

She managed a little smile at her own little joke. Trust Zaphire to somehow lighten the mood, even though she was hurting like hell. It wasn't about me breaking the rules, it was purely her feelings for Eliza that had riled her so much. Eliza meant a lot more to her than I had thought. Poor Zaphire.

"Thank you. That means a lot to me and I won't let you down. Trust me."

I really felt it, but it was going to be difficult. I knew for a fact I had undeniably and irrevocably fallen in love with Eliza.

I glanced over to Eliza, smiling but didn't like what I saw. She sat frozen on the sofa with a thousand mile stare. Zaph rushed over and I let her take charge of the situation.

CHAPTER 49

I hardly dared move whilst Zaphire was talking to us, afraid to lose control once again. Not sexually but emotionally. I just wanted to scream and scream. I could not make sense of any of my own feelings and everyone else's emotions were physically hurting me. My head was pounding, my stomach was churning, my body was aching with excruciating stabbing pains. I couldn't actually work out what my own feelings were or which belonged to the twins. I owned them all and it was driving me insane. My whole body felt heavy and hot. I couldn't actually hear what was being said any more. It felt like I was falling, spiralling out of control.

"Eliza...Eli...are you okay?"

I heard a voice trying to emerge above the noise and fog in my brain. I couldn't make out who it was, but then I felt two cool soft hands cradling my face, and two beautiful eyes boring into mine. It was Zaphire.

"Eliza. Come on. Regain control. Shut down your other senses, just listen. You're fine. You just experienced a bit of sensory overload. You're safe. Relax. Everything is sorted sweetheart. I have you."

The pain fell away and I suddenly felt as light as air.
I slumped into Zaphire's arms, grateful for her not to
reject me. I wasn't sure if she'd forgiven me, but she
was here for me now and that felt good.

"I'll order us some drinks and food." I heard Zack
whisper to Zaphire who nodded, without letting go of
me.

"How do you cope with this crap, Zaphire? It's
exhausting fighting with my senses like this."

"You will learn, babes. You'll develop a coping
mechanism. We can't keep letting other people's
emotions cripple us like that. You'll get there. Believe
it or not, experiences like this will only help fine tune
your control over them. You'll learn to shield better
and if that doesn't work, you'll develop a greater pain
threshold to absorb other people's emotions. Look
now, you got out of it. Well done."

She smiled her mesmerising smile with her
luscious lips. *Don't even go there.* I berated myself.
It felt like I had turned into a nymphomaniac or
something!

I couldn't make myself move so I just sat on the
sofa, leaning into Zaphire who was all too happy to
just sit there. In the mean time, Zack had wisely kept
himself out the way, and didn't speak to us until our

order arrived. I wasn't feeling hungry, but I doubted the twins would let me get away with just picking at the food. There were some nachos, chicken fajitas, corn on the cobs and some fruit and as expected Zack put some of everything on my plate. I resigned myself to trying to eat as much as I could as I couldn't muster the energy to argue. Besides, it would probably do me good anyway.

When I started eating I realised how hungry I was as we never actually got to eat in the end. Rick had forced me to leave the pub before we'd had our dinner. Zack and Zaphire also wolfed their dinner down as they had also skipped food due to the mission.

After dinner I slunk back to the sofa and Zaphire followed me. Zack cleared up our mess and made himself scarce again. We watched a bit of tv and then after an hour or so Zack did pipe up and told me to go and get some sleep. Zaphire still mostly ignored Zack, but gave me a kiss on my cheek, to say goodnight.

"Don't worry about the meeting with Markus tomorrow, my sweet. Even though I'm furious with Zack, I know he's got your back, and there is no one better to have on your side."

"Thanks Zaphy, will you be there too?" I needed to know.

"No, it's a closed meet. Just you, Zack, Markus and

Frank. But I will see you afterwards, okay?"

She nodded in encouragement and I nodded back. Then she left, leaving me feeling awkward with being with Zack on my own. I'd have to get used to that pretty quickly again though.

I climbed over his bed with a sigh.

"Can you move this already. It's getting on my nerves and it's totally unnecessary." I said a bit prickly.

"That's for me to decide Eliza, and it will stay exactly where it is. You're likely to be wandering around again and I can't risk not noticing and you disappearing off or getting hurt." he grumbled.

"Just go to bed."

Which I did, expecting fully to lay awake for hours with all the events of the evening still raging inside me. To my surprise, however, I fell asleep almost straight away and woke up the following morning feeling quite refreshed.

Zack was up already and the smell of coffee in our room was divine, which reminded me of the joy of having super enhanced senses. It truly was a gift.

I noticed Zack looked absolutely shattered. He clearly had not enjoyed a good night sleep.

"Bad night?" I enquired to be met by a scowl.

"You could say that. I'm surprised you are so

sprightly this morning."

He took a swig from his coffee and sighed.

"Do I even dare ask?"

I tried to smile a little at him, but to no avail. I knew he was alluding to my supposed night time activities, but I had no recollection of them whatsoever and didn't suffer with any ill after effects either.

"And you wanted to move my bed yesterday. No chance." he scoffed.

"You might have slept better if I didn't have to climb over you."

I tried again against my better judgement. He didn't even afford me an answer, just a warning stare.

"Just go and get yourself ready, will you." he said instead, still grumpy.

"We'll have to go in three quarters of an hour."

I poured myself a coffee and made some toast. My life was so surreal. Yesterday I met my father alone for the first time since I was little and probably condemned him to death with my revelations to the Sensorian leaders, was grilled by my superiors over it and nearly went too far with Zack, upsetting Zaphire in the process. Now, I was having breakfast as if nothing had happened. It was weird and felt wrong somehow, but I felt amazingly fine. I seemed to find it quite easy to put it aside and look ahead. I hoped it wasn't going to bite me in the backside at some point. Maybe I worked it all out at night, hence keeping Zack awake. My subconscious has always worked overtime at night.

"How are you getting on? Nearly ready?"
Zack disturbed my musings whilst looking me up and down and he knew I hadn't actually changed from my pyjamas yet. He, on the other hand, had put on a shirt and tie and despite looking like a train wreck only ten minutes ago, now looked professional and not to mention stunningly handsome.
I groaned and sighed out loud but got up, sauntered over to my wardrobe and stared blankly at the contents of it. I could literally feel Zack's impatience burning a hole in my back and it spurred me on to just grab a top and trousers which looked relatively smart. They would just have to do the job for the impending meeting with Markus.
Though I had a good night sleep and felt refreshed, the meeting made me feel lacklustre. I didn't want to go over all of it again; I'd rather focus on what they wanted me to do next, if anything at all. I hated the fact they didn't fully trust me and felt I would have to prove myself again before they would regard me as one of their own. I decided to voice my worries to

387

Zack.

"I don't understand what else they want to know. Couldn't they see yesterday that I did everything I could to make the mission successful? I wished you had listened to me and got him. Maybe I would rather have the physical pain of having my legs blown off then feeling like a failure and mistrusted by everyone."

"Don't be fucking stupid. That would have definitely been the worst outcome and I would never have forgiven myself for that and neither would your mum!" he retorted angrily.

"I know, I know. I just feel a bit rubbish about the whole thing. I can't help it."

"Yeah, I can tell. You need to try and get a grip and cover up your feelings a bit more. You're an open book at the moment and remember that everyone around you can sense your feelings and it's fucking tiring for those involved."

"Well, that's making me feel a whole lot better, Zack." I said, not managing to keep the sarcasm out of my voice.

"I was looking for some support or sympathy, not another telling off!"

"I'm just saying it as it is, Eliza. You should be used to that by now. We haven't got time to pussyfoot about." he said, equally annoyed.

388

This wasn't going well this morning.

"Right. Well. I'll do my hair and brush my teeth. Ready in a minute." changing the subject, willing myself to ignore Zack's grumpiness.

I had to focus now, regain control over my senses and think positively.

"I can do this." I desperately tried to encourage myself.

CHAPTER 50

When Eliza finally appeared looking just about smart enough, we made our way up to Markus' office. I wasn't particularly looking forward to this meeting. I was going to try my damned hardest to turn the meeting into planning our next move, rather than going over yesterday's events again. I knew I was going to be scrutinised as Frank would have given Markus a detailed report on my actions. I felt fairly confident about my decisions, but there were a couple of things that could've gone better and I knew Markus would damn well pick me up on them.

"Come in." Markus answered my knock on the door immediately.

"Eliza, you go with Frank first. He's just going to go over your statements from last night and check them with you to see if there's anything else you remember."

Eliza was ushered to the little room on the side and I felt her anxiety rise. At least there was a window, so I could keep an eye on her body language and I gave her a nod and a smile, as she was looking back over her shoulder for my encouragement. I heard Frank making some small talk to make her feel at ease, all designed to get the most information from her. At least he would do it gently and she wouldn't feel so harangued.

"So how do you feel the mission went overall, Zack?" Markus started.

I couldn't make out his mood completely, but something was bothering him so it didn't bode well. I steeled myself and answered.

"It was a partial success. We know Rick's plans and that it's of the utmost importance we find him and deal with him. I would've liked a less dramatic ending and some way of being able to track where Rick is now. Also, I would've preferred Kas to have been detected earlier so he could have been dealt with before he arrived at the cafe the other day. Most importantly, I would've liked Eliza not to have put herself in danger."

I paused there and tried to gauge his reaction, which was difficult as he was heavily cloaking.

"Hmm...yes."

Still not giving anything away.

"Frank said he was impressed with you. You had to make some difficult decisions and you kept in control. Well done for that. However, when I first heard about the Kas situation, I was furious with you for missing it. It could have blown everything. Frank said you dealt with it well and the only way you could have given the situation, but it was risky and could have been prevented."

"I had words with the surveillance team about it, Sir. It shouldn't have happened." I tried to defend myself.

"I know you've bollocked them, but they came to me and said you hadn't given them specific instructions to look out for Kas, so the buck stops with you, Zacharya. Though, I told them in no uncertain terms not to try and shift blame and they should have thought about it themselves. I didn't want to undermine you. However, you need to learn from your mistakes and always look for every eventuality yourself. You are not to rely on others when you're in charge. You're ultimately responsible."

He was stood behind his desk, leaning on his arms with a grave expression on his face. Imposing and in no mood to be argued with.

"Yes, I know. Sir. And I apologise for that mistake."

I was about to attempt to move the meeting on to what to do next, but he wasn't quite finished with me.

"You need to talk to your team again. Tell them you are aware you should have given more specific instructions, but that you expect more from them too. They knew the score, they should have used their initiative." he carried on.

"Yes Sir." I said simply, hoping we could now get down to business, but he still had more questions.

"How are you going to deal with Eliza? She put herself and others in danger, even though you ordered her to bail if that was going to be the case. I know she got valuable information from doing just that, so were you wrong to give the order or was she wrong to defy you?" he challenged.

I feared he'd ask that question.

"Sir, I have to be honest and say I don't know. I can't have been wrong to try and keep her and everyone else safe. She didn't follow my order so there has to be a consequence for that. Had she listened to me we still may have been able to follow Rick and keep him under surveillance, but it was a hard call to make for her and she thought she was doing the right thing. So, I don't want to be too hard on her. She's already hard on herself, feeling she has failed anyway."

Markus slapped his hands on the table. He wasn't happy with that answer. I didn't have to be a Sensorian to work that one out. His frustration seeped through every part of his body and he wasn't cloaking at all. It hurt.

"Zack, you have got to stop making allowances for her!" he growled, barely keeping his voice under control.

"She disobeyed you. You said yourself we could still be in a position of knowing where Rick is, had she listened. She has got to learn to follow orders, and that's the end of it. She's not experienced enough to make a decision to disregard an order!"

"Yes Sir, I know but..."

"No. No buts." he interrupted.

"You are the mission leader and her trainer. Deal with her. Don't get me wrong, she did her best and we're grateful for the information she got. I'm impressed with her courage and improvisation. One day she will be an asset to us, but it's up to you to train her. Don't give her any slack, it's not going to benefit her in the long run. I don't blame her for the choices she made, she did the best she could with her level of training. But I would be incensed with you if you don't make her the best Sensorian she could be, due to misplaced sympathy."

He regained some control over his frustration and my body started to relax slightly, not having to try and shield as much. It was bloody painful to cope with

394

Markus' outbursts, physically and emotionally.

"I want you to test her loyalty to the full." he added, emphasising 'full'.

"Well?"

He stared at me, demanding a response impatiently.

"I'll do my best, Sir. I hope my best will be good enough." I just about managed to sound calm.

"It better be." Markus said uncompromisingly.

Fuck it. It was going to be damned hard and I shoved it to the back of my mind for the moment. I just didn't want to think about it.

I glanced over at Eliza in the other room. Her body language looked relaxed. Frank was brilliant with people, always managing to get to his goal without making people feel miserable. However, he was allowed that freedom as Markus made sure it was possible. Frank used him literally like the proverbial stick. If it wasn't for Markus' strict discipline, Frank wouldn't be able to get anywhere either. Typical good cop, bad cop scenario. Anyway, I was glad Markus had chosen to speak to me and not Eliza. It wouldn't have ended well for either of us I don't think.

I was waiting for Markus to decide to move on. I

felt in no position to broker it as he was clearly not in the best of moods with me, so I just stood silently. It looked like Frank was done with Eliza as he looked over to check with Markus who gave him the slightest of nods. I guessed they would come in soon, which couldn't come quickly enough for me.

CHAPTER 51

That meeting hadn't gone half as bad as I thought it was going to go and I felt quite good now. Frank had been perfectly amenable and had managed to make me feel less of a failure. I could still detect a hint of distrust though, and I was sure he was cloaking as hard as he could. But then I suppose, they had to be careful who to trust and they have only known me for just over a month. So I made my peace with that and hoped I could convince them of my loyalty in due course.

It took one glance over to Zack to determine he hadn't had the best meeting. When we entered the room the stench of frustration hung heavily in the air and it stemmed from both of them. Frank raised his eyebrows at Markus, but he gave nothing away, instead asking us calmly and quite pleasantly to take a seat around the table.

"Hey." I mouthed to Zack, trying to catch his mood.

He threw me a little smile but then looked towards Markus again, giving him his full attention.

"Right, let's get down to it." Markus started.

"Last night, the leadership team have discussed at length how to proceed from here. We have decided to dedicate all our available Sensorians on the task of locating Rick and then monitoring him. We need to know exactly who he's in contact with and who he has recruited already. We're going to have to deal with each and everyone he has got involved in this. It's going to be a huge operation, Rick must be caught at all cost. He's endangering all of us with his actions and he has to be stopped."

Markus paused and both Frank and Zack nodded in agreement.

"What's my role going to be in this?" I dared ask.

Markus glanced at Frank who turned to me to speak.

"You will be instrumental in finding out information from him and eventually capturing him. You're our way in. Part of him is still hoping you'll join him in his delusional revolution and we could use that to our advantage. We hope that he'll approach you again and you'll let him persuade you to join him, giving us the insider information we need to discover who's involved."

Frank waited for a moment to scan for my initial reaction before carrying on. I agreed, I did think my father desperately wanted me by his side, though I wasn't sure of my own ability to deceive him. It was going to be a difficult and dangerous task.

"However, there is a big 'but' in this. It all depends how your next month or so will go. Whether you can prove to be a loyal Sensorian and, trust me, you will be severely tested. If after that time you still wish to help us and be part of our community, then that would be the best outcome for all of us."

Ah, that explained Zack's mood as I guessed it was going to be down to him to 'severely test' me and I could tell he wasn't particularly looking forward to that. And neither was I! I didn't really know what to say to that apart from *shit shit bollocks shit,* but I didn't think that would go down too well. So I just nodded, hoping that someone else would take the attention away from me. Zack obliged.

"Yes Sir. Markus informed me briefly about this earlier and I will see to it. I'm confident Eliza will do her utmost best to prove her worth and loyalty to us."

He gave me an encouraging nod, which made me feel good. Whatever he had to do next, I knew he had my back. He trusted me and I would try my hardest to prove him right. I hoped to God I would remember this in the undoubtedly difficult time ahead.

Have we got any leads as to where they went last night?" Zack enquired, eager to find out anything, even if it was the tiniest thing, hoping he hadn't

399

completely lost them.

"A few unconfirmed sightings which we're looking into now. As soon as we can confirm them we have something to work with." Markus answered.

"Well at least it's something I suppose. Let's hope for some good news then."

Zack looked mildly happier. Losing Rick had been heavy on his mind. He didn't like it all and I knew he partly blamed me for it, even though he hadn't quite voiced that to me yet. It was sure to come.

"Any other questions?" Markus tried to wrap up, but I had one other thing I wanted to know more about.

"Well, yes, I do. When you said you have to "deal with" all the people involved in Rick's organisation, what exactly does that mean? What are you going to do?"

I wasn't really expecting a proper answer but Frank was uncharacteristically straight up about it.

"If they're a normal civilian, well, you've seen what happened to Kas. They take the secrecy deal, or else. If they're from our community however, it will most likely end in long term imprisonment or, if they're instrumentally involved, death."

I couldn't help but gasp, even though I knew that was the consequence for betrayal. It's just so brutal and I couldn't get used to that. It also reminded me that's exactly where my own father was heading and it hurt like hell. All three of the men were staring at me and I realised I must have been emitting a massive spike in my emotions and remembered to try and cloak the best I could. I didn't want them to think I couldn't cope with it, plus Zack has already been annoyed with me earlier this morning for not being in control of my emotions and I didn't want to irk him again.

The men carried on talking without paying me much more attention. They were planning a big meeting with all the Sensorians to warn them about Rick and that he might approach them. Everyone was to be urged to let the leaders know immediately if that happened or if they suspected someone had been approached but was keeping it to themselves. Everyone was to be reminded about the severe consequences that would befall them if they were to step out of line, or help Rick in any way. Zack chipped in saying that the leaders must make sure that everyone understands that if anyone has any complaints work wise or has issues with their personal life, they should be encouraged to speak up about it.

"We must make sure there's nothing Rick can tap

into to turn any one of us. If there's a feeling of dissent amongst us, like Rick seems to think there is, we must find it and deal with it. We must have a clean house; that is of utmost importance." Zack added and both Markus and Frank nodded in agreement.

"I'm not aware of anything, but then we haven't been looking in house much so it's probably worth setting up a team which can actively go out and talk to people and making sure issues are being dealt with appropriately with satisfactory outcomes for all." Frank suggested.

"That makes sense. Good plan. Laura will head that team up." Markus decided.

I realised I was made privy to all of this purely on the back of being Zack's trainee. I actually thought they'd forgotten I was there and I kept very quiet. I felt strangely exhilarated seeing the three in focused work mode. Then, as if Zack had read my mind, he looked over at me and instantly decided I shouldn't be there. He turned towards Markus and Frank and announced our leaving.

"I'd better take Eliza back. We need to discuss what happens next with her training."

Markus and Frank acknowledged Zack's decision and they both gave me a nod.

"Good luck." Frank whispered in my ear as we walked past.

My feet suddenly felt very heavy and my stomach turned. I took a deep breath to steady myself. I wasn't sure if I wanted to hear what Zack had in store for me but there was no way around it. It had to happen.

CHAPTER 52

"First, I am going to take you to lunch, Eli. I will text Zaphy and the others to see who can join us. Try and make the most of it. Have some fun as it may well be a while before you can do this again."

I looked at her face, which lit up a little compared to the doomed expression she wore a second ago. The prospect of having a bit of fun definitely cheered her up somewhat and to be honest, I could do with some distraction as well.

Brody couldn't make it, but Ned, Sam and Zaph all texted back eagerly with a positive reply. They all piled into the cafe as if they'd been waiting for the text. Zaphire came up and hugged Eli, she'd clearly forgiven her but I was still on the receiving end of her icy stare. Sam picked up on it straight away, but I shook my head to tell her to ignore it for now. Ned also gave Eliza a big hug and told her how proud he was of her. She was beaming.

"No really, Eli. Well done!"

He insisted as she was about to minimise the compliment.

"You are basically a newbie and you pulled it out the bag. I know you'll be told all the things that went wrong and what you could've done better (as he poignantly glanced at me), but you're back, alive and well and you got the information you were asked to get. So, in my book that is a job well done."

Sam and Zaphire both agreed in unison.

"Trust you to get the award for the most dramatic first real mission, though!" Sam jokingly remarked, punching Eliza's arm.

"It was bloody tense, disarming that device! I learned a lot. Thank you very much!" she carried on, still half joking, but she meant it.

They didn't have to put their skills into practice very often in a real life situation and Sam was still in training.

"No worries, I will try my hardest to give you some more practice in the future!" Eliza laughed.

"You'd better not, crazy girl." I chipped in shaking my head but smiling.

Everyone was in a buoyant mood and jokes went across the table for a while yet. Until Nurse Kate arrived with one of her patients. It caught Eliza's attention straight away.

"What on earth happened to him?" she enquired shocked but curious about the rather battered looking man Kate was pushing in a wheelchair into the cafe. It brought us all back to the, on occasion, dangerous realities our jobs presented us with. Ned took it upon himself to explain it to Eliza.

"Yeah." he said slowly and sighing with it.

"That's what can happen when you get caught out on a job. It's Rob Saunders. He was working on a case where he tried to infiltrate a paedophile ring of rather influential people. They managed to work out his cover story was false and those guys take no prisoners. They basically hired a mob to 'teach Rob a lesson'. He was in hospital for a couple of weeks, but luckily recovered well now and, I heard, determined to get those men prosecuted."

"Things like this occur occasionally, but it reminds us to always be alert. The risk is always there and it's good to be confronted with it. Keeps us on our toes." I explained.

It had brought our exuberant mood down somewhat, but we carried on having our lunch and soon everyone was chatting and laughing again.

I took the opportunity to observe Eliza for a while and drink in all her little quirks, her cute pink cheeks, glowing with excitement and her beautiful grey eyes shining with pleasure. I loved the sound of her voice, usually warm and a little husky but with occasional little squeaks when excitement spilled over. I was going to miss all of them over the next month or so, having to test her with one of our more severe punishments. I knew I had arranged this lunch as much for my benefit as hers, eking out a bit more time to enjoy her, when she was in a happy mood.

I had forced myself not to push Eliza on her VH status. She clearly wasn't ready to tackle that yet, but I really had to work hard to reign in my enthusiasm over it. It was huge, and if she was able to properly control it, it would be an amazing skill to have. I hoped she would be open to being trained in it. I had already contacted Rob Saunders over it, as he's a VH too. Like me, he was eager to help her develop her potential skill and promised to talk to her after the month was up. If she decided to stay, that was.

I had to warn Zaphire what was going to happen with Eliza over the coming month. It was only fair. I signalled for Zaph to come over for a minute, removing myself from the group somewhat. She reluctantly left Eliza's side and came over, her face dark as thunder.

"What do you want, brother." she grumbled angrily.

What I had to tell her wasn't going to improve her mood at all, but I hoped she would appreciate the heads up at least.

"You're not going to like this, Zaph, but my hands are tied. The leaders are expecting me to test Eliza's loyalty to the full, before they'll accept her on the next mission. We need her, but they unanimously decided that if she isn't completely loyal to us, they won't trust her. They worry that Rick will be able to get under her skin and lure her to his side. And I don't blame them, you know as well as I do, the familial bond is extremely strong."

Zaphire's demeanour changed from not only hostile but despondent too. She knew what it meant but still asked.

"I won't be able to see her, will I." It wasn't a question. I shook my head.

"I'm so sorry Zaph. I know what she means to you. It's not forever. You're strong."

I tried to sound as empathetic as I could, knowing she wouldn't quite see it that way.

"That's easy to say for you. She'll still see you. I bet part of you is actually pleased she's out of my reach so you can work your magic?" she bit back.

"Yeah, she's really going to fucking love me, isn't she." I answered sarcastically.

"At least you're the innocent bystander who she can pour her heart out to afterwards. She'll fucking hate me, Zaph!"

I sighed, feeling frustrated.

"Just go and spend some time with her now, before I have to take her."

I rather roughly pushed her back to the group, where of course everyone had noticed our argument, though desperately trying to hide their curiosity.

Zaphire sidled back next to Eliza, and I noticed an instant spike in Eli's heartbeat. Clearly not unaffected by Zaphire's attentions, to Zaph's delight. She glanced at me, smirking somewhat. I really didn't like that we were competing over this girl. I needed to get a grip and lock my feelings away. It was going to be tough, but necessary. I had to let my sister and Eliza sort their feelings for each other out first, that was only fair, especially for Eliza as she was confused enough as it was.

I didn't want to be fighting with Zaph, she was my soul mate and my only family. Being twins, the bond was so much stronger than any other family bond and this friction wasn't doing either of us any good.

I gave them another half hour, and Zaph didn't leave Eliza's side during that time. They were deep in conversation, having eyes for no one else. I noticed Sam and Ned were checking my state of mind regularly, but I was in full control now and gave nothing away. Instead, I was fully immersed in their company.

"Don't forget it's fitness test time tomorrow." Ned helpfully reminded me.

Bollocks. Had to fit that in as well somehow. Great.

"I do need to have words with Markus about that again, I tell you." I sighed, annoyed.

"Forget it. You tried before. It's useless. He won't change his mind." Sam shrugged her shoulders in defeat.

"Well, maybe. But with Laura heading up this new team looking for in house mutterings, airing some of those grumbles could work to our advantage." I said with a glint in my eye.

"Jeez, don't start stirring Zack. If that comes back to you, Markus will give you hell!" Ned exclaimed.

"I'll just have to be clever about it then, won't I? Not a word from you two!" I threatened, though I already knew I could rely on them a hundred percent.

"On that note, I will leave you in peace. Get back to work. Say your goodbyes to Eliza. You won't see her for a while." I added.

Sam and Ned looked at each other and me with raised eyebrows, about to question me.

"Don't ask." I sighed and called Eliza over.

"Time to go, crazy girl. Give everyone a hug."

She looked at me, pain in her eyes. She knew whatever was coming next wasn't going to be good or easy.

CHAPTER 53

Walking back to our room I felt like a lamb being brought to slaughter. Zack wasn't talking so I was left to my own thoughts, which to be honest weren't the most upbeat. I needed to gain control over them because I was imagining all sorts of bizarre scenarios as to how I was going to be severely tested. I'd hear all about it soon enough I told myself over and over again, until we got to our room.

"Sit down. We need to talk."

Zack looked extremely serious and seemed eager to get it over and done with. I nodded and took the seat opposite him. There was nothing left of the jovial, relaxed Zack that he was when surrounded by his friends, he was just my unrelenting trainer now, intent on 'dealing' with me.

"Look. The mission was a partial success and on the whole you did well. I'm proud of how you dealt with the precarious situation you were in and the courage you showed."

He paused for a second.

"Uh, thank you, Sir." I mumbled, unsure if he expected an answer.

I started picking up some agitation from him, although very subtle, barely noticeable.

"However, you made one big mistake. Can you tell me what you think that was?"

I'd been expecting this. I knew he wouldn't let it go.

"I didn't manage to use the signal to tell you it looked like it might become dangerous and to get me out."

I had thought carefully about how to phrase it, hoping to make it sound like I'd wanted to make the call, but wasn't able to. Zack wasn't impressed though. His voice turning icily cold, but in total control.

"Bullshit. Don't make me angry, Miss Mankuzay. Try that again. Last chance."

"Okay, okay. I didn't follow your order to use the signal when a dangerous situation threatened to unfold. But..." Zack interrupted.

"No buts. You disobeyed an order. One that I made very clear before you set off. That decision put yourself and others in danger. You took it upon yourself to make a call on something that you're not experienced enough to do. You thought you knew better and as a consequence of your actions, we lost him. Had you obeyed my orders we would still have tabs on him."

He sighed in frustration.

"Ned's story obviously didn't make much impact on

you so maybe you should experience the
consequences yourself."

He leaned forward, our faces just centimetres
apart as I didn't dare move back.

"What do you think, Miss Mankuzay? Think
carefully before you answer."

He leant back into his chair and folded his arms.
Mask fully on now. I couldn't read his feelings at all, or
what he expected. I could hazard a guess though. Of
course he was right. I had done exactly what he
accused me of. At the time I thought it was the right
call, but I shouldn't have done it. I did get it. Though
inside me there was still a little voice saying that we
wouldn't have all this information had I bailed out.

"I'm waiting for your reply, Eliza." he prompted.

Even though I knew he was right I still wanted to
scream at him. *How is this fair! I did what I thought
best and it paid off'. How does that not count for
something. Aaaaaargh!* But I knew that would be
totally counterproductive and probably make my
predicament worse.

"I suppose I should, Sir." I started, but Zack's
eyes turned dark immediately, he stood up shaking his
head, giving off the scent of frustration now.

"I mean, yes I should, I should bear the
consequences. Sir." I hastily rephrased, lowering my

414

eyes, nodding my head.

That worked as he sat back down again.

"Okay. So you understand you have to go in isolation."

It was more of a statement than a question, so I simply nodded my head.

"You know I've been tasked with testing your loyalty by our leaders. That means I'm going to make you endure our severest form of isolation. It will last at least four weeks, depending on your behaviour and I'll explain what is expected of you."

He paused to observe me for a minute. My heart was racing and I felt sick to the stomach. *A month of isolation!* How was I going to cope with that? I sincerely didn't know if I could. Zack carried on regardless of my distress that he surely had picked up on as I wasn't making any effort to cloak.

"You will have no contact with any one apart from me. You will not be able to talk apart from answering questions with either yes Sir or no Sir. You stand up when spoken to. You will get one hour outside, accompanied by me alone. You'll be given an exercise regime at the gym, one hour at 6am and one at 8pm. You will study for your exams and sit them whilst in isolation. You are allowed one hour of television a day plus you can have books other than

415

your study books, but those are privileges which can be lost if you choose to break any rules. Lights out at 10pm. Do you have any questions?"

Zack's eyes inscrutable as he scanned my body language. I felt empty. It was worse than I had expected and I just wanted to cry.

"Will I get a chance to see my mum before I go in? Please?" I pleaded, resenting my voice cracking. I wanted to at least appear strong.

"No." Zack simply stated.

"You can see her afterwards and spend some time at home. You can then decide if you want to stay with us, and become the best Sensorian you can. Have a fulfilling life with us where you won't have to hide your gift, but can use it to do good. By then, you will know within yourself if you can be loyal to us and submit to our rules."

Zack didn't show any empathy for my plight. There were no encouraging words, no sympathetic squeeze of my hand not even a reassuring nod. Absolutely nothing. I desperately needed a little sign, anything to show he was still on my side.

"Zack, I don't know if I am ready for this." I tried to elicit some reaction.

"You have no choice, Eliza. This is it. Your time to prove you can bear the consequences of your actions and come out a better person. Stronger. More accountable. Don't let me or yourself down. We'll be here for you afterwards. Zaphire, and everyone else."

He got up and finally I sensed a bit of emotion in him, a litter glimmer to show he cared. It was enough for me. I could do this.

"There's no need to pack a bag. No personal items are allowed apart from your books. Tomorrow you can write a list of books you might want to read. Everything else is provided. You'll have to strip down in your cell and get changed in the clothes made available to you."

"Am I going now? Straight away?" I asked slightly panicked.

Everything was moving so fast.

"Unless you have another question?" he offered.

I desperately tried to think of something to procrastinate. Stretching the time I was still able to talk and have relative freedom.

"What about the fitness test tomorrow? Am I still doing that?"

He looked at me incredulously.

"Of course. It's obligatory. At 6am."

"Oh my God! Why so frigging early?" I couldn't help but exclaim to Zack's obvious annoyance.

"Better get used to it as I already said you have

exercise every morning at 6 am." he said grumpily.

"Anything else?"

I needed to come up with another question quickly to postpone the inevitable just that little bit longer. I didn't want to start my time in solitude.

"What happens when I feel ill? How am I going to let you know if I can't talk?"

Zack just snorted. Stupid question of course. He would sense if something was wrong with me. *Duh*.

"If there's anything serious you need to talk about, you may write a note. I will either respond to it or not, depending on the issue. However, don't abuse that privilege because it will be retracted. Then you would just have to speak and be punished for it, however urgent it is."

Zack moved towards the door. I felt my time was up and I capitulated. I got up from my chair and followed him out with heavy legs. This was it now. A month of isolation ahead. I sincerely hoped I would come out stronger. Not broken. I wanted to help them find my father. Stop him from exposing every one of us and stop his stupid plan to take over society. I had to prove to them I was ready for it, prove my loyalty to Zack, Zaphire and all of the Sensorian community. But most of all I had to prove it to myself.

ACKNOWLEDGEMENTS

First of all I'd like to thank my husband Steve for encouraging me to start writing this book and giving me the time to do so, plus his sometimes not so patient, but always given, IT support. Lots of withering looks were banded about in the process. He's not read the book yet as I think he's scared he might think it's rubbish and wouldn't want to tell me! Also thank you to my children Nienke, Bentley and Hanneke who had to sometimes put up with a very absent minded mum or asked to 'hang on a minute' whilst finishing a sentence or two. Hanneke needs a special mention as she was a more than willing audience to having my book read out loud to her, to check if everything made sense to a teenager (and to pick out some more little mistakes!). Some valuable lessons were learned and consequently changes were made to the book that I'd otherwise would have missed.

My biggest thanks goes to my friend Clare, who read all my rough first drafts and had to endure listening to me ramble on about it on our dog walks together. Her comments, help with English, and constructive criticism have been invaluable. Without her I probably would never have finished it or dared to let anyone else read it.

Also thank you to my other Guinea Pigs; my sister Margot, her partner Miquel, my friends Annemarie and Carol who read it and again came back with lovely encouraging comments plus some valuable criticism and advice on grammar and spelling. They and some of my other friends, Denise, Nic, Becky and Emma and my daughter Nienke were also extremely helpful in helping to write the blurb which I found an almost impossible task.

Another big thank you goes to Lauren, who was 'volunteered' by my husband to check spelling and grammar once more, giving it its last QC. It was definitely necessary!

Last but not least I'd like to thank Miquel for his awesomely stunning front cover design. You can see more of his work on www.lumigo-film.com

AUTHOR PAGE

I hope you enjoyed reading this book as much as I have enjoyed writing it.
If you have, I would be super grateful if you could leave a comment on Amazon. I would love to hear your thoughts!

The second part of The Sensorians trilogy is called Trust and will be out soon. Watch this space...

For up to date information check out my instagram account brigitte__books

Printed in Great Britain
by Amazon